THE GOOD GIRL

THE GOOD GIRL

CHRISTY BARRITT

WhiteFire
Publishing

This is a work of fiction. All characters and events portrayed in this novel are either fictitious or used fictitiously.

THE GOOD GIRL

WhiteFire Publishing
13607 Bedford Rd NE
Cumberland, MD 21502

ISBN: 9781939023025 (print)
          9781939023932 (digital)

*The book is dedicated to all of the good girls out there.
May God's grace and favor rest upon you,
and may the hard times only serve to make you stronger.*

"For it is by grace you have been saved, through faith—
and this is not from yourselves, it is the gift of God—
not by works, so that no one can boast."
~ Ephesians 2: 8-9

1

Forrest Gump was known for saying that life was like a box of chocolates. You never knew what you were going to get.

Grandmother Griffin had a different saying. She said that life was like a Bible story. You didn't always get a happy ending—at least not here on this earth.

For years, I didn't believe Grandma Griffin. After all, she honestly thought that "cleanliness is next to godliness" was in the Bible. I mean, I was a Christian, so life was supposed to be blessed. And blessed meant that life was full of unconditional love and feel-good moments and abundance. Right?

Wrong.

Now, I have my own sayings. One is that life is like a beautiful apple. Sometimes you don't know it's rotten until you bite into it. Other days, I thought life was like the solid wood coffee table that my uncle fell on—revealing it was actually made of particleboard, thus my saying, "You never know what you're made of until you're broken."

I'm Tara Lancaster, and I come from a family of missionaries, preachers, and Bible college professors. One could never be too righteous in this clan. I was right on track in my family tree, following a path that would have made Mother Teresa and Billy Graham proud.

That was, until two years ago.

It's taken me a long time to figure things out. First, I had to battle a ghost, question my faith, consult a psychic, and fall in love with someone who wasn't my husband.

It's a long story. It's a story about a good girl gone...well, I can't tell you. I will say this: Life is like a movie. Just when things seem perfect, the movie ends.

And that's where my story starts.

2

Where does a twenty-something go when she's lost faith not only in God, but in mankind?

She goes to a middle-class neighborhood in St. Paul, Minnesota to dog sit, that's where.

At least, that's where I went.

I'd been here all of one hour so far—most of that spent in the airport—and already things weren't going according to plan.

I walked from the curb toward my sister's house, glancing back for long enough to see the yellow taxi cab turn at the corner of the picturesque neighborhood. The houses resting on the neat blocks had character with their nooks and arches and detailed trim work. Each property was dotted with looming, established trees that seemed to root the area in a *Leave It to Beaver* type of aura. My sister Lana lived on Elm Street, a street name that conjured up images of cozy cookouts and friendly neighbors...or men with razor-sharp knives attached to their fingers, depending on which picture your mind wanted to conjure up. I'd stick with the cozy one.

I squeezed my cell phone between my shoulder and ear, all while trying to drag my suitcases up the cement steps of my sister's cozy bungalow. My mom's voice, usually soft, sounded like a megaphone in my ear, and as much as I tried to tune her out, I couldn't.

"Are you sure you're going to be okay there? I wish you were back here in Florida. Certainly Lana's dog would be okay in a kennel for a few weeks."

Little did my mom know that I saw this trip to Minnesota as an escape from the nightmare surrounding my previous life. Anywhere was better than Florida, even if it did mean I was running from my problems. I decided not to tell her that, though. She worried enough without me dropping bombshells like that. I knew my mother. She'd automatically think "depression." I didn't want to add anything else to her already growing list of "things to pray about for Tara Lancaster."

I leaned my suitcase against my leg and fumbled with my keys, trying to find the one Lana had mailed me. I grabbed the shiniest one and jammed it into the lock, just as a high-pitched bark began repeating on the other side of the door. That would have to be Doggie Gaga, a Maltese/Poodle mix and the sole reason for my existence for the next four weeks. I would give the dog food, water, and walks, and in return she would listen to me babble on and on for hours about how I hated my life.

"I'm going to be just fine, Mom." I made sure my voice was even and light.

"I love you, Tara." My mother sounded so sweet and kind. People used to say I was just like her. It was strange how life could change in the blink of an eye. A few years ago, I'd have all kinds of platitudes to tell myself at moments like these. Not long ago, I'd written all of those clichés down and ground them up, one by one, in my paper shredder. The moment was supposed to be symbolic and healing. Instead, I'd felt a bit psychotic.

Maybe the evil, maniacal laugh I'd forced out during the entire process—a laugh meant to break an otherwise tense moment—had been a little too much.

A motorcycle roared behind me. Between my mom, the dog, and the motorcycle, a headache began pulsating at the back of my head. I glanced over my shoulder at the rider, wondering why he'd stopped in front of Lana's house.

"I have to run, Mom. I'll check in with you later."

"Tara?"

"Yes?"

"Everything's going to work out just fine. I know it's hard to see now, but it will. Just keep trusting God."

How many times had I heard that before from well-meaning Christians? I loved my mom, but she just didn't understand. She'd lived a flawless life. She'd been my example, and I'd planned my life to be the same.

I'd failed.

I told her good-bye before snatching the phone from my shoulder and jamming it into my purse. No sooner had I opened the door than I heard a footfall behind me. I twirled around, having visions of the paparazzi standing there camera in hand, ruining my plans.

Instead, a woman dressed in black—all the way from her finger-nails and lipstick to her clothing—stood there. The only "accessory" not black was her hair, which was toilet bowl blue. A helmet rested in the crook of her arm, and a cool, aloof expression saturated her gaze.

"You Tara?"

I paused, hand on the doorknob and muscles tensed. Could I run inside and slam the door fast enough if this conversation went down-hill? It might mean abandoning my luggage for a while—perhaps even having it stolen—but I could handle that.

"Depends on who's asking." I heard the suspicion in my voice. I was a new girl in a new town. I had to use some caution here.

"I'm Candy."

Candy? Black licorice maybe, but the woman definitely didn't look sweet. Or did she? Beneath her edgy exterior, soft features and a petite build peeked through. Sure, her appearance screamed, "Look at me!" but her eyes hinted at something deeper. "I was supposed to pick you up from the airport."

I pointed to the motorcycle on the street. "On that? With luggage?" I shook my head, deciding to forgo pondering the woman's sensibilities in favor of ending the conversation succinctly and sweetly. Besides, minding my manners was Good Girls Rule #21. "It's okay. I called a cab. No harm done."

The woman didn't move. Her gaze traveled up and down as she

looked me over, making me feel like a lamb being sized up by a hungry villager. "So you're Lana's sister?"

I nodded, drew in a deep breath, trying to gather some patience and recall what Lana said about Candy. I remembered Lana mentioning something about a Katy Perry wannabe with an aversion to animals and some crazy story about an unfortunate encounter with a chicken as a child. Why my sister had told me those random factoids and why I'd actually remembered was a mystery to me. "And you're her new best friend? The one who's allergic to dogs?"

"That's me. Hair stylist by day, Internet celebrity by night."

Lovely. My sister never failed to surprise me, although this shouldn't come as any shock. Lana had been deemed "Party Girl" after a stint on reality TV. Most people said that Lana and I were polar opposites, and they were right. Lana was the rebel, I was the good girl.

The thought of being the good girl caused nausea to roil in my stomach. I'd been guilty of being a people-pleaser my entire life. I'd disappointed people to such a great extent recently that I didn't know who I was anymore. Not a good girl. Not an atheist necessarily, but not a Christian either. All I had to define me right now were the facts that I loved Golden Oreos, I had a mad addiction to *Dancing with the Stars*, and I was insanely disappointed in myself and approximately half of the people who used to be in my life.

Candy scrutinized me. "Has anyone ever told you that you look like Natalie Portman?"

"No." I crossed the squeaky wooden floor, soaking in the walls of windows coming at me from two sides, and deposited my suitcases by the cheerful yellow sofa. Gaga turned crazy circles at my feet, that high-pitched bark filling the room until I finally scooped her up into my arms.

"Well, you do. You know, from some of her sweeter roles. Not the crazy *Black Swan* movie." Her nose twitched, and I wondered if her nose ring was bothering her or maybe the dog.

I soaked in Lana's house. Magazines cluttered the corners, a coat stand overflowed with colorful garments, a CD organizer was stuffed with plastic cases, and various brown-leafed plants littered any free space. Despite the clutter, something about the space felt warm and way too normal for Lana. Maybe my sister had left me the wrong house key?

Photos confirmed this was the right place. Pictures of my sister in a bikini, raising a beer bottle in a toast, kissing her latest boyfriend while the sun set behind them. Totally Lana, uninhibited and free.

So different from me.

Maybe we could trade lives for a while. After all, St. Paul, Minnesota was hundreds of miles from Miami. I already liked it here, most of all because no one knew me.

No one knew that I was the girl who had perfect Sunday school attendance for sixteen years, the record only broken because at seventeen I had pneumonia and my mom forced me to stay home so I didn't infect anyone else. No one knew that in high school the church council nominated me as the Teen of the Year for the entire state of Florida, and that I won. Mothers had wanted me to marry their sons. Teachers had said I was their favorite. My outspoken stance on purity had inspired my peers. Oh, and my pious legalism had also led me to create the Good Girl Chronicles, a blog where I daily—and naïvely—told teen girls all over the country how they should live. As if I'd had a clue.

Nor did anyone here know how royally I screwed up. I had gained firsthand knowledge about the domino effect of bad decisions. One wrong move could make everything around you tumble downward.

Being in St. Paul was my new beginning. I'd had twenty-six years to grapple with my inadequacies, but despite my best attempts to accept all my flaws, I still failed and longed for that perfection.

The sound of a digital camera clicking distracted me from the strange smell mixture of stale pizza and apple-scented jarred candles. Candy's cell phone was aimed at my feet.

I hid one foot behind my leg and balanced precariously on the other. "What are you doing?" Anxiety bubbled up in me. Who was this woman, and what was she up to?

"Taking a picture of your shoes. They're so cute."

I glanced down at my loafers and then back up at Candy. Her fingers moved across the phone's screen with precision as she spoke in sync with her keyboarding. "My new pal Tara's rad shoes. Must get a pair."

I stepped closer, trying to peer at her touch screen. "What are you doing?"

"Putting it on Facebook."

"That's just...perfect." I forced a smile, trying to conjure up ideas on how to get her out of the house, so I could get on with my total and complete introverted seclusion, pity party, and quite possibly the remaking of Tara Lancaster. I'd only decided on two of the three options for sure, but all were appealing. "Look, I appreciate you stopping by, but I'm okay. I'll adjust to being here just fine."

Candy put the phone down, and a grin stretched across her face. "I know you will, because I'm going to help you."

I shook my head. "No, no. You don't understand. I'm like...I'm like..." What was I like? With my fingers, I drew an imaginary circle around myself. "I'm like an island." I smiled, pleased with my explanation.

Candy looked at me a moment and then snorted. "An island? Really? Lana said I needed to look out for you, show you around town. That's what I'm going to do." She punched my arm. "You little island, you."

I didn't come here to see the town—or to be made fun of, for that matter. I came here to hunker down in a cave and disappear from the world. Was that asking too much? I was divorced, humiliated, and I'd nearly caused the mega church where my father was pastor to split. And that was only the beginning. My heart still twisted at the thought of the train wreck back home.

Candy walked toward the kitchen, and I had no choice but to follow. Good Girls Rule #14: Be nice to guests, even the annoying ones who won't leave. "I'm going to grab some water from the kitchen before I hit the road. You don't care, do you?"

She breezed past me, and I caught the scent of cigarette smoke. I glanced at her retreating figure and frowned. The woman had a swagger, even in her platform shoes. I was pretty sure Candy was the type of person who didn't care what anyone thought. On second thought, maybe I *should* hang around her. I could use a few tips in that area.

She stopped in her tracks at the kitchen door. "Whoa." She muttered the word in a low voice, a touch of awe to it.

My muscles tightened. I didn't like the sound of that. "Whoa?"

"I knew Lana had a wicked sense of humor, but wow."

I pulled Gaga closer. What? A dirty kitchen? Fake dog poop? Twenty pages of instructions on how to care for Gaga? I peered over her shoulder and into the cozy, small kitchen where early afternoon sunlight poured through two windows. Gray walls. Stainless steel appliances. A butcher knife standing devilishly on end in the wood cutting board.

A butcher knife? Standing on end?

I looked closer. A piece of paper lay like a corpse underneath the knife.

I pushed past Candy and glanced at the words scribbled there. *I'm still here.*

"I'm still here? Who's still here?" Shivers shimmied down my spine.

Candy's eyes widened, some of her cool confidence leaving for a moment. "You're asking me?"

I looked at her, suddenly realizing she might be my only friend here in St. Paul. "Is Lana still here?"

"Nope, she's definitely in Tuscany. Sent me a picture this morning." Candy peered at the knife again. Her gaze changed from fearful to curious. "I'm totally getting this on video."

She already had her phone out and aimed at the cutting board.

"Absolutely not." My hand went to my waist—an assertive stance, if you asked me—as realizations began to click in my head. "Are you guys punking me or something? I know Lana is amused by the strangest things, but really?"

"Punking is so 2006. I, Candy Cornelius, am all about today and being on the edge of all that is cool and worthy. This would be perfect for my YouTube channel." She held up her phone again. "And no, I had nothing to do with this. I'm fame hungry, but not when it comes to stuff this twisted."

"Any idea who might have left this?" I kept my voice even, as if I'd played detective a million times before. I hadn't. But I had been questioned by detectives before, so maybe some good would come out of that experience as I tried at the moment to imitate them.

Candy shrugged, shoving her phone back into the pocket of her tight black jeans. "I have no idea. There was that weird stalker guy who Lana told to get lost."

Weird stalker guy? Why hadn't I heard about him? Was I really that wrapped up in my own little world? I already knew the answer—yes, I was.

"Stalker? What stalker? And more importantly, was this stalker violent?"

She shrugged. "He seemed more like a pitiful little puppy dog to me. I can't imagine him doing this, but who really knows?" She paused and straightened her head. "Are you sure I can't get this on video?"

I had to draw on every ounce of strength and politeness inside me not to scream. You know, Good Girls Rule #5: Practice patience even when you want to throttle someone. The last thing I needed right now was some stalker sneaking into the house where I was staying and leaving notes underneath a terrifyingly sharp knife. I was no Nancy Drew. I had no desire to add a little mystery to my life. I just wanted to grasp that ever-elusive peace that dangled just out of reach.

I cleared my throat, deciding to try a different approach. "Listen, it's like this. I hate video cameras. All cameras, for that matter. Like, I really hate them." They'd followed me around for months as my face had been splashed across the news. Lana promised me that she hadn't told anyone here about what happened.

Candy stared at me a moment. Did she know about my past? My cheeks reddened at the thought. She crossed her arms. "Fine. I won't make you an instant celebrity after all."

"I'm thinking I should call the cops. The note by itself may not be that threatening, but the knife definitely sends a message." As I looked at it again, fear trickled down my spine until I shivered.

"I agree. Can I stick around long enough to see what they say?"

"Aren't you allergic to Gaga?" I looked down at the perky little dog who sat at my feet.

She flicked a piece of lint from her shirt. "No, I just told Lana that so I wouldn't have to dog sit. Of course." She shrugged as if that was the most natural explanation in the world.

I sucked in a deep breath, considering my options. Finally, I settled with, "No pictures."

She grinned. "Deal."

This was one deal I hoped I didn't regret.

3

I'd envisioned coming to St. Paul, being dropped off on Lana's doorstep by one of my sister's semi-responsible friends, and fading into blissful oblivion. If I haven't already mentioned it, things were not going according to my plan. The same could be said for my entire life, I supposed.

I'd followed all the steps and done everything correctly. Kind of like the time I'd built a model airplane, one of my dad's favorite pastimes. I'd followed all of the directions. At the time, I couldn't see my work turning out to be an airplane, but I told myself I needed to finish before I'd see the big picture.

The final product looked more like a Transformer than a FW 190.

A Transformer that had been destroyed by the Decepticons, at that.

Little did I know that my life would parallel the building of that model airplane—I'd followed the rules but the end result was nothing like the picture on the box.

The police had been here fifteen minutes—an unglamorous fifteen minutes, at that. There was one uptight, middle-aged officer who'd taken my statement. Along with him was a younger guy with spiky hair and a shirt that read CSU. He was snapping some photos and dusting for fingerprints.

What had I just walked into? What was going on in Lana's house? I knew things here couldn't possibly be as normal as they first appeared, and I was right. Something was seriously *not* normal.

Why would someone leave a message like that? And who? Had Lana made someone seriously upset before she left on her trip? The message had to be intended for her. All of my "enemies" were back in Florida and preferred the public humiliation brand of justice to the "scare you out of your mind" kind.

Maybe this was a joke. That's what it had to be, I decided.

The doorbell rang, bringing me back to reality. I stomped across the room and jerked the door open, thankful for the opportunity to get away from Candy's delightful chatter with the crime-scene guy. All I'd heard was something about an opportunity she might have to be an extra on the TV show *CSI* and could he give her some pointers? I'd tuned the rest out.

I blinked at the man on the stoop and quickly took inventory of him—early thirties, short brown hair, defined biceps, trim build, and at least six feet tall. He wore faded jeans, a plain white T-shirt, and a tattoo peeked from the edge of his sleeve.

He was the kind of man women noticed—not me, of course. I mean sure, I guess by the strictest definition I had just "noticed" him, but *not noticed* him noticed him. I mean, why bother? I had no hopes of a happy ever after. My last relationship had left me tattered and bruised and done with love. Besides, in a neighborhood like this, one filled with two cars in the driveway and swing sets in the backyard, most people were married and living the American dream with two-point-four children. It was that kind of community.

He extended his hand. "I'm Cooper. Ben Cooper. You must be Lana's sister."

Ben Cooper. Lana had mentioned him. That's right. He'd taken care of Gaga since I couldn't get here until a day after Lana left—thanks to a meeting with my attorney. And he was the only other person I could think of who had a key to Lana's place. "I'm Tara, and you're just the person I want to see. The police have some questions for you."

He raised his eyebrows, his blue eyes widening. "The police?"

18

"I'll let them explain." I extended my hand, inviting him inside, and nearly slapped Candy inadvertently in the process.

Cooper stepped in the house. I caught the brief scent of sawdust and gasoline, as if he'd been working in a garage somewhere. The smell was surprisingly pleasant. The uniformed officer greeted him and pulled him aside to ask questions.

"He's Lana's hottie neighbor," Candy whispered, wagging her eyebrows up and down. From the way he'd simply nodded to Candy, I assumed they hadn't met before, that she'd simply admired him from afar.

He was handsome. He also had a wedding band on his finger, which was no surprise. Middle-class neighborhoods weren't exactly a hub for singles. No, they were a hub for tandem bikes with baby seats on the back, and adorable little tricycles left haphazardly on sidewalks filled with chalk drawings and wildflower bouquets picked by chubby little hands.

I edged closer, wanting to hear what Ben Cooper had to say. Maybe he had some of the answers we needed. I could hope. Candy edged closer with me. Perhaps digging deeper into her character study for a possible role on *CSI*? Or was Candy simply the type of person who liked to insert herself everywhere and anywhere she had the chance?

Cooper's hands went to his hips as he addressed the officer. "I stopped by this morning. I didn't go into the kitchen. I just unlocked the back door, let the dog out, and then put her back inside a few minutes later."

The officer shifted. "Nothing appeared to be out of place?"

Cooper shrugged. "I didn't go poking around, but no. Everything seemed normal. The dog didn't seem agitated or give any sign of distress."

"And the door was locked when you arrived, and you locked it before you left?"

"That's correct."

"Have you seen anyone around the neighborhood acting strangely?"

Cooper shifted, his fingers still splayed across his hips. "As I'm sure you know, we have had a couple of break-ins in the area recently. Last I heard, they hadn't caught the guys who did it."

The officer closed his notebook. "You'll be around if we have any more questions?"

"Absolutely."

After they wrapped up, Cooper strode back over to me. "What a welcome to the neighborhood. Lana know about this yet?"

"I tried to call her, but she didn't answer. Maybe it's just as well."

"I'll be right next door if you need anything while you're here."

I couldn't help but smile. "I appreciate that." But I wouldn't be needing anything except some alone time.

At that precise moment, my contact lens began half-burning, half-popping out of my eye. My eyelid fluttered as I struggled not to lose the lens. Cooper stared at me, his head tilted and eyes narrowed in confusion.

What if he thinks I'm flirting with him? The thought made me sputter, all while my eyelid continued to blink with rapid-fire precision. Certain that my cheeks were red and that Ben Cooper thought I was the world's worst winker, I nodded toward the hallway and mumbled something about dust.

I escaped into the bathroom and flipped on the lights. I stepped toward the vanity and stopped cold.

I blinked—partially on purpose, certain I was seeing things.

There, on the bathroom mirror, waited another message. I peered closer, ignoring the signals that caused alarm to burst like boiling water in my head. The words looked to be written in slime—runny, oozy, gooey slime.

Help.

A handprint smeared beside the word, like someone had tried to reach through the mirror in desperation. My moment of courage wore off, and trembles claimed my muscles. I took a step back and fell against the toilet, knocking off a small city of cosmetics before sliding to the floor.

"Uh, guys, you're going to want to see this."

Candy swung around the doorway, her eyebrows knitting together as she spotted me. "I'm going to want to see you looking like an *island* in the middle of a sea of overpriced cosmetics?" She deadpanned the question, her lips parting in confusion.

I shook my head, my cheeks heating again as I realized my head was resting on the back of the toilet and various bottles laid around my shorts-clad legs—which needed to be shaved—all while my eye fluttered and watered, probably sending mascara down my cheek.

I nodded behind her. Her gaze landed on the mirror.

She gasped and stepped out of the bathroom. Her eyes were wide—with fear or in awe? I wasn't sure.

She pointed to the mirror, her voice trembling. Fear. Definitely fear. "I never thought I'd see that with my own eyes."

Chills continued to seep into every fiber of my being. "See what?" Leftovers from the Kid's Choice Awards on Lana's bathroom mirror?

"Ectoplasm."

Ectoplasm. As in ghostly, paranormal ooze?

I closed my eyes, suddenly not caring about my contact or my legs or the mess around me. It was like some kind of wicked game of Clue was being played, and I'd been forced to participate.

It was the ghost in the kitchen with a butcher knife, I heard myself saying.

4

The police ushered me out of the room so they could do their thing. Candy lingered close to the bathroom, her phone out as she probably updated her social media sites with ectoplasmic photos or, at least, some great tales that were sure to entertain others at my expense.

Which left me in the living room with Ben Cooper and Gaga.

"I'm sure there's a logical explanation," he said. His tone acknowledged that he knew how lame he sounded. What exactly did you say to comfort someone in a time like this? I had no idea, but assuring someone that there was a reason for the crazy around her was a good start.

I nodded. Another Good Girls Rule, of course. Better to bite your own tongue than to say something that will come back and bite you later. "A logical explanation. Of course."

"Scare tactic?" His gaze looked earnest as he rubbed his chin in thought.

"Why would someone try to scare me? No one knows me here."

He stared at me another moment, his crystal blue eyes still sincere as if he honestly wanted to help but came up blank. "They're trying to scare Lana and didn't realize that she's out of the country?"

"Unfortunate timing for me, then."

"Just lock your doors tonight."

Lock my doors? Did ghosts care about locks? Now I was thinking like a crazy person. Never would I admit it, though. "I will."

He nodded toward the door and took a step back. "I've got to go pick up my son, Austin, from his friend's house. Remember, I'm right next door if you need anything."

I nodded, understanding that he wanted nothing to do with this mess. I couldn't blame him. "Got it."

When the police left a few minutes later, Candy followed them out the door, mumbling something about having to go to work and that she'd see me on Sunday.

See me on Sunday? I didn't even ask. Nope. I closed the doors, locked them, and then stared at the house. What now? Wasn't this what I wanted? Time alone?

So why did I feel so freaked out then? Why did I actually, just for a moment, miss Candy's chatter? Should I go to a hotel for the night? Or should I tough it out at Lana's place? I would tough it out, I decided. If I could survive what I had in Florida, certainly I could survive a ghost in Minnesota.

Right?

I paced over to the bookshelf and looked at a picture of Lana and me from when we were teens. I missed those youthful days when our futures seemed so bright. When I was determined one day to be a teacher, a wife, and a mother. When I just knew my life would turn out perfectly.

There was also the small factoid that I wasn't even sure I was a Christian anymore. My doubts about God had simmered beneath the surface for a long time. Each time they tried to emerge, I shoved them down with a vengeance.

But now I was in St. Paul. Now it was time to let them boil to the surface.

My cell phone rang. I grabbed it and answered. Lana. I sank onto the couch, propping my feet up and letting my head fall back.

Her perky and loud voice sounded worse than an alarm clock right now. "What's going on, big sis? How do you like the place?"

"It's nice, Lana. Very unlike you." I'd expected something sleeker for my ever-in-vogue sister. Maybe a new condo decorated in cool tones of gray? A grungy apartment in downtown? An industrial loft near the Mississippi? She was the type of woman who'd drop $400 for a trendy new purse, all while forgoing paying her rent, so a house this normal seemed like it'd be the bane of her existence.

She laughed, the sound carefree, just like Lana. "I know. It is, isn't it? That's why I decided it was perfect."

I stared at the white ceiling and remembered the threatening note. "Listen, there are a couple of things I need to tell you."

"Me, too. Tara, you'll never believe this—Nate popped the question last night. We're getting married!"

A foreign emotion filled my chest. I realized I needed to react and forced out a congratulations. She went on and on about how he proposed and when they would get married. They'd probably have a perfect life together. Lots of children and laughter and love.

That's the way it worked for my sister. She never followed the rules. She lived for herself completely, and life had been all rainbows and blue skies.

"Tara? You still there?"

I snapped back to reality. "I'm really happy for you, Lana."

"Thanks, big sis. Listen, take care of Doggie Gaga for me. Nate and I might extend our vacation, make it more of an early honeymoon. Are you okay with that? I know we planned to spend some time together when I got back, but sometimes these things happen."

"I'll be fine, Lana. Don't worry about me." Gaga jumped in my lap, and I stroked her soft white fur.

"And don't let the ghost scare you away."

I remembered the eerie messages I'd found and stiffened. "Ghost?"

Lana laughed. "Yeah, there's a rumor that a ghost haunts the place. That's why I got the house at such a good price. Some woman died there or something. That's what the story is, at least."

I swallowed, though my saliva didn't want to go down. "Is that right?"

"Crazy, isn't it?"

"Not so much, Lana." I hugged Gaga to my chest. "Do you have any enemies?"

"More than I can count. Why?" She said it without a care in the world. Nope, she didn't give a second thought to what people said about her. Must be nice.

I told her about the note and the message on the mirror.

"Really?" She screeched, sounding fifty-percent excited and one-hundred-percent intrigued. "That's crazy. Who would do that?"

"I was hoping you could tell me that."

"I have no idea. It's creepy." She paused. "I have a couple of pretty sick friends. I'll call them and make sure they're not behind it. In the meantime, if you have any trouble, my friend Candy can help you out. She did pick you up from the airport, right?"

"I did meet her." I didn't want to sound like a tattle-tale.

"And there's this guy named Mark I want you to meet. He's super cute and just the RX you need right now."

"Not interested." I picked some stray dog hair from my shirt and shook my head as if Lana could see me.

"Oh, come on, Tara. One day, you'll have to start dating again."

"Not really. Being single isn't that bad. It beats subjecting myself to more heartache." I mentally "amened" myself, even throwing in a "you got that right, sister." Who needed actual friends when I had a whole choir in my head backing me up?

"You picked a bad one, Tara. You've got to face that. Peter was no good. Don't let him ruin your future."

Lana did not understand. At. All. "Call it what you want. I don't think I can ever trust a man enough to have a relationship again." *Girl, we don't blame you. We'd be the same way.* I loved my mental choir.

"Well, just in case you change your mind, I'll call Mark and ask him to keep an eye on you."

"Lana..." I threatened.

She laughed. "What?"

"Don't play matchmaker."

"Don't get your knickers in a knot. Sometimes you've just got to let your hair down and live a little."

I couldn't even argue with her. My mental chorus of support disappeared. "Maybe you're right."

She gasped. "Are you admitting that I could quite possibly be on to something? This is a first. Listen, sis, I've gotta run. Give Gaga a big kiss for me."

I set the phone back on its cradle and stared at it. My sister...I shook my head and laughed. Could we be more opposite?

Don't let the ghost scare you away...

My laugh faded. Ghosts? They weren't real.

Despite my logic, I really wished Lana hadn't told me that.

I yawned and pushed myself back into the couch. I'd wasted three hours flipping through TV stations, staring blankly at inanimate objects and otherwise feeling bored out of my mind. My sister subscribed to three magazines: *Vogue, TV Guide,* and the *National Enquirer.* None were really my thing. So, instead, my thoughts had done their daily replay of all of my mistakes, faults, and missteps—a nightly routine, it seemed. Some people counted sheep; I counted my mistakes one by one.

Finally, I stood. It was time for bed, that dreaded time of night where sleep made you vulnerable to the world around you. Ever since I was young, darkness and nighttime had frightened me. Still, to this day, my fears could get the best of me, especially when I was alone. Fears over creeps and crime and home invasions. The events of today only made my fears more real. Someone had been inside my home. Would they come back?

I turned off the light in the kitchen, then moved into the great room and tugged both lamps off. It was June, and I was too stubborn to turn the AC on. After all, I'd escaped the stifling heat in Florida, where opening the windows up made the house feel like a sauna. The weather here in Minnesota beckoned me to enjoy it. During the day, the house had felt perfect after I'd cracked the windows and let a gentle breeze roll through. Right now, the house was warm, but I didn't dare keep any windows up. The thought of someone cutting the screen and sneaking inside as I slept was too vivid in my mind.

Not that anyone could sneak up on me with these squeaky wooden floors, I comforted myself. The oak-stained planks might be beautiful as they stretched across the entire level, but they were old—original to the house maybe?—and every other step I took was announced with a squeak or a groan.

The light from my bedroom illuminated my path. I cracked one window by my bed, only because there was a safety latch that allowed it to stay open a mere three inches. No one could fit through that opening. A crisp breeze crept inside.

I stripped down to my underwear and a tank top, threw back the thick comforter, and crawled between the cool sheets. Once I was settled, I calmed myself by taking inventory of Lana's bedroom decor. Lana had probably been thinking of a summery white when she decorated the monotone bedroom. It boasted an alabaster comforter on a silvery, metal bed, billowy ivory curtains, paintings of pasty white roses in pale frames, a snowy-colored rug on a light oak floor. The gang at HGTV would be proud of her overall look. To me, it was all... spooky, ghost-like.

I ignored my shivers and hesitantly reached for the light by the bed. My fingers lingered on the twist. I held my breath, then turned the plastic knob and ducked under the sheet before I had time to stare the blackness in the face. My heart raced, and I listened for any suspicious sounds.

A car zoomed past on the street outside. A dog barked. The alarm clock hummed on the nightstand. The house creaked. It was just settling, I told myself. Old houses did that.

I'm still here.

The words from the note echoed in my mind. What if someone was still here? What if they were hiding in the basement or the attic or the garage? Had the police considered that? Had they checked those places?

The sheets still covered my head. I should move them down, act like a grown woman. Instead, I breathed in and out. My breath hit the silky fabric around me, warming my nose and cheeks. My hair tickled my face. My heart pounded in my ears.

I closed my eyes, willing myself to think about something else.

My hand skimmed across the empty space in the bed beside me, and I thought of Peter. It was a toss up which subject was less appealing—ghost or ex-husband. But my thoughts went where they went.

Though we'd only been married for two and a half years, I still felt like Peter should be beside me, protecting me from anything the world threw our way. That's what marriage was about, right? Being there for each other in the good times and bad. In sickness and health. In times of peace and in times of ghostly hauntings.

Everyone said we were cut from the same cloth, a perfect match. Unfortunately, they were right. We'd both cared too much about what people thought of us. When Peter had the chance to distance himself from the disaster surrounding my life, he'd done just that. I, on the other hand, had been stuck with myself.

At one time, I'd thought Peter was charismatic, confident, and righteous. Somewhere along the road, those qualities had morphed into being flighty, arrogant, and judgmental. Funny how your perspective changed with experience.

I had to admit, I hadn't been the easiest person to live with after I'd been arrested. I'd withdrawn. Bottled up my emotions, trying to hide the fact that I felt sorry for myself. I did feel sorry for myself—I'd just decided not to let anyone else know that.

Yeah, that's me. Good Girls Rule #23: Always appear strong even when your muscles are jelly. Kind of similar to wearing a girdle to look skinny and then taking it off and letting your flab flounder.

I wish now I'd cried more, opened up more, saw the counselor more than once.

Maybe things would have turned out differently if I hadn't been in denial about my problems and my marriage.

Tears wet the pillow in my cocoon, and I knew I should peek my head out of the covers. Thinking about Peter was not a good alternative to thinking about the creepy things that had happened today. But I was frozen.

The same fear haunted me every night. The fear of someone breaking into my house, watching me while I slept. I couldn't get the image out of my mind before, and I certainly couldn't now.

I forced my breathing to steady. This fear was just my overactive imagination, after all. There was nothing to be scared of. Gaga would protect me.

The thought made me smile. I tugged the sheets down and let the fresh, cooler air fill my lungs. But I still found myself holding my breath again.

On the count of three I'd open my eyes.

One.

Two.

Three.

I yanked my eyes open, and the stark-white room came into focus. It was empty. No spooky ghouls or unwanted visitors were staring at me from the foot of the bed.

The clock on the nightstand read 12:28.

I tried to relax against the mattress. When would I ever get over this childhood fear? I turned over, dug my head into the fluffy, feather pillow, and searched for the sleep that felt so elusive.

Metal clanged outside.

I tensed and gripped the covers. Was it just my imagination? No. This wasn't my imagination. Something clicked and squeaked and groaned.

I sucked in a deep breath. I knew exactly what the noise was. It was the rusty gate leading into Lana's backyard. I'd heard it earlier in the day when I'd let Gaga outside. I distinctly remembered fastening the stubborn thing. Someone was either going into or coming from my backyard.

Logic told me to peek out the window. Fear told me to freeze. Fear won.

Why would someone be entering or leaving the backyard at 12:30? Why would someone be going into the backyard at all?

I forced myself to practice yoga breathing for calm. There had to be an explanation. Maybe Cooper's little boy had tossed a toy into the yard and Cooper was going to retrieve it. That made sense.

But not at this hour.

Maybe he'd thrown something into the yard earlier and Cooper just now found the time to get it.

I convinced myself it was a plausible possibility. Tomorrow, I'd ask Cooper and he'd explain it. Then we'd have a good laugh. I'd chide myself for being so silly.

I pulled the covers tighter, listening for any more telltale sounds. It was silent. Shivers attacked my limbs as the note continued haunting me.

I'm still here.

Who? I wondered. Who was still here?

Would I live to find out the answer?

5

Lying in bed the next morning, I watched as gray turned to orange outside. The tropical colors eventually morphed into a hazy, lazy white. I remained under the covers, wishing I'd doze off again.

My head felt as if it were stuffed with tiny lead beads. When I'd finally drifted off to sleep, somewhere around 2:30, Gaga had jumped in bed with me. Of course, I'd thought it was an attacker. My heart raced for the rest of the night, yet some invisible chain had kept me in bed and unable to move.

I glanced around Lana's room again. The white did look pleasant in the sunlight. In the daytime, everything seemed so much friendlier and my fears seemed so unfounded. Still, there was the butcher knife, the note, the supposed ectoplasm, and the squeaky gate. Add that to my already-in-place fears, and I was done for.

Gaga barked at my feet. "What? You need to go outside?"

She barked again. I threw on some shorts and a robe and followed Gaga to the backdoor. The morning sunlight looked so glorious that I couldn't resist stepping outside.

My gaze meandered over the grass and patio set and garage. My perusal skidded to a halt when I saw the gate. The open gate. The noises last night hadn't been my imagination. Someone really had been in the backyard. A shiver zinged up my spine.

I walked barefoot down the brick sidewalk and closed the gate, thankful I'd followed the dog outside. Otherwise, Gaga might have run away and Lana would never forgive me. Sure, my sister acted like the dog was an accessory half of the time, hauling her around in rhinestone-studded bags and buying her designer clothing. Sometimes I thought Paris Hilton was her role model. But I did think that deep inside, the dog was Lana's baby. Otherwise, she wouldn't have left me a note, asking me to tell Gaga a bedtime story every night—not that I would ever actually do that.

I had closed the gate yesterday, hadn't I? I stared at the latch, remembering how difficult it was to force down. Yes, I'd definitely closed it.

And some ghost had opened it while I was sleeping.

"Good morning."

I half-gasped, half-screamed and threw myself back toward the house. My foot landed on a sharp rock in the process. I grabbed it, rubbing the indention. When I looked up, Cooper stared at me from the fence, amusement dancing in his eyes.

"Didn't mean to scare you."

"You didn't," I started. I dropped my foot and shook my head. "Well, you did, but not by any fault of your own."

He raised an eyebrow. "Everything okay?"

I nodded and pulled the robe closer. Though I was wearing shorts and a tank top, I felt exposed. "Fine. You?"

"Just enjoying some coffee and watching the sunrise."

"You're an early riser, huh?" When I stepped outside, it had been nine a.m. The sun probably rose three hours ago, at least.

"It's ingrained from my days as an Army Ranger."

I nodded. "You seem like a special ops guy."

"Is that a good thing or a bad thing?" Cooper raised his chunky blue mug to his lips and took a sip. I needed some coffee, I realized. As soon as possible, for that matter. It was my wonder drug, just as addictive as all those other substances I'd cautioned those younger than myself to stay away from. My urge to pump some caffeine into my system nearly had me plotting to snatch away Cooper's to take a sip. A good girl would never, ever do something like that, though, as per rule number 41. We'd just fantasize about it instead.

Cooper tilted his head, his eyes still twinkling.

"A little of both," I finally answered.

He chuckled. "At least you're honest."

I pulled my arms over my chest and drank in the fresh morning air. "Nice neighborhood. You said there'd been some break-ins?"

"A few, which is unusual for this area. I've always felt safe. I know you might have a totally different impression based on your start here. That's generous that you can dog sit for your sister. Your job must be very forgiving."

If he only knew. "That's the nice part about having the summer off from teaching." It was true. I was a teacher, and I did have the summer off. But I'd also been fired prior to that. I cleared my throat. "How about you? What do you do for a living?"

"I'm a security systems analyst. I test out security systems to see if they're as solid as they claim to be."

"Sounds interesting."

He smiled. "I enjoy it."

I cleared my throat, knowing I needed to ask him something that might make me sound like a lunatic. I decided to ask anyway. "You didn't go in my backyard last night, did you? Like at midnight or a little past?"

"I try not to make it a point to sneak into my neighbor's backyards at night."

"Is that a no?"

He smiled. "It's a no. Why?"

Because a ghost just might be haunting this place after all. I didn't say that, though. Instead, I shrugged. "Just wondering."

"Maybe your friend opened the gate when he left last night."

All moisture vanished from my throat. My eyes. My entire head, for that matter. "My friend?"

His smile disappeared, and he squinted, almost as if he were trying to read me. "I saw someone leave your porch, probably around eleven or twelve. He didn't appear to be sneaking around or acting suspiciously, so I thought you'd had someone over."

My hand went to the fence. I had to hold on to something so I wouldn't fall over from the fear that threatened to seize each of my muscles. Cooper must have thought I was a party animal like Lana. Not me. "I'm not like my sister, and I don't know anyone in Minnesota."

His blue eyes remained on me a moment, again appearing like he was trying to figure me out. Finally, he nodded slowly and decisively. "Considering everything else that's happened since you've been here, I'd be careful, Tara." There was no tease or lightness to his voice. No, this man I hardly knew looked genuinely concerned.

That realization caused chills to whiz up my spine.

What if someone had found me here? What if they were trying to scare me off, to get me out of their safe little neighborhood? Was that what this was all about?

I cleared my throat. "So this man...he just walked off my porch? Did it look like he came from inside?"

"I couldn't tell." He shook his head sympathetically.

My childhood fears seemed to come to life. "Okay, I'm sufficiently freaked out now. What should I do?"

He tilted his head. "Get a security system."

I sighed. Cooper probably had just the right one to recommend to me, too.

I'd spent most of the day catching up on my work as a virtual assistant. Since leaving the school where I'd taught, I'd been helping my father with his radio show and my uncle with his mission organization. I did things like Twitter updates, blog entries, and other online campaigns. The work had kept me out of the public eye, allowed me to earn some money, and gave me something to occupy my thoughts. I'd continue working while I was here in Minnesota.

After I'd finished my work to-do list, I'd cleaned out Lana's refrigerator, dusted the house, and swept her wood floors. I'd opened the windows and let fresh air flood inside. I'd done crossword puzzles and taken a shower.

It was only five o'clock, and I was completely out of ideas of what else to do, so I sat at Lana's kitchen table with a half-eaten peanut butter sandwich in front of me. Two dead yellow daisies had begun to wilt in a jar on the table, the sight strangely gripping. Sometimes I felt like those daisies. I'd once been cheery and bright, but the life was slowly draining out of me. I couldn't bring myself to throw the flowers away when I cleaned. Instead, I slid one from the glass jar holding it and twirled the flower between my fingers.

Had Lana's boyfriend given these to her before they left? I hoped that she'd found someone who would make her happy, who would treat her right, because being treated poorly by a spouse ranked high on my list of the quickest ways to bruise someone's spirit.

I ran my fingers down the row of petals, causing a few to flutter to the floor. Gingerly, I plucked one of the yellow petals that had still been hanging on.

"He loves me," I whispered, dropping the delicate leaf to the ground.

I plucked another one. "He loves me not."

I went through several more and then glanced down at the confetti-like petals at my feet. I didn't bother to pick them up—not now, at least. I would in a few minutes because I was a self-professed neat freak who liked everything to be in place. I liked my house clean, my outfits neat, and my schedule planned.

Peter had never understood my need for order. He said I just didn't get it. In all truthfulness, I still didn't get it. I didn't get how we went so wrong so quickly. I didn't get how the only thing I've ever failed at was the one thing most important to me.

I plucked another petal. "He loves me."

All I'd ever wanted was to get married. I wanted to be a mom with lots of kids and a minivan. I wanted to clip coupons and sort through hand-me-downs.

After high school, I'd gone off to a Christian university to get my degree in education. I'd had big dreams of meeting my husband there, and I figured he'd be someone like my dad—strong, committed, and respected. While in college, I began volunteering with a youth organization that promoted abstinence before marriage. That's where I'd met Peter.

He was a volunteer also. He was a business major at a secular university an hour away. He'd been introduced to Christ through a

Christian organization at his school. God had turned his life around, and he'd jumped right into whatever his cause-of-the-moment was. It had worked to my advantage at the time because transforming himself from his old life of worldliness to a new life of purity had been Peter's one goal.

I'd embodied that purity as I'd been an outspoken promoter of saving yourself for marriage. Peter had never lived a wild life before he'd become a Christian, but he'd lived by a different set of values—values that led him to drink and begin keeping a list of all the women he'd ever been with. He'd turned himself around, though.

We'd dated the standard year and had a respectable six-month engagement. I shook my head as I remembered our early days together. Peter wasn't a bad person. He didn't grow up with the same foundation I had. His parents had been divorced. They didn't go to church. He'd never been shown what to do when the going got rough.

Maybe I should have seen the signs. Just because we'd made so much sense on paper didn't mean we'd actually work in real life. He'd always had a bit of a temper underneath his smooth exterior. He liked to jump around from job to job, from commitment to commitment. That should have given me a clue.

No one ever thought that I would get divorced. I had a good head on my shoulders and a bright future ahead. Peter fit right into that future, and everyone said we made the perfect couple.

I dropped a yellow piece of the flower to the floor. "He loves me not."

Then life had fallen apart. Until then, I'd always considered myself a little better than everyone else—the rule breakers. No, I never told them they were sinners or that they should have tried harder to do right. I never told them they were living halfheartedly with one foot on both sides of the fence. But in the secret room of my mind, I'd thought it. I knew God loved me just a little more because I followed all the rules. I was a good girl.

I rubbed the velvety flower between my fingers. "He loves me."

Now I knew what people thought of me. I knew they thought they were just a little better than I was.

I guessed they were, and I guessed I deserved every one of their judgmental thoughts. I dropped the final petal. "He loves me not."

No, I wasn't talking about Peter's love.
I was talking about God's.

The living room at the front of the house had no curtains, just unadorned windows that exposed my train-wreck-in-progress life for all to see. I felt like a goldfish with no place to hide in my fish bowl, a feeling that should be familiar given that my dad was a pastor.

As evening fell, I turned my thoughts to those windows. I should put some sheets across them. Even the thought of getting that close to the glass, of not knowing what lurked in the darkness on the other side of those panes, made my breathing shallow. Visions from the slasher movie *Friday the 13th*, the scene where the killer had jumped through the window at the end, wouldn't leave my thoughts. It had been my sister's idea to watch the movie and now, fourteen years later, I still couldn't get it out of my mind.

Then again, maybe it wasn't what was on the outside of my windows I should be worried about. Maybe it was the ghost living inside these walls.

I rolled my eyes. Ghosts were for people who believed in hocus-pocus. Not me.

Still, a cold shiver breezed down my arm, and I swallowed, imagining an invisible being watching my every move, prickling my skin with its presence.

Had someone really died in the house? If so, how? What was it that Lana had said? They were murdered?

I shuddered and pictured a woman sleeping in bed at night, waking to find a man standing over her. Before she can react, he's strangling her. Panic rips through the woman. She gasps for breath but finds none. Worst yet, she recognizes the man. She knows her killer—

Pounding sounded in the distance. The woman! She'd come back to find the person who took her life. I shrieked and jumped behind the doorframe.

"Tara? It's me. Cooper."

Slowly, my grip loosened from the molding around the door. I straightened, feeling foolish.

Of course it was someone knocking on the door, not a spirit from the afterlife. What was wrong with me?

I brushed my hair out of my eyes and gathered my wits. The floor squeaked as I went to let Cooper inside. When I pulled the door open, my neighbor stood there with twinkling eyes.

"Everything okay?" He leaned against the door with his arms crossed, looking at me as if I belonged in a loony bin. Maybe I did.

"Everything's just fine."

"I hope I didn't scare you."

"Scare me? Why would you think that?"

"I thought I heard a scream."

"Interesting." I gulped and opened the door wider. "Would you like to come in?"

He stepped into the house, his gaze scanning the living room as if he thought I really did have a stash of guys hiding somewhere, just waiting to sneak out past midnight. "I thought, just to be safe, that I'd come and check things out while my son is playing with the neighbor across the street." He shrugged, his eyes back on me. "You know, with everything that's happened and all."

"Feel free."

He began walking the perimeter of the house, checking to make sure the windows were latched and the doors locked properly. "You use these deadbolts at night, correct?"

"I wouldn't dream of doing otherwise."

He examined one. "They look sturdy. A criminal would have a hard time getting past one of these." He continued on. "You might want to consider trimming the hedges in front of the house."

"I was thinking about tearing them out." I had to do something to occupy myself while I was here, and re-doing Lana's flowerbeds just might to do the trick.

He sent me a glance over his shoulder. "Not a bad idea. It also keeps varmints away from your house. Mind if I check out the basement?"

"Be my guest."

He thumped down the steep steps and ducked his head to avoid hitting it against the low overhang. I followed behind, dreading the voyage down. What was it about basements that were so spooky? The dim lighting, the low ceilings, the various nooks and hiding places, all made my imagination race. I could already feel hands reaching for my ankles as I crept downward. I could picture a madman jumping out as I opened a storage door. I could smell the decay of rotting flesh buried behind a hidden plank.

A shrill scream rang out. I thought of a demon escaping from hell and shrieked myself. Then I realized it was just Cooper opening a window. He raised an eyebrow.

"You're kind of on edge tonight, huh?" The hinges of the narrow window screamed again as Cooper pulled against them.

"You could say that." I covered my warm cheeks with my fingers. I remained where I was while he checked the rest of the basement. I pinched the bridge of my nose, forcing my lungs to expand and deflate evenly.

Cooper approached after jiggling the last window. "Everything looks safe. There are a few extra things you could do for security measures, though."

I moved my hands away from my face and raised my chin, determined to appear normal. I cleared my throat. "Such as?"

"You could get an outside motion-activated light." He started back upstairs and I followed. "You could also get window film to put over the glass. It makes it difficult for intruders to break the glass."

"I've never heard of it."

He paused at the top. "Of course, your biggest alert system is going to be this floor. You can't take a step on it without being heard."

"That's both comforting and disturbing."

Cooper turned to face me. "You going to be okay?"

Instead of pouring out all my nighttime fears, I nodded. "I've got squeaky floors. What more could I ask for?"

"Look, I don't know who that was walking off your porch last night. I wouldn't lose too much sleep over it. Besides, if you need anything, I'm right next door." He handed me a business card. "Or you could just call me."

"Thanks for everything, Cooper."

He smiled, and wrinkles creased the corners of his eyes. "I'll see you later, Tara."

The smile faded from my lips the moment the door shut and Cooper was gone. Silence surrounded me, and the bare windows stared at me like a peeping Tom. I took a step toward the couch and the floor groaned.

My pace quickened and I dove for the couch, nestling myself between the cushions and pulling a blanket to my shoulders.

What exactly did my sister mean about that ghost she mentioned? What had gone on between the walls of this house? Most importantly, did I really want to know? Probably not.

I turned the TV on and flipped through the stations. Eerie music from a made-for-television mystery floated from the surround sound. I quickly flipped stations and found a sit-com. I watched it until my eyes began to lose the fight to stay open.

I clicked the TV off, and silence surrounded me like a hungry pack of wolves. After crossing the room, I flipped the lights off and darted into my bedroom, Gaga right on my heels. I peeled off my clothes and crawled into bed, treasuring the security from the light on the nightstand.

Gaga jumped in bed with me and nosed under the covers. I stared at the light, knowing if I left it on I wouldn't sleep, but if I turned if off I wouldn't catch any Zs either. My arm felt bound with weights as I reached toward the switch. As it flickered out, I pressed my head into the pillow.

I felt more like a six-year-old than a twenty-six-year-old.

I closed my eyes. The craziness of yesterday was behind me. Certainly, the rest of my stay here would uneventful. Certainly.

I drew in a deep breath, trying to will some calmness into my thoughts.

That's when I heard the scratch at my window.

6

Each scratch tightened my nerves. Was that someone trying to cut the screen and get inside? Tomorrow I had to turn the AC on. No more of this crazy, enjoy-the-fresh-air ideology. No, I needed Freon-charged cool air blowing through these vents and each window locked down tightly and securely. Just because the neighborhood looked all perfect didn't mean it was.

Especially if there was a ghost.

I shook my head, noticing the sweat across my forehead. A ghost? Did ghosts scratch at windows? I doubted it.

The *Ghostbusters* theme song began repeating in my head. *Who you gonna call?*

That was my problem. I had no one to call. No family here, no friends, not even some crazy local ghostbusters. I sighed. This was getting me nowhere.

I suddenly didn't want to be alone. I'd never wanted to be alone, but right now especially I'd do anything to have a friend with me, so I could talk through this crazy situation. I felt like I was being pulled into some kind of dark abyss. My soul was flailing and reaching for help that wasn't there.

I took a few deep breaths. I was going to get through this. I just needed to control my thoughts and stop singing that stupid *Ghostbusters* theme song.

I closed my eyes, beyond frustrated with myself. I needed help. Serious help.

And answers.

Ghosts couldn't plunge knives into cutting boards or unlock gates or scratch windows...could they?

But a burglar could. Or some sicko bent on scaring someone. Like Lana's stalker. Like the people who'd chanted "crucify her" back in Miami. I mean, I had gotten some death threats. Had someone followed me here? If so, they'd been smart. I could disappear here in Minnesota and no one would notice for days.

The scratch raked across the window screen again, stretching my nerves tight. And immobilizing me. Some people might check out the sound. Not me. I couldn't move. I could hardly breathe.

A loud boom cracked the air. I screamed and pulled the covers over my head. Gaga also panicked and nosed under the covers with me, letting out a small whine.

Thunder. That was thunder. I laughed but only for a moment. My heart had sped and now slowed—but not to a normal beat. Its rhythm was still erratic, and the fact that I was so aware of each beat only increased my anxiety.

I pulled the covers down, just below my eyes. I could hardly hear anything else over the pounding of my heart in my ears. I thought of Poe' story "The Telltale Heart." My own heart was telling its own tale right now, a tale of living in fear.

Lightning lit the room in an electric shade of blue-white. I half expected the light to reveal someone standing in the room, staring at me with ghastly white skin, a hollow look in their eyes, and a butcher knife in their hand.

I should have never let Lana convince me to watch all of those scary movies, movies that I'd claimed had no effect on me. Obviously, they did because my subconscious pulled them to the surface at the absolute worst times. Like now.

Thunder boomed again, causing another squeal of horror to escape. At least Cooper wasn't around this time to see or hear me embarrass myself. No, he was probably at home, cuddled in bed with his wife. Had Austin woken up and ran to jump in bed with them?

The thought twisted my heart. That's what I had wanted. A warm, cozy little family.

Instead, I was hiding like a nine-year-old in a haunted house—alone. Without anyone to tell me things would be okay. Without faith in God that everything would somehow work out for the best.

How pathetic.

Thunder rumbled. Lightning flashed. Rain pounded the roof. I straightened at another sound. What was that?

Music?

The sound was soft. A guitar maybe? Playing a little lullaby?

But where was the music coming from? It almost sounded like it came from the guest bedroom.

I shook my head. No, not the guest bedroom. That wouldn't be possible.

Chills prickled my skin, fear tightened my lungs and sent my heart racing.

And what about the scratching? What was the scratching? Should I call the police? And tell them what—that a ghost was haunting my home?

I looked like a ghost myself when I glanced into the mirror the next morning. Okay, it was actually closer to noon than morning, but who was keeping track? Bags hung beneath my eyes, and my skin looked pale.

At least there wasn't an eerie message on the bathroom mirror. I'd count the victories, however small they were. And, right now, that was a victory.

I splashed water on my face, dried it, and then stepped into the short hallway. I stared at the door on the other side. It was the guest bedroom. I hadn't been in there yet. I'd had no reason.

But I had heard music last night, and I didn't know where it came from. That room was my best guess.

Even though the storm from last night was long gone and bright sunny skies lit the house, I couldn't escape my fear. But pride wouldn't allow me to escape the problems of this house either. I was stronger than this. I'd been defeated in a lot of ways.

But I wouldn't be driven away by a ghost. No, if I could face this ghost here then I could also face the demons of my past. Even if it killed me.

Speaking of demons…I shook my head, squeezing out the images of Satan's minions and spiritual attacks. I couldn't go there.

No, there was a logical explanation for all of this. Not a supernatural reason. A *logical* one.

I put my hand on the doorknob, wondering what waited on the other side. Nothing. Nothing waited there. I'd just been hearing things. Or a car had parked outside and its music had drifted into my home in between bursts of thunder. Maybe an alarm clock, programmed to play music, had gone off in the middle of the night.

I drew in a deep breath. There was no better time to find out than now. I twisted the knob and the door creaked open. Creaky floors and creaky doors.

My throat felt dry as I got a glimpse of the room. *Look for a radio. A radio.* My gaze scanned the furnishings. A spare bed. Spare dresser. Clear plastic tubs full of clothes. A bookshelf stuffed with hardbacks.

No alarm clock.

No radio.

My breathing labored as I crept across the floor. That stubborn floor gave out another squeak, as if just to spite me. I touched the closet door. Last place to check in the room. Why did I half expect someone to fly out as soon as I opened the door? Or to see a penetrating blackness on the other side, a darkness so deep it might reach out and grab me?

Get a grip, Tara. Open the door. Get it over with.

Before I could psyche myself out anymore, I yanked the door open. I released the breath I held as I saw the space was jammed full of clothes.

I laughed at myself, at my foolishness.

I'd never realized just how big of an imagination I had.

I started to close the door when, for good measure, I shoved a few dresses and suits out of the way. Shoes at the bottom of the closet came into view. One final nudge in the corner stopped me cold.

I dropped the dresses and took a step back. It couldn't be. But it was. A guitar.

7

At that precise moment, a knock sounded at the front door. I rushed from the room, knocking off a vase in route. The crystal container crashed to the floor and shattered into hundreds of pieces. I'd clean that up later. I reached into the bathroom, grabbed a robe to throw over my scant pajamas and yelled, "Coming!"

Would this be more bad news? The police coming to confirm that some extraterrestrial being had left the knife and that the slime on my bathroom window was nothing of this world?

Or perhaps my ever-present fear of the paparazzi would be realized?

Nope. It was Candy, standing at the door popping bubbles with her chewing gum and twirling her hair.

"Hey, Bermuda," she muttered with a grin. "Wassup?"

"Bermuda?"

"You know, an island." She grinned.

"Funny," I mumbled.

"You ready for Sunday brunch?"

"Sunday brunch?" I'd planned on working on my sister's flowerbeds today, then cleaning her baseboards and alphabetizing her DVD collection.

Candy shrugged. "It's a weekly tradition."

"Having brunch with Lana is. Lana is in Tuscany."

"Yeah, but you're here."

I thought about my options. Stay here in the house with a guitar that plays by itself at night or go to brunch with Candy. I nodded, decision made.

I rushed back into the bedroom, threw on some clothes, and hurried through everything else I had to do—minus the shower. Finally I met Candy at the door. I glanced at her motorcycle as I stepped out. "We're not taking that."

"No, we can walk, actually. The place we frequent is just a few blocks over on Eighth Street."

I'd noticed a gift shop, a sandwich joint, and a coffee place, part of a row of businesses as I pulled into the neighborhood. I'd hoped I might have the opportunity to frequent some of them before I left. The high-rise buildings of St. Paul rose in the distance. The cab driver had told me that the Mississippi wasn't that far away, either. I had to give Lana credit. She'd picked a great location.

I glanced back at Cooper's house as we started toward the sidewalk. His car was gone. Church maybe? I wondered if he was the church type. I'd be lying if I didn't admit that I felt a little guilty not being at church myself. I just couldn't bring myself to go because, if I did, it would simply be out of obligation, to keep a long-standing tradition going. That was no reason to attend church, and I knew that. I dreaded the eventuality of watching my mother freak out when I confessed.

The sun warmed my skin, but a breeze made it bearable. My loafers hit the cement, a soft thud compared to the clack of Candy's spiky heels. I supposed that in church circles, Candy would be known as "worldly." And I supposed in Candy's circles, I'd be known as a prude.

Candy popped another bubble with her chewing gum. "I totally tried to friend you on Facebook last night, but I couldn't find you."

I'd deleted my account. "Yeah, I consider social media a big time waster."

"I do believe you're the only person I've ever met in her twenties who's said that."

We walked into a little dive with only eight tables and a breakfast counter. The outdated decorations left a lot to be desired, but at least the place looked clean. We sat at a corner table and ordered our food.

"So, any more ghostly sightings or evidence?" She took a long sip of her orange juice, her eyes lit with curiosity over the rim of the glass.

Now that she mentioned it, I could really use someone to chat with about what I'd experienced. Candy already seemed crazy, so maybe I wouldn't feel so off my rocker if I told her about the music. I wiped the corners of my mouth with a napkin. "Something strange did happen."

Her eyes widened. "Tell, tell."

I licked my lips, gathering my courage before admitting what was sure to sound unbelievable. "My first night here I heard someone open the gate leading into the backyard. Then last night when I was in bed, I heard someone playing the guitar in the other room."

She plunked her glass back on the table and her lips parted slightly as she stared at me. "What do you mean playing the guitar? Like, someone snuck in and just started playing?"

I shrugged, wishing I had an explanation. "I don't know. It was weird, but I clearly heard some strands from a guitar. I didn't even know Lana had a guitar in the house."

"Are you sure she does?"

Chills danced up my skin again. It was the AC, I told myself. Just the AC. "I found it in the guest room. In the closet."

"She's never mentioned that before."

"I'll ask her next time she calls. She told me something about a lady who was murdered in the house. You know anything about that?" Tension mounted between my shoulders as I waited for her answer.

Her bottom lip dropped and she shook her head. "No way...I can't believe Lana didn't tell me that. Are you for real?"

"That's what Lana said. Maybe she was yanking my chain."

Candy leaned closer, as if conspiring some devious plan. "You know, I have a friend who's one of the producers for *Ghost Chasers*. I could call him, see if they could come out to your house and do an investigation."

Ghost Chasers? The TV show? I shook my head forcefully. "No, absolutely not."

"Why not? They can do these thermal heat imaging tests and these electronic voice recordings that will prove whether or not a paranormal being is living in Lana's house with you."

"A paranormal being?" I realized I started to consider the possibility and stopped, shaking my head. "No. There's an explanation. Something logical." I just had absolutely no idea what it was.

She raised her eyebrows as the waitress set down plates of steaming eggs, bacon, biscuits and hash browns. Not good for my waist, but extremely good for my appetite.

I started to bow my head and pray but stopped myself. Old habits. They were like an ex-boyfriend that wouldn't go away. Or a ghost. Or a bad reputation, for that matter. The list could go on and on.

"You should seriously think about it. It would be crazy fun to have them come out. I've never done a paranormal investigation before."

"No." That just sounded like a bad idea any way I looked at it.

"Think about it."

"Fine." I took my first bite of over-easy egg, ready to put that conversation behind me. "So, if you're this into all of this Hollywood stuff, why do you live in Minnesota?"

"I decided I wanted to be the big fish in a small pond. I've done lots of local commercials and I'm really active on the Internet. *Access Entertainment* actually featured me once as an Internet celebrity to watch out for."

Impressive. I took another bite of egg and realized it needed some salt. I quickly remedied that problem. "What kind of stuff do you do on the Internet?"

"I've done lots of stuff, but I'm mostly known for doing parodies and man-on-the-street interviews. I've organized two flashmobs. My blog and YouTube channel are called iCandy."

"I'll have to check out some of your stuff sometime."

Candy studied me for a moment as she tore off a piece of her bagel. "Your sister said you're a blogger too? Something about ten-thousand followers or something. Not bad for a novice."

"I used to be a blogger. Not anymore." I'd taken the blog off-line, and, most likely, I'd delete it completely. I just couldn't bring myself to do that yet. That blog had been my masterpiece, my legacy. At least, that's what I'd thought at one time.

Someone stopped beside our table. I looked up, expecting to see our fifty-something waitress standing there. Instead, my gaze continued climbing upward at the six-foot-plus man standing there with a broad grin across his face. And he was staring at me.

Candy slapped her hands on the table and stood. "If it isn't Mark Champion."

"Hey, sugar." He gave her a hug, but his gaze lingered on me. "Who is this fine piece of work with you?"

"This is Lana's sister, Tara. You gotta remember Lana telling us that she was coming."

He stepped back and extended his hand. "I'm Mark. Pleasure to meet you."

Fine piece of work? Was that a compliment, or had the women's movement just traveled back in time several decades? I reached for his hand, fussing at myself for the flutters I felt in my stomach.

Mark Champion. The man Lana wanted to fix me up with. He was certainly handsome enough in a big, overblown way. Meaty muscles, tight T-shirt, gelled hair, a smile that I was quite certain showed off veneers. I cleared my throat. "Same here. Nice to meet you also."

He nodded with approval. "Tara. I like that name."

Why was I blushing? "Thank you."

"Sorry to stare. I'm sure you're used to it, aren't you? Someone as pretty as you."

Where did this man come from? Was he always so over-the-top when he flirted? Even scarier, was it working? "It's been awhile, actually." The last man who'd hit on me had been a weirdo who recognized me from the news. He'd actually enjoyed the negative coverage I'd been receiving.

"That's too bad." Mark nodded toward the kitchen area. "Listen, I'm about to start my shift. I'll see you two tonight at the rave, though, right?"

You two? A rave? What in the world was he thinking? I shook my head. "I'm not a rave type of girl." What was a rave exactly? A big party with electronic music and dancing and lots of alcohol?

He smiled again. "You could be. You should give it a shot. It would be fun."

Fun? Wasn't fun making cookies for the residents of a local nursing home? Or going on mission trips and leading children in Mexico in songs about how much God loves them? Or sitting around a campfire and talking about Jesus?

Fun was certainly not a rave.

He winked. "You should come hang out. We'll be gentle on you your first time."

"Gentle on me?" I'd reduced myself to repeating everything he said.

"Think about it."

I would not be thinking about it, I thought as he walked away. Even with my failures, I still had some standards to live by.

As soon as he was out of earshot, Candy raised her eyebrows at me. "That was fast."

"What was fast?" Me rejecting the rave?

"That you caught his eye. He's a hot commodity in the area, you know. Businesses have actually paid him to show up at their parties."

"Why in the world would they do that?"

"If Lana is Party Girl, then he's Party Boy. He has an entourage with him wherever he goes. He brings in crowds."

"Why?" I wiped my mouth, suddenly fearful that I had toast crumbs on my chin.

"Did you see him?"

"Handsome faces are a dime a dozen."

She rolled her eyes. "Sure. Okay, it's like this. He played college football for a while. He got canned because of some knee injury or something. I don't know. Then he was cast on one of those survival shows. He didn't win but he did get some endorsement deals from it."

"Why is he a waiter then?"

"The party lifestyle isn't cheap. He blew through all of that money pretty quickly. Don't worry. He'll get more deals and quit this job. When that money dries up, he'll find some more part-time work. It's the nature of the business."

I leaned back and chewed on her words. His story wasn't that much different than Lana's, I supposed. Lana was the type of girl who got noticed wherever she went—she always had been and always would. Sometimes that came out in positive ways—like when she was a cheerleader. Other times it came out negative ways—like when she danced on tables at restaurants on a dare.

In college, she auditioned for *Sunset House*, a reality TV show where people lived and partied together for three months while cameras captured their every drunken move. She became an instant sensation when her cutthroat abilities and unwavering deception pushed her to the top and she won.

She stayed in L.A. for a few years, trying to keep her reality TV star shining bright, but it had eventually dimmed. She followed a boy out to St. Paul. Their relationship ended after a year, but she found a job as a receptionist for a publicity and marketing firm. Then she started doing a lot of local gigs, including her biggest one as the spokesperson for a local car dealership. She'd gotten the Hummer out of the deal. She'd also done some other jobs and gotten herself jewelry, clothes, and a lifetime supply of dog food.

I had to work twice as hard at being the good daughter to make up for Lana's "heathen" lifestyle. That was only the start of my problems, though. I'd worried about everyone else when I should have been worrying about myself.

Had Lana really thought I'd be interested in someone like Mark? Sure, he was handsome. But he was the opposite of my type.

Which was probably why she thought I should go out with him. She'd always thought I was too uptight. She was probably right.

I pushed my plate away and looked up at Candy. "Ready to go?"

"We should probably pick out your outfit for the rave tonight."

I shook my head. "It's not happening, Candy. I'm not going to the rave."

"It's gonna be fun." Her voice sounded singsong.

Still, I shook my head. Nope, a girl needed standards. End of argument.

Who needed standards? Maybe I should go to the rave. Look where standards had gotten me so far. Nowhere.

That's all I could think about as I held the corner of a bed sheet up to the window frame and pressed a tack into the wall. Instant curtains, right?

What would it be like to go to a rave? I wondered as I pulled another fabric corner to the edge of the window. Why shouldn't I? I mean, it was just like one, big party, right? And I'd already been accused of being a fuddy-dud. What would it be like to step outside of my comfort zone?

No. I could never do something like that. There was walking away from my faith, and then there was embracing a hedonistic lifestyle. I needed to waver between them and not simply embrace everything I'd ever preached against.

Maybe it was time to get out of my comfort zone, to try new things. Maybe I should hang out with Candy and Mark and go to parties and "let down my hair a little," as Lana had said. I didn't have to go crazy, but I could be a casual observer. A lukewarm heathen.

I reached farther, the corner above the window barely out of reach. The stool beneath me wobbled. I shifted my weight, trying to keep my balance. I wondered if ghosts could knock stools out from underneath people's feet. They could apparently play guitars.

I shivered at the memory. Being in this house wasn't exactly working out the way I'd envisioned, which seemed to fit in with the rest of my life. But unlike the rest of my life, this house would *not* defeat me. It would be the ultimate showdown, "Tara's Last Stand" I'd call it. This would be the place where I proved I was strong.

The stool wobbled again. I'd move it closer to the window, but an overstuffed chair and iron plant stand blocked the floor. All I needed was to balance myself....

Too late. Gravity pulled me downward until I sprawled on the floor. I grabbed my arm as a burning sensation whizzed across it. When I pulled my hand back, blood stained my fingers. The plant holder. I must have scraped the edge of it on my way down.

So much for Tara's Last Stand...

I grabbed a wad of tissues from the box on the table and pressed it against my cut. *I will not freak out. I will not freak out.* Blood always had that affect on me.

First-aid kit. I needed a first-aid kit.

I kept my arm raised, trying to remember something about the dangers of bleeding out, while I ran to my sister's bathroom. I searched the cabinets, under the sink, beside the toilet. Nothing. Not even a Band-Aid. Where else would Lana keep a first-aid kit?

Arm still in the air, I searched her closet and the kitchen. Still nothing.

My wound began to ache. I sucked in a deep breath and pulled the tissues back. What I saw made my head feel light enough to float away. Blood. Lots of blood. A three-inch cut that looked deep enough that I could see things I'd never seen before.

I couldn't let this go untreated. No, I was going to have to drive to the store and get something to clean this with.

Except I felt like I could pass out.

Think, Tara. Think. There has to be another option.

Call 9-1-1? Nah, they'd just laugh at me.

Call Candy? Did I even have her number? I didn't think I did.

That's when the answer smacked me in the face. Ben Cooper. He seemed like just the type to have a first-aid kit. A really good first-aid kit, at that.

I grabbed some paper towels, covered my cut again, and then exited the house to walk toward Cooper's. My hands trembled and my knees suddenly felt weak as I pounded on his door. I thought about Jesus dying on the cross. It might seem weird, but it was my coping mechanism. Whenever I was dealt some kind of physical pain, I thought of what Jesus endured and it made me realize that things could be worse. Despite my wavering faith, thoughts of Calvary still comforted me.

A moment later, Cooper answered the door, and I forced a smile. "Do you have a first-aid kit?" I held up my arm, and my head swam when I saw blood dripping down my elbow.

He leaned in closer, moving the paper towels again and touching the skin around my scrape like he knew what he's doing. "We need to get that cleaned up."

"That's what I thought, too."

My knees suddenly felt weak. I sagged against the railing of the porch, trying to keep my balance. Pain screamed from my elbow, and wooziness circled my head.

"You okay?" Cooper cupped my other elbow as if he knew I might pass out.

I pushed myself away from the porch railing. On top of putting things in perspective with thoughts of Calvary, I also tried to avoid drama at all costs, even if it meant pretending to be okay when I wasn't. Call it a character flaw, but having a drama queen for a sister had made me like this. "I'll be fine."

I followed Cooper into a neat-as-a-pin house. I could have stepped onto the pages of *Better Homes and Gardens* the way the place was decorated. This man definitely wasn't a bachelor. Maroon walls, a lush animal print rug, and a sleek dark brown leather couch and loveseat were welcoming and homey. A little boy, probably four or five years old, played on the rug at the center of the room. He must be Austin.

I didn't have time to introduce myself now, especially not since I could pass out at any minute. Cooper waited at a hallway on my right, past a walnut, mission-style table. The room smelled of citrus-tinged linen. Any minute now, I expected Mrs. Suzy Homemaker to step from the kitchen with perfectly coiffed hair and a dishtowel draped over her shoulder.

I stepped across the hallway toward a small bathroom. Cooper waited at the sink. He turned glorious blue eyes on me and pointed to my arm.

"Let's run some water over it for a minute." He turned on the faucet, and I took a deep breath before stepping into the small space.

The scrape was deeper than I thought, and the spray from the bathroom sink burned. I wanted to squirm, but I had to keep steady, to hide the fact that blood caused me to tremble. Weaknesses were a personal no-no for me.

"You okay?" Cooper held my arm as if he knew I might jerk it away.

I nodded, as I always did. I was always okay, no matter what headed my direction.

Whatever. Even I couldn't fool myself with that way of thinking anymore.

"Squeeze my arm if you need to. I know this can't feel good."

I had no intentions of touching Cooper and definitely not squeezing his arm. My mom called it having scruples. While my arm was under the water, he rummaged around the medicine cabinet and pulled out some hydrogen peroxide.

I soaked in his features again, now that he was closer, and confirmed my earlier assessment that this was one handsome man. Where was his wife? At work? Out of town?

Before the man caught me, I looked away. Good Girls Rule #2: Never stare because it makes you look freaky.

"This might sting." He unscrewed the cap and began pouring solution down my arm. Pain burnt from my hand to my elbow. I squeezed his arm. His very muscular arm. I scolded myself for noticing—and for squeezing.

"So who's older—you or Lana? You guys could almost pass for twins."

Except that Lana liked her clothes short and tight, had a mouth like a sailor, and was rarely seen without alcohol in her hand. "We're eleven months apart. I'm older."

He smiled, the action nice and calming, as he continued to examine my wound. "So how'd you get this cut?"

"The windows. They needed shades. You know. I tried sheets instead." I wasn't sure what was wrong, but I'd lost my ability to speak in complete sentences. Maybe it had something to do with the pain screaming at me from my scraped appendage.

"Sheets?"

"Sister. Has Hummer. Not ready. To drive."

He smiled again, but it faded when he pulled out tweezers. "There's a paint chip—"

I closed my eyes, unable to watch, and squeezed his arm again. "Don't tell me. Just do it. Whatever. I don't need to know."

"There's a Target not far from here. You could probably pick up something pretty cheap there. You know, since the sheets didn't seem to work out."

I didn't open my eyes, but I was quite certain from the lilt of his voice that he was smiling. "I'll have to try that." Although, if I'd injured myself with sheets and thumbtacks, what would I do with screws and actual tools?

Note to self: Pick up first-aid kit at Target while buying shades.

"Probably a good idea to cover up those windows. You don't want to be too exposed."

Exposed. Exactly. That's how I'd felt. At least someone understood.

Of course, if I put up shades, I probably wouldn't have time to go to the rave. Not that I was going to go anyway. Some kind of curiosity made me want to go and see what it was like, to see what I was missing out on.

And it would give me some time away from the ghost living at Lana's.

Cooper dug at my arm.

"Ouch!"

He displayed the tiny sliver of paint between the tweezers. "Got it."

"Praise God," I whispered. My face immediately flushed. "And I'm not saying that in vain. I mean it with every ounce of my being."

Not that this man probably cared. Most people didn't anymore, so I didn't know why I explained myself. I wasn't even sure if I cared. But I had cared for so long. The fact was that I even confused myself on matters of spirituality right now, so explaining my feelings to anyone else would be a lesson in foolishness.

"I just need to bandage this up and you'll be set."

In gentle, swift motions, he wrapped white gauze around the wound. I noticed for the first time that he smelt like spearmint and baby shampoo, a surprisingly nice combination. "You'll need to check this every day for infection, just to be safe. You have had your tetanus shot, right?"

"Every seven years."

"Good girl."

"That's me," I mumbled.

"All done."

Our eyes met for a moment, and I realized there was something about Cooper I liked. His eyes were kind and steadfast. He was the kind of neighbor anyone would want to have.

I cleared my throat and turned my attention to little Austin, who was playing with a fire truck on the rug. "Cute boy."

"I think so."

I scanned the pictures on his bookcase and spotted a snapshot of Cooper, a baby, and a blonde. She was just the type of woman I expected to see with a man like Cooper—tanned, thin, and gorgeous. "Your wife is beautiful."

It seemed Cooper tried to smile, but failed. "Thank you."

I wondered about his reaction. Maybe they were separated, and

I'd put my foot in my mouth. "I should go and see if I can maneuver the tank my sister insists on driving."

He leaned against the bookcase, his arms crossed over his chest in a relaxed manner. "We'll drive you to Target if you want."

"Really? You don't have to do that. It's totally imposing on your day."

"You're not imposing. Besides, there are a few things I need to pick up."

"That's...really kind of you." I shifted, not wanting to ask the next question but feeling the need to anyway. "Would that be weird for your wife, though?"

Cooper looked away for a moment. "No, she's..."

Austin looked up at me with wide eyes. "She's with Jesus in heaven."

My heart dropped, while at the same time being clutched with grief. "I'm so sorry."

"You didn't know. It's okay." Cooper straightened and shoved his hands down into his pockets. "So about Target...?"

My cheeks flushed at my mistake, but Cooper didn't seem to have any hard feelings against me. Besides, I really needed to go to Target. "Yeah, that would be great. I'll grab my purse and be right out."

8

"How have your first few days here been?" Cooper leaned back, his hands draped through the steering wheel as we headed down the road in his extended-cab pickup truck. Austin sat in the backseat and had traded his fire engine for an airplane.

Cooper seemed like the type who never worried, and being around him made me feel the same way. Even as he wove in and out of the crazy drivers buzzing around us, I felt safe, like he was in control and could handle it.

Just like he'd handled his wife's death and seemed amazingly well adjusted now. I wondered what had happened? Car accident? Sickness?

He'd asked me a question, I remembered. My first few days here? They'd been terrifying, stressful, and confusing.

"Relaxing. Fun. Slightly boring. But boring is good." There I went again, not able to talk in complete sentences. I drew in a deep breath. The truck still had a newish smell to it and, as I glanced across the dash, I noted how clean it was. He'd obviously taken the time to keep the truck looking clean. Type A me could appreciate that.

He glanced at me, those ever-perceptive eyes at work again. "Boring usually means things are under control."

The pressing need for answers had me abandoning my desire to appear sane and even respectable. "Did you know the people who lived in the house before Lana?"

Cooper kept his eyes on the road. "As a matter of fact, yes, I did."

"What were they like?" I tried to sound casual and laid-back—two things I wasn't exactly known for being. As extra initiative, I relaxed my shoulders but ended up feeling like I had bad posture. I straightened again. If there was one thing I could say about my upbringing, it was that my parents had taught me about Jesus, church, and good posture.

"The Millers?" He drummed his fingers against the steering wheel a couple of beats then stopped.

I watched his controlled movements, the easy stretch of his muscles as he maneuvered the steering wheel while navigating through thick traffic. I soaked in his masculine profile and the spectacular balance of his features. He dressed casually in a black T-shirt and jeans. His hair had a slight touch of curl, but was cropped tightly and had a natural, messy look to it. Ben Cooper was not just good-looking. He was really good-looking, the type of man who seemed like every girl's type. He'd make some woman very happy one day.

Before he caught me staring, I looked away and focused on the vehicles zipping across the bland highway all around us. "Yes, the Millers. What were the Millers like?"

He shrugged. "They were a young couple. They actually found the house through an Army buddy of mine, Jimmy. He knew them from high school. They moved down here and were looking for a place to live. I told them the house next door was for sale."

I nodded, licking my lips and willing my hands to remain still and not give away my anxiousness. "Did you know them very well?"

"We had dinner with them a few times. I wouldn't say I knew them, but we were acquaintances. We just didn't connect with them, I guess. We didn't have much in common."

"What were they like?"

Cooper stared straight ahead as we bounced down the road. The sun hit his wedding ring, and I realized with clarity that Ben Cooper still loved his wife.

"They were an interesting couple. Danielle, she was into crystals and psychic readings and tarot cards, and Jeremy walked around with a permanent scowl. Sunni always said they freaked her out."

Sunni. She must have been Cooper's wife. My heart panged with sadness again. I thought divorce was hard, but having your spouse die...I couldn't even imagine.

"Why'd they move?" Either Cooper was trying to be nice and not tell me what had happened at the house or nothing had happened. I was rooting for "Nothing had happened" so that I could put all of this behind me.

Cooper drug in a deep breath and glanced in the backseat at his son. "They didn't. She...died."

The hairs on my arms bristled. "Died?"

"Died as in her husband's the number-one suspect, but the police don't have enough evidence to charge him." His voice sounded low, like he was telling me a secret. I knew he just didn't want his son to get freaked out, and I couldn't blame him.

"So he...?" I couldn't bring myself to say *killed her*. I feared the answer. I feared what had taken place in the house where I now slept. I feared believing in something I knew wasn't true. "Wow."

Cooper nodded. "Yeah."

All the moisture left my throat. So what Lana had said was true. Someone had died in that house. I needed more information. I needed to put my questions to rest. But exactly how would I do that?

"Where are all of these questions coming from?"

I shrugged and shook my head. "Would you believe me if I said I was just curious?"

"No, not really."

"I didn't think so." I heaved in a deep breath while formulating my answer. "Someone's just trying to mess with my head." I fluttered my hand in the air, trying to look like it was no big deal. "You know, the butcher knife, the note, the ectoplasm, the gate opening." I could go on, but what I'd told him was sufficient.

"What's that have to do with the Millers?"

Uh... "Nothing."

He cast another glance my way. "Nothing?"

I shrugged, one shoulder at a time while wobbling my head back and forth. "I mean, there's been speculation."

"You believe in ghosts?"

"No! Of course not." I sucked on the side of my cheek for a minute. "I mean, not normally." I sounded pathetic, and I knew it.

"Tara..."

I buried my face in my hands for a moment, feeling vulnerable and...slightly loony. "Don't judge me."

"I'm not judging. I agree that some crazy things have been happening at your place. But the cause is most likely of the human variety."

"I agree. It's like I said, someone's just playing with my head."

"Your house isn't haunted."

"Of course not," I agreed. "Ghosts aren't real."

No, they weren't real. What kind of person in their right mind thought they were?

Maybe ghosts were real. With my belief system turned upside down, maybe I should consider all possibilities. If they were real, these blinds would do me no good.

Cooper insisted on helping me put them up. Thank goodness. I know I should be all female-independent, G.I. Jane and all. But I really didn't feel like it, not at the moment, at least.

Cooper, on the other hand, seemed to know exactly what he was doing as he stood on the step stool and expertly attached little thinga-ma-doodles to the window frame and inserted the blinds between them. He'd already done three.

I watched him from the couch a moment before turning to Austin who sat next to me. "Are you in school yet?"

"I'm going to kindergarten." The blond-haired boy grinned up at me, his blue eyes sparkly and worthy of many melted hearts.

"In the fall," Cooper added.

I smiled at the boy. "You're old enough to go to school?"

He flashed a toothy grin. "I'm a big boy." He held up four fingers then popped his thumb out. "I'm five."

"Five years old? That's quite the milestone."

Austin let his Army helicopter hover over the coffee table. "What's my stone?"

"Milestone," I pronounced the word carefully. "A milestone is an important point in life."

The helicopter swooped toward the seat. "Do I get to put my stone in my room?"

"Not quite." I shared a smile with Cooper.

The bookshelf against the wall at the far end of the room had been bugging me since I got back to Lana's place. At times, I could rival the OCD TV detective Adrian Monk with my attention to details. I excused myself and walked toward the shelf, unable to ignore it any longer.

I stared at the pictures. They'd been rearranged.

I squinted, questioning myself for a moment. No, they were definitely not like I left them. Who would have rearranged the pictures, though? What was going to happen next? Would my face have a big, fat X through it?

I swallowed. Should I tell Cooper? No, I decided. I'd just sound crazy. Unease had me rattled, though.

"Last one's up." Cooper stepped back. "That should do it."

I put on my game face and looked up at the shades. Really, they were more like eye patches. Those windows had made me feel like someone's eyes were watching my every move. Finally, maybe I could have some peace. "I deeply appreciate your help today. And yesterday, for that matter. How can I repay you?"

His intense gaze, broken up with a rascally sparkle, caught mine. "Come have dinner with us tonight."

I blinked, unsure that I'd heard him correctly. "I can say thank you by eating with you?"

He grinned. "That's right. I know you're new in town, and I just happen to have enough chicken marinating that I can be a good neighbor. What do you say?"

I say that I'm a mess and that if you heard about what I'd allegedly done, you'd want me to stay far away. But the man had been kind since I'd been in town, and I didn't want to insult him as he tried to be a good neighbor. Besides, if he didn't know what people had said, then my presence at his house shouldn't offend him, right? Dinner couldn't hurt.

"I say okay. That sounds nice."

Cooper herded Austin out the front door, and I promised to be there in an hour. As soon as they left, I began second-guessing myself. Why was I feeling guilty for something I hadn't done? When would the guilt ever stop hounding me? I wasn't sure which haunting was worse—my past or this house.

I glanced up at my windows again. The shades made me feel better. I only wished it was that easy to strap blinds over my life so no one would see the mess inside. I knew that as I got to know people, I wouldn't be able to keep them from seeing the disaster my life had become. But I wanted to keep those disappointments at bay for as long as I could.

I sank into the couch and crossed my arms over my chest. Being in the house alone made me feel cold. I still couldn't shake the eerie feeling that something wasn't right here. Someone had died on this property. Been murdered even? But that didn't mean a ghost was haunting the place. No, it could very easily be a human with a sick sense of humor.

But what kind of person would do something like that? Candy? Maybe. The woman wanted attention, and this could be a way in for her.

Lana's stalker? Another possibility.

Who else would have something to gain by doing this?

That's when a horrible thought smacked me in the face.

Who else would have something to gain? How about someone trying to sell you a security system?

9

I was halfway through the cookout at Cooper's house and I still couldn't stop thinking about Cooper's possible role in all of the craziness going on at my temporary home. He'd had a key to Lana's. He could easily come and go or hide outside the window without looking too suspicious. He could be running some kind of "security experiment" on me.

But then I'd look at him and see the way he interacted with Austin, his tenderness with the boy, and question myself. Certainly he would never do anything like that.

"You look lost in thought."

I snapped my gaze back to Cooper, who sat across the table from me. Empty plates that had once held chicken, baked potatoes, and salad scattered between us, as well as some cups of soda. My contribution to the meal—a package of Golden Oreos that I'd brought with me from Florida—sat partly devoured, closer to me than Cooper. Austin played on a swing set in the yard as the sun sank low in the sky.

What could I tell him? That I was wondering if he was vile enough to scare me all so he could make money or test some security system out on me? I didn't think so. So I shrugged. "Sorry."

His gaze led me to think that he already knew me better than to believe my answers, like he could see through my façade more quickly than nearly anyone else in my life had been able to. That thought scared me, made me want to run back home and close those blinds.

It didn't matter, I reminded myself. He still had a wedding ring on. He was still in love with his dead wife. I glanced back at him, curiosity clawing at my thoughts. I couldn't go there. I couldn't be that nosy. Instead, I went with a safer subject. "So you were an Army Ranger?"

"Yeah, I thought joining the military would give me a chance to see the world."

"Did it?"

"I was over in the Middle East for Operation Enduring Freedom. After I got out, I decided to ride my Harley across the U.S."

A Harley? He and Candy should get along great, then. "I didn't see you as the motorcycle type."

"I'm not anymore. I got rid of it when I got married."

"Too dangerous?"

He pulled up the sleeve of his T-shirt and showed me a two-inch scar on his shoulder. "This is from my third accident."

"Ouch." I tried to keep my gaze on his scar and not his defined bicep. "Why'd you do it? Ride across the country?"

The sparkle left his eyes. "I think I was searching for something. I had no plan on where to go or what I was going to do on my journey, which I think reflected the state of my spirit. I thought the next town, another job, a different woman would make me happy. I was restless. The things I'd seen in the Middle East still haunt me."

"What made you stop and settle down?"

"Sunni, my wife. I came to St. Paul for a job interview, wondering if I should put an end to my journey. I met Sunni in a grocery store. We were both buying avocados and started talking about how to tell if you were buying a ripe one."

I smiled, despite the stab of sadness I felt, and made a mental note to never eat avocados around him. "Did you ask her out right then and there?"

"We left the grocery store together." A mournful smile grazed his lips. "We got married three months later."

"Love at first sight, huh?"

"Love is a nice way of saying it." He looked at me, a half smile on his face. "I'm pretty hopeless, huh?"

I shook my head, my reaction surprisingly honest. "It's refreshing, actually. Most people try to cover up their pasts, to smooth over any rough edges. Either that, or they flaunt it. You seem authentic, and I appreciate that." I could use some pointers, for that matter.

"I've made my share of mistakes. Had my wild days. Done plenty of things I regret."

I held my hands up as if displayed the grand prize on a game show. "But look at you now."

"Still messed up but saved by grace." A winsome smile flashed across his face.

"Can I be nosy for a moment, Cooper?"

"I'm an open book. Go ahead."

I shifted. "What happened to your wife?"

He looked off in the distance. A breeze swept through and ruffled his hair and brought with it the scent of our leftover food. I just stared at Cooper, waiting to hear his story. Not many people in their early thirties were widowed already. The notion seemed tragic. The notion *was* tragic.

He still didn't glance at me as he started. "When they did the C-section they found a tumor the size of a baseball. The doctors tried to remove it, but it was too far advanced. She died four weeks later." Though he said it with the utmost control—even tones and relaxed shoulders—I still saw his pain. I wanted to reach out and touch his hand but didn't. I didn't know him well enough.

"That's awful." It was all I could think to say.

He leaned back, finally turning toward me. "It was awful, but she's in a better place now. A place with no pain or suffering." He glanced back at Austin and smiled. "And I still have Austin. His smile reminds me of Sunni."

"Life can really throw curve balls sometimes, huh?"

"You speak about it like you know."

Half of my lip tugged up in a knowing smile. How did he see

through to me so easily? "I do." How much did I tell him? He'd just shared a heartbreaking story, so I had to say something. "I'm divorced," I finally offered.

"How long?"

"One year and nine months since we separated. Eleven months since the divorce became final." I'd refused to sign the papers for a long time, until I finally realized I had no choice. I had to let go and give up on the hope that things would somehow work out for the two of us. I had to accept my failure.

"Any children?"

"No. We were only married two years."

"Two years isn't a long time."

"No, it's not. But it was long enough for my ex-husband to decide he didn't love me." The words still stung, even after two years. I looked away, ashamed that I'd said the words aloud. I've always tried to brush things over, make it seems like the divorce didn't affect me. Admitting that my ex had stopped loving me sounded pathetic. I wished to take the words back but couldn't.

"What really brings you to St. Paul? I'd guess it was to visit your sister, but your sister is halfway across the globe. Certainly she could have found someone else to dog sit..."

I hesitated. "There's no easy answer to the question, actually."

"In life, there rarely is." His gaze held mine for a moment and understanding passed between us. No, Cooper hadn't staged everything that had happened as a way to manipulate me into using his business. He wasn't that type of guy. Guilt assaulted me that I'd even thought he might be.

A voice drifted from the distance and cut our conversation short. "Hey, Fiji! Are you home?" Without seeing any faces, I already knew who it was. Candy.

If she described me as an island, maybe I should describe her as a different sweet treat based on her mood. Today, since she'd shown up unexpectedly and without invitation, made her seem like a cheap box of chocolates brought by an unwanted pursuer.

Cooper looked at me, and I shrugged again. What was she doing here? Didn't normal people simply knock quietly and leave when no one answered? I sucked in a breath, trying to figure out what to do. Ignore her? Or see what she wanted? I shouldn't be so torn, but I was.

Before I could fully decide, I heard the squeaky gate cry out in all of its agony. And there was Candy, walking into the backyard with... Mark Champion beside her. She wore platform boots that stretched up to her knees and a short mini-skirt. All black, of course. It was like the cast of *Jersey Shore*, only in Minnesota. She spotted me before I could say anything. Her hand went to her hip and her head tilted dramatically to the side.

"You're not wearing that tonight, are you?" She nodded up and down at my outfit, her lips pursed.

I looked down at my T-shirt and shorts. Respectable. Modest. Comfortable. "What's wrong with what I'm wearing?"

"That's not how you dress for a rave." Her know-it-all gaze caught mine.

The rave. Of course. I shook my head, suddenly wanting to crawl underneath my chair. "I'm not going."

Her head tilted to the other side. "Oh, come on. You've gotta go. It'll be fun." Her gaze lasered in on Cooper. "You can come, too."

Cooper raised his chin nonchalantly, not at all flustered by the invitation. "It's not my scene, Candy, but thanks for the offer."

"You'll miss out if you don't." Candy's voice sounded singsong and teasing, like a girl who was used to getting her way.

Cooper smiled. "Then I'll have to miss out."

"I promise I'll watch out for you, Tara." Mark's deep voice resonated across the lawn and all the way to the tips of my fingers, which unwillingly shivered in delight. "Like I said, we'll be gentle on you your first time."

My cheeks heated. "Guys, I have other plans. I can't go."

Candy made her best pouty face. "You're being a party pooper."

"We just want to show you a good time," Mark muttered.

"I'm actually having one of those right now." I tried to keep my voice soft, as to not insult either them or Cooper.

Mark shrugged. "Have it your way then."

They turned and walked back toward the street. When I looked up, Cooper stared at me. His gaze was filled with questions. "A rave?"

"I had no intentions of going." Though I did seriously consider it for a few minutes. I didn't mention that.

His gaze remained on me, serious and...concerned? "I'm not trying to tell you what to do, but I wouldn't hang around with Mark Champion if I were you."

I straightened, curious now. "You know him?"

"I know *of* him. And not good things, at that." His gaze didn't break mine. "You're a big girl, but I just wanted to give you fair warning. That guy's bad news."

Now what did he mean by that? I wanted to ask but didn't. Instead I nodded. "Thanks for the heads up."

Besides, I had bigger fish to fry.

Because there was either a ghost in my house or I was losing my mind.

Neither possibility seemed good.

When the sky was filled with more gray than blue, I decided it was my cue to head back to Lana's. I'd much rather camp out in Cooper's backyard—and I wasn't a camping kind of girl—than go back to that house and face the eerie happenings there.

I stood and brushed imaginary crumbs from my shorts. "I appreciate dinner. It was great." I began gathering dishes. "Let me help you with these before I leave."

"Don't worry about it." He flipped his hand in the air as if shoeing me away. "I'm just glad you came."

Austin ran across the lawn toward me. "Ms. Tara, I left my helicopter in your house." His lips pulled downward in a frown.

I bent down to his level. "How about you guys walk me back home and I'll look for it?"

"Can we, Dad? Can we?"

Cooper smiled. "Of course."

Relief filled me that I wouldn't have to walk into that house alone. I really had to get a grip on these fears. But every time I closed my eyes, I heard the guitar music again. I felt those unseen eyes watching me.

I unlocked the back door, scooped up Gaga, and waited for Cooper and Austin to file inside. "I think you had it on the couch, right?"

Austin nodded.

I stepped into the living room, my gaze on the floor. Usually, tension filled me when I walked into that room. But I remembered the shades I bought and the tension left my shoulders.

Until I looked around me.

All the shades were gone.

10

I backed up until I hit a wall and pointed, words failing me.

My shades. Someone had stolen my shades. I blinked, certain that my eyes were deceiving me. But they weren't. The windows were exposed, just like my life.

"Tara?"

I couldn't speak. I just pointed. Reality hit me. Someone was watching me. They knew about the shades and didn't like them. They wanted to keep an eye on me. Even worse, they'd been inside my house.

Were they still inside my house? My eyes widened at the thought.

Cooper grasped my arm. "Tara?"

"The shades are gone, Daddy." Austin pointed also.

Cooper's gaze swept the walls. He dropped his hand from my arm—and I missed his touch—as he walked toward the windows. From the wrinkle between his brows, I'd guess that he was just as perplexed as me. He touched the facing, looked out the glass.

Finally, he turned back toward me. I hadn't realized that I'd gravitated toward Austin, but my arm had gone around his shoulders as some kind of instinct came out. I wasn't sure if that instinct was to protect Austin or comfort myself, however.

"I think you should call the police."

"They'll laugh at me. I mean, who reports stolen blinds?"

"In light of everything else that's happened, I think they'll be rightfully concerned. Someone is coming and going around here like they own the place. That's something to take note of." He stared up at the empty brackets on the window frame. "Why would someone do this? I've never seen anything like it."

I knew the answer, but I said nothing. Instead, I walked to the phone and calmly reported the crime. The dispatcher said they'd send an officer over.

Cooper had been wandering around the house as I was on the phone. As I hung up, he stopped in front of me. I could tell something was on his mind by the slow rise of his chest and the unflinching steadiness of his eyes. I twisted my head around to observe him better.

"What's wrong, Cooper?"

He crossed the floor until he stood in front of me. "There's no sign of forced entry."

"What do you mean?"

"Usually, if someone breaks into a home, there's evidence showing where he entered, how he got in. There's jimmy marks by the doorjamb or a broken window." He paused, and his stare bored into me. "There wasn't anything here."

The sinking feeling in my gut sunk even lower. "Then how did he get in?" *Please don't say it was a ghost. Please don't say it was a ghost. Please don't say—*

"Someone must have a key." He shook his head. "I'm going to have all the locks changed for you, and I'm going to put in a security system."

A key. Of course. What had I been thinking?

I didn't argue with him about the locks or the security system. If I was going to continue staying here, both of those options weren't options. They were necessities. Staying here was also a necessity. I couldn't bare another failure in my life. I *would* conquer this house, if it was the last thing I did.

And it just might be the last thing I did, the way things were going so far.

"Thanks, Coop." I huddled with Austin on the couch.

The police arrived—the same two guys from before—and asked some questions and dusted for prints. Cooper's lips were set in a straight line and his eyes looked permanently narrowed as he stomped around with his hands on his hips. Austin and I remained huddled on the sofa, watching everything, until at about nine p.m. when Austin snuggled against my arm and drifted to sleep. Finally, the police left and Cooper stopped by the front door to look at me.

I pushed myself straighter on the couch, careful not to wake Austin. Cooper's eyes wandered down to his son. The boy's chest rose and fell evenly, and a soft purr escaped from his lips. Then I felt that gaze on me again. "I don't feel good about you staying here tonight by yourself."

I didn't feel good about me staying here by myself tonight either, but what were my options considering I knew no one else in this town except Cooper and Candy?

"Do you have someone you could stay with?"

I shook my head. "No, not really."

His lips pulled into a tight line until he finally said, "How about if I camp out on your couch? You'll have a security system tomorrow and be okay."

A lump formed in my throat. Theoretically, there was nothing wrong with that idea. But I knew it would look bad for two unmarried singles to sleep in the same house, even if there was a little boy with us. I could still hear my old youth pastor talking about purity and the appearance of being virtuous. But should I really care about appearances when my safety could be on the line?

"I promise not to try anything."

Startled, I looked up at Cooper. I realized how he interpreted my silence, and my cheeks warmed. "No, it's not that. I just don't want to make you bend over backward."

"I'd feel better if someone was here with you, at least until you got new locks and an alarm."

I suddenly realized that God must think it ridiculous that I tried to rule myself so much by the laws of opinion. And wasn't that what I'd been doing all of my life? Maybe I'd cared more about what other people thought of my Christian walk than I'd cared about what God thought.

"If you want to put Austin in the guest bedroom, I'll grab some blankets and a pillow for you." I didn't mention that the room might be haunted.

Cooper nodded and gently lifted Austin from my arms. I tried to ignore the ache in my chest as I saw the tenderness in Cooper's eyes. As they disappeared into the back bedroom, I let Gaga outside before rummaging the linen closet. I found what I needed and tucked a sheet over the couch cushions and draped a blanket over the back.

I let Gaga inside and wandered back into the living room. I crossed my arms over my chest as I waited for Cooper to emerge. I stared at the black fingerprint dust covering the window frames. Then my gaze traveled to those windows. I shivered, feeling unseen eyeballs following my every move again. I backed up, closer to the wall, away from the outside edges of the house.

"Whoa!" Hands grasped my arms from behind.

I twirled around and swallowed a scream. "Cooper. Sorry."

His gaze traveled the room and he must have figured out my thoughts. "You want to put some sheets up over those windows?"

"I don't think Lana has enough to cover all of them."

"We'll buy you some more shades tomorrow." One of his hands remained on my arm, his grasp firm and protective. In the brief amount of time I'd known Cooper, I'd come to rely on him way too much.

"Can we talk for a few minutes?" Cooper asked.

I nodded, my arms still pulled over my chest. With that anchor of a hand still gripping my arm, Cooper led me to the oversized chair next to the couch. I lowered myself there and pulled my knees to my chest. Cooper sat on the couch across from me.

I stood, unable to sit still. "I just don't understand."

"Understand what?"

"Ever since I started house sitting, I've felt like someone was watching me. I know it doesn't make sense, but this house just gives me the creeps. There's something about it. At first, I just thought it was paranoia, but now..."

Cooper's jaw flexed. "You need to be careful, Tara. I know it's probably hard for someone like you to believe, but there are people out there who hurt ladies like yourself just for fun."

The end of his statement fell on deaf ears. All I heard was *someone like you.* What did that mean?

"Tara?"

I forced my chin up. "Someone like me?"

"I didn't mean it like that." His eyes softened.

"How did you mean it?"

His expression was unwavering. "Tara, I see a lot of bad stuff all the time."

"And I come from the world of Pollyannas who wear rose-colored glasses?" I'd heard it before. People thought I was sheltered. Naïve. Innocent.

"Tara—"

"It's okay, Cooper." I stood and stepped away. "I'm going to bed now. Thanks for everything."

I hurried to my room and shut the door before he could say anything else. Maybe I shouldn't have reacted so harshly. Maybe I should have done what the old Tara would have done—swallowed my true feelings in favor of being polite. But sometimes, I was so tired of the old Tara.

I changed clothes and crawled under my covers. I stared at my closet door, wondering if someone lurked behind it. Cooper said he checked everything out. Still, fear rippled through my bones.

I dug down deeper into the comforter, wondering why some material with cotton stuffed between it made me feel protected. I prayed that sleep would come quickly. But my mind still raced at Cooper's insinuation.

I know it's hard for someone like you to believe...

I knew there were bad guys out there. The Bible was the ultimate tale of good and evil. You couldn't believe in the good without knowing about the evil. Sure, I'd never been wild. I'd never gotten myself into trouble or hung out with the wrong crowd. But that didn't mean I was blind to what was happening in the world. I knew bad things happened to good people. I knew pain didn't favor only the poor. I knew loving someone could be the scariest thing in the world.

I sighed and flipped onto my back. I stared at the fan on the ceiling and the elegant glass light fixture beneath it. I visually traced the intricate swipes of plaster that decorate the white ceiling.

I'd spent the last couple of years feeling sorry for myself. Even coming to St. Paul to get my new start, all I'd done was dwell on what happened a thousand miles away. I'd let people who didn't know me have this strange power over my life.

Suck it up, Buttercup. It's what my internal voice constantly told me.

I was going to make some changes. Lots of changes, for that matter. And Candy Cornelius was just the person to help make that happen. In the morning, I was going to find her number and give her a call.

11

The next morning, I sprang forward in bed, my heart racing. Sunlight flooded through the windows. Quiet surrounded me.

I blinked, wondering what I was missing. I'd slept all night, and I hadn't heard a thing. And this was after my window shades went missing. One would have thought that eerie reality would have kept me up all night.

Then I remembered Cooper sleeping on my couch, and the truth fell over me. I'd slept better only because there was someone else in the house watching out for me.

Slowly, I threw my legs out of bed and tiptoed to the door. I cracked it open and scanned the hallway. Nothing appeared out of place. I crept forward until the living room came into focus. The empty living room.

I frowned. Where was Cooper? All the blankets and pillows I'd pulled out for him were now neatly folded and placed on the sofa. But no Cooper.

I glanced at the clock. It was nearly nine o'clock. Of course he'd had to wake early and go to work, get Austin to the sitter's. And I hadn't heard any of it?

I shook my head. That only confirmed the fact that someone could sneak up on me during the night and I'd be oblivious.

My gaze scanned the rest of the room. The windows were still uncovered, causing my gut to twist. Who had ever heard of someone stealing your blinds? Someone either had a sense of humor. Or they really wanted to watch everything going on in this house. Other than those windows, nothing appeared out of place.

The fact that nothing had happened should comfort me. Instead, I felt even more suspicious.

I was really quite the contradiction. I was certain ghosts weren't real, unless I wasn't. I didn't want to believe in God, but my thoughts always came back to him. I certainly couldn't understand myself, so I didn't expect anyone else to.

Especially not Ben Cooper.

After taking a shower and wandering into the kitchen, I found a note from Cooper. "Stay safe. Can we talk sometime?"

I crumpled the note, threw it in the trash, and poured some cereal. What was there to talk about? Nothing. He had an opinion. I didn't like it. And that was the end of it.

Still, I frowned. Why did I care what he thought of me? I'd only met the man two days ago, and it wasn't like he was going to be a lifelong friend or anything. I only had a few weeks in Minnesota. Let people here think whatever they wanted. I'd be gone soon.

Which made me feel empowered to do things I'd never done before.

I grabbed my cell phone and called my sister to get Candy's number. She answered on the first ring, giggling at something in the background. We did our preliminary chatting about her trip and my stay. Then I brought up her stalker.

"I'm glad you asked, because I did some checking on Travis White, my stalker. His company transferred him to India, so he's not in St. Paul anymore."

I guess I could rule him out. That realization was both comforting and disturbing. I was glad a deranged stalker wasn't hanging out around the house, but if not Travis then who?

"Weird things still happening?"

I filled her in.

"Oh Tara, that is creepy. I wish I knew what to tell you." Serious and sincere Lana had landed. It didn't happen very often, but I was glad it had happened now. When Lana wanted to, she could be the most well-mannered, charming person this side of the Mississippi. Other side too, for that matter.

Lana, the rule-breaker, had always been my father's favorite. I, on the other hand, was like the older brother in the story of the Prodigal Son. I was always there, always faithful, and basically ignored. But none of that mattered right now.

"When did you start playing the guitar, Lana?"

She paused. "Guitar? I don't play guitar."

"You have one in the closet of your spare bedroom."

"No, I don't."

Cold fear crept in me again. "I see."

"Look, Tara, Nate's telling me we've got to leave for this tour we're doing. I hate to leave the conversation here."

"Don't sweat it." I got Candy's number from her and hung up.

Just where should I start on my quest to remodel Tara Lancaster inside and out?

After sticking my cereal bowl in the sink, I called Candy, who promised to be over at one o'clock. That left me a little more than four hours to get a few things done on my own.

I plopped down at Lana's computer, located in the guest bedroom. After doing a little more work as a virtual assistant, I did a search for Danielle Miller.

Finally, I saw an article I could use, detailed, "The Psychic House Murder."

Psychic house? Was the lady doing palm readings in the living room? The house was close enough to the main road that it could have been used as a business. I closed my eyes and pictured a woman with curly red hair piled high on her head, big, dangly earrings, a flowery robe, and a crystal ball.

When Danielle's picture appeared, I was surprised at how normal she looked. Almost pretty even. Her face was wide and her eyes a little close, but her smile looked genuine. Jeremy was skinny with dark hair and a beak-like nose. Did he really kill his wife?

I skimmed the article. Danielle's body had never been found, but apparently there was evidence of a lot of blood in the front bedroom. In the room where I slept. Jeremy claimed he came home from a boy's night out and found his house a mess. He panicked. Began trying to clean up the blood. Then he came to his senses and called the police.

Though his friends agreed he was out with them, there's unaccounted time. The gang was watching a football game at a restaurant about fifteen miles from this house. No one saw him for an hour—just enough time to go home and do the deed. Others said the two were having marital problems. Jeremy had been charged once with disorderly conduct for getting into a fight while in public. Apparently, he was tired of his wife's fascination with the occult. There was no body and no murder weapon.

So, where was Jeremy Miller now?

Another article profiled a fellow psychic who claimed Danielle's spirit couldn't cross over to the other side until she had a conclusion to her murder.

In other words, she was roaming Lana's house.

Great.

Would I have to find her killer before she'd leave me alone? Not exactly my cup of latte.

Then again, whoever plagued the outside of my house and stole my blinds wasn't a ghost.

I dropped my head to the table. What was a girl to do?

I read a few more articles that didn't give me any new information. I noticed the same reporter wrote most of the news pieces about the murder, so I jotted his name on a kiss-shaped notepad belonging to Lana. I also took the name of the psychic who claimed Danielle still roamed the earth, unable to cross into the netherworld. Maybe I'd talk with her. Maybe I wouldn't.

I glanced at my watch again. I had just enough time to go knock on a few doors before Candy got here. I started with the neighbor's door across the street, and a kindly older woman answered. She introduced herself as Winnie. She was heavyset with a poof of styled gray hair curling back from her round face and a sweet smile.

I pointed my thumb behind me. "I'm Lana's sister, Tara, and I'm in town for a while. I think someone was in my house yesterday while I was out, so I just thought I'd check with a few neighbors and see if they saw anything out of the ordinary. Did you, by chance, see anyone creeping around my house at around six or seven?"

"You mean while you were over at Cooper's?" The woman's voice was so high-pitched that she almost sounded cartoonish. It only added to her sweet aura, though.

I raised my eyebrows. "That's right."

She smiled. "I watch Austin sometimes for him. Such a nice little family."

I didn't know what to say, so I smiled, swallowing all of the negative emotions that rose when I thought about my conversation with Cooper last night. "Did you happen to see anything else?"

"I saw a girl with blue hair and hooker boots. There was a man with her."

I hid my smile. "That was Candy." My smile slipped. Would they have had time to slip inside? Could this all be some kind of publicity prank? I hadn't thought to ask Candy if she had a key, but she very well could.

"I'm really not as nosy as I sound." She laughed nervously.

"Nosy neighbors are good neighbors. Isn't that how the saying goes?"

She rubbed her hands. "I think you're right. I didn't see anything else."

"No suspicious cars or anything?"

"Sorry, dear. I wish I could help you more."

If Winnie hadn't seen anything—and she seemed pretty attuned to what was going on—then what was the chance that someone else had? Or was the most obvious answer the right answer—that Candy was behind this?

The house right next door to Lana's was vacant, complete with a for-sale sign in the front yard. I'd already talked to Cooper. But, there were still a few other houses where the neighbors might have seen something.

I knocked on three more doors. One person wasn't home. One was a stay-at-home mom who didn't notice the stray curler left in her hair, so I doubted she'd notice any strange cars. At the last house, a man in his forties answered. He had blond hair that was gelled away from his face and revealed a harsh receding hairline. The only place he seemed to gain fat was in his stomach, which bulged like he was pregnant. However, it was the look in his eyes that made me step back. His gaze was intense and cold.

And from the second story of his home, he'd have the perfect view of Lana's place. Shivers wracked my body at the thought. Could this be the person responsible for everything going on at Lana's?

The man partly leaned against the doorframe and partly leaned toward me. "Can I help you?"

I glanced beyond him. A woman stood in the background, her eyes as wide as saucers. She halfway hid behind the wall, as if too afraid to come any closer. She had milky brown skin, and her eyes seemed to beckon me.

Was she this man's wife? Then why did she look so frightened?

"Ma'am?"

I glanced back at the man and forced a tight smile. The last thing I wanted was to tell this man I was staying at that house alone—even though he might already know that. But my mind drew a blank as to what else I might say.

I licked my lips and fidgeted. As my grandma might say, I'd gotten myself into a real pickle. "You're not Marvin Henderson, are you?"

"Marvin?" His eyes narrowed.

I raised my palms in confusion, going into airhead mode. "I think I have the wrong house. Someone else's mail was put in my box, and I'm new in the area. I thought you might be Marvin."

The man looked at my hands. "So where is it?"

"Where's what?" I blinked, having no idea what he was talking about.

"The mail?"

Another stab of cold fear clutched my heart. "Oh, the mail. It's at my house. I didn't want anyone stealing it or anything. Isn't there a law against that or something?" What in the world was I talking about? I had no idea. I swallowed and took a step back. "I gotta go. Sorry to bother you!"

I ran back across the street and into Lana's house, locking the doors behind me. Why had that man scared me so much? It didn't make sense. On the other hand, it was all about sense—my senses, my gut feeling. That guy just gave me the creeps.

And I couldn't stop thinking about the woman standing in the distance. Was my imagination working overtime or was that woman frightened?

The doorbell rang and I gasped, nearly jumping out of my skin. *The doorbell. Just the doorbell, Tara.* I scolded myself for overreacting.

I looked out the peephole and saw Candy standing on the other side. I pulled the door open and ushered her inside.

"Hey, Jamaica. I'm glad you called." She had her normal attitude. Today, she'd be known in my mind as Hubba Bubba since she smacked her gum with the best of them.

"I'm glad you're available." I ran over a list of things I wanted to do. It might drain the little bit of savings I had, but I didn't care. Being responsible had gotten me nowhere.

"So, are we taking the motorcycle or the Hummer?"

I thought about it a moment. "The motorcycle. Definitely the motorcycle."

Candy grinned. "First stop?"

"The police station."

"To talk to detectives?"

I shook my head. "No, to fill out some paper work."

12

My gut told me this was going to be the not-to-miss episode of *Extreme Makeover: Tara Lancaster Edition.* Candy hadn't let me look in the mirror all day, and I was anxious to see the final result of all of our work.

We arrived back at my place at seven after stopping at the police station, the mall, and Candy's place. I'd found a note from Cooper, asking when he could stop by to upgrade the house's security. I'd crumpled it up, trying to put Cooper out of my mind. I didn't need him or his help.

Candy didn't seem to notice the scowl across my face as she chattered on and on in the background. I had to admit that I'd enjoyed getting to know Candy today. She had a genuine smile that emerged on occasion, she never scurried around the truth, and she was totally comfortable in her own skin. Wherever we went, she got lots of looks, but she kept her chin up—unless she was looking at her cell phone or posting Facebook updates. Today, she'd been less of an Atomic Fireball and more of a Bit-O-Honey.

I'd discovered through our conversation that she'd been in one national advertising commercial—it was for feminine hygiene products. Perhaps it was in honor of that commercial that she'd dyed her hair toilet bowl blue? The Iowa-native had gone to college for two years and studied acting, but dropped out because of too much partying. Her goal was to one day be famous enough to be on *Dancing with the Stars*, one of my favorite shows and a fact that made me instantly like her. I'd also discovered that she had an amazing ability to quickly and accurately text message someone using only one hand.

As she led me to the bathroom mirror at Lana's, her lips curled into a curious grin. I held my breath before stepping into the small room. Would this be the start of *How Tara Got her Groove Back*? It wasn't seeing myself that caused me anxiety—it was the fear of seeing another eerie message left on my mirror.

I glanced at it. No, not today. Thank goodness.

She shoved me in front of sink. I blinked. Instead of ectoplasm, I saw the reflection of someone I hardly recognized. Me.

"What do you think?" Candy stood in the doorway grinning.

I studied my skin, which now had an instant tan. Red streaks now ran through my hair—not red as in auburn, but red as in fire engines were now put to shame. A small nose ring, no bigger than a freckle, sparkled, and I'd bought some new trendy clothes that didn't scream "Church Lady" as my others apparently had.

Gone was the safe Tara and in her place...someone who wasn't afraid to try new things. Now maybe people couldn't say, *someone like you wouldn't understand*.... I could single-handedly thank Cooper for giving me that final bit of initiative to make some changes.

I nodded. "I like it."

Candy stared at me in the mirror. "I think you look totally hot. Cooper's going to think you look totally hot also."

My lips parted in surprise. "Cooper? I don't care what he thinks."

"Really?" She raised her eyebrows in doubt.

I touched one of my new red streaks. "Yeah, really. Why?"

One of her shoulders lifted. "You two just looked pretty content over there on his deck last night."

On the deck. Yes, that's when we were content. Then he'd let it slip what he really thought of me. "Friendly's about all there is to it. Nothing else."

She crossed her arms across her chest, Bit-O-Honey gone and Atomic Fireball back. "You should think about Mark then."

Normally, I would have said no right away. But that was the old Tara. Maybe the new Tara would go out with Mark. The new Tara would have the Bad Girl Rules, starting with Rule #1: Whatever you would have done in the past, do the opposite.

"Mark? He seems..." What? What did he seem? "Buff." I shrugged, no other descriptors coming to mind.

A question had been nagging at me all day, but I hadn't wanted to ask Candy until after I was home safely and she'd done my hair—no one wanted an angry hairstylist working on him or her. We moved into the living room. Candy helped herself to one of Lana's leftover bottles of beer. She offered me one, but I declined. I'd already had enough excitement in my day without adding any alcohol to the mix.

"Do you have a key to Lana's place, Candy?"

She shook her head. "No, why?"

"Just wondering."

"Oh, come on. We both know there's more to your question than that."

I told her about the shades.

Her eyes widened. "You've got to be kidding me?"

"I wish I were."

She moved from the chair to directly beside me on the couch. "I talked to my friend with *Ghost Chasers*. He said he'll come out and do some tests for you. In fact, he's going to be out in this area on Friday."

"I don't know..."

"It would be fun. Maybe you'd finally get some answers you've been looking for. And if you don't believe in ghosts, then what could it hurt to have him out? He'll get his kicks, and you'll have some funny stories to tell people once you get back home."

Home. Was that Florida? Was I ever really going to go back there? Was there any place I'd truly ever feel safe and comfortable again?

The old Tara would have said no to *Ghost Chasers*. My new Bad Girls Rule echoed in my mind. Which led me to Rule #2: If in doubt, do it. "He can come. Do the tests and see what happens."

"Really?" She squealed. "He's not like one of the main guys on the show. He's actually one of the technicians, but he knows how to use all of the equipment. Can I film it for my YouTube channel?"

"As long as I'm not on the video." Me showing up on the Internet was the last thing I needed. If the angry mobs knew where I was, they might show up at my door with pitchforks in hand. Maybe not pitchforks, but, at the very least, they might have restraining orders or a big, fat Scarlet Letter to strap across my chest.

"It's a deal!"

I sighed. Was this one deal I was going to regret?

Candy left an hour later, and I sat alone in my eerie little abode. My gaze fixated on the windows and wondered if someone was watching me. I stared back.

Until I remembered the creepy guy across the street.

I should have called Cooper and taken him up on his offer to replace those locks and install a security system, but my pride stopped me. He wouldn't be over here tonight, sleeping on my couch. It would just be Gaga and me. How was I ever going to get any sleep?

I reached into my purse and pulled out a Glock. Yep, a gun. I'd filled out an application down at the police station. I didn't have a right to carry this anywhere, but I did have a right to keep it in my house, right beside my bed. I'd been all set to go to the gun shop and purchase something, but Candy said I could borrow hers.

I stared at the black metal and ran my hand down its smooth edges. I guess I should learn how to shoot. Ghosts were pretty bulletproof, but intruders weren't. This was how I was going to sleep tonight.

In theory, at least.

I stood and started toward the hallway, bypassing my own bedroom in favor of the spare. I sat down at Lana's computer and pulled up the Internet, doing a quick search for Candy Cornelius. Pages of results popped up.

I clicked on a few of her videos and smiled at what I saw. Candy doing random man-on-the-street interviews. Candy videoing herself on a roller-coaster. Candy not caring what anyone thought of her. People loved it. Some of her videos had more than a million hits.

My fingers hovered on the keyboard. *Don't do it, Tara. Don't do it.*

I did it anyway. I typed my name into the search engine, something that always caused my emotional state to be declared a disaster area for days afterward.

Pages of articles appeared.

Against my better judgment, I clicked on the first one. The story was called "Saint Turned Sinner," and it detailed my life growing up as the daughter of a prominent mega-church pastor. It highlighted all of the accomplishments of my past and how I'd taken a job at the Christian school affiliated with my father's church. It mentioned my marriage to a respected man in the Christian community.

Then it showed my mug shot, the picture taken when I was arrested for taking indecent liberties with a minor. The image still crushed my heart. When I thought of the blatant lies said about me, tears pushed their way out.

Not only had one of my seventeen-year-old students accused me of having an inappropriate relationship with him, but the firestorm that had erupted afterward broke my heart and my spirit. My dad's church nearly split over it. Those who didn't believe I could have done it stayed. Those who thought I was a child molester had left.

I felt like the main character in a million different Bible stories. I was Job facing hardship after hardship. I was Daniel in the lion's den. I was David, staring down my own Goliath.

The difference was that the people in the Bible had conquered their trials. I'd been stoned and died. I'd tried to walk on water but sunk. I'd looked back and turned into a pillar of salt.

People had either believed me or they hadn't. Most of what I said didn't have any affect. People's minds were already made up. *It's always the sweet ones you have to watch out for. You never know what a person's really like. Even her husband thinks she's guilty.* I'd heard the whispers.

Even though there had been no evidence to convict me, I'd been deemed guilty by the community. My face had been splashed on newspapers all over Florida. One national news show had even picked it up. Websites that profiled women pedophiles listed me.

The strain the scrutiny caused put a burden on my marriage. I could have done better. I should have done better.

People saw Peter's departure from my life as more evidence that I was indeed guilty.

I knew I wasn't guilty, but I still *felt* guilty. I still felt like I'd done something wrong.

Zack Morris was seventeen years old. He was able to enroll at the Christian school on a need-based scholarship. He had a single mom who didn't make much money. His mom, his younger brother, and Zack had moved to Florida from the Midwest after the divorce.

Zack was always a little standoffish from his classmates. He was a good-looking boy with short brown hair and an athletic build. He'd had a steady girlfriend of four months, a cute girl who played the clarinet in the school's marching band. Zack had always seemed like he needed a father figure in his life, and he'd struggled some with the rules of the Christian school.

Even though I taught elementary school, I'd been asked to head up the drama club, mostly because I'd had the lead in a couple of productions when I'd been a student at the school myself. Drama wasn't my passion, but I told them I'd do it for a year, a decision that had been pivotal in my decline. If only I could go back and say no. I'd traded my happy ever after for hopes of impressing my principal and a sad performance of *The Sound of Music*.

I'd set my own boundaries about not spending any time alone with students of the opposite sex. But, unlike other parents, Zack's mom never picked him up on time. I'd talked to her about it, and she'd broken down in tears, telling me about how hard it was to be a single mom. My heart had caved with compassion because she'd seemed truly broken.

Even after that conversation, she continued to be late. One Thursday in May I'd been anxious to get home. The day was sunny and I had dreamed all morning of sitting in my backyard reading after I got home from work. Peter was out of town for a few more days on a business trip, so I had some time to myself. The end of the school year had been so busy and stressful, and I needed some downtime.

All the other cast members had gone home after play practice, and I'd waited an hour for Zack's mom to arrive. I tried to stay occupied with grading papers and organizing my desk. Zack had stayed in my classroom working on his homework. He'd seemed nervous, and I thought it was because he sensed my agitation.

Finally, I'd offered to drive him home. We'd chitchatted about the play and school athletics on the drive home. He'd mentioned how bad things had been for his family after his dad left them—money was tight, his mom was always emotional, his brother was always in trouble. I'd felt for him. I really had. I remembered making a mental note to talk to the principal about ways we could help his family out.

I pulled up to his house, a run-down building that needed some major TLC. There were no cars in the driveway, which didn't seem unusual after what he'd told me. Zack had grabbed his book bag, gave me a wave, and went inside his house. I'd driven away. End of story.

At least, it should have been the end of the story.

The police came and arrested me two days later. Zack had told his mom that I went inside the house with him. He accused me of making advances at him, not just once but on several occasions. He even alleged I'd asked him to stay late so we could have time together. But then he changed details of his story a couple of times, which reduced his credibility.

With Peter out of town, I'd called my parents to bail me out. My mom wouldn't stop crying, and my dad was even worse—he was simply quiet. We'd approached a family friend and one of the best attorneys in the area about representing me, and he'd refused. That's when I knew I was in trouble.

Thankfully, between the lack of concrete evidence like DNA, text messages, or pictures, the district attorney's office couldn't meet their burden of proof.

It was Zack's word against mine, which wouldn't hold up in a court of law. But it was more than enough in the court of public opinion.

Even with the charges dropped, there was no formal "clearing" of my name or closing of the investigation. Any day could turn up a new lead, and I could be hauled back for more questions, more accusations, and more humiliation.

In Christian circles, there were a lot of things that merited forgiveness. Embezzling money. Divorce. Pregnancy out of wedlock. But not this.

Even I had to admit that what I'd been accused of was heinous enough to justify people ostracizing me.

My career working with children was now marked DNR. I knew employers would find excuses as to why they couldn't hire me, and I couldn't blame them. I wouldn't even hire me, and I knew I was innocent.

Police had searched for more victims, asking the public to come forward with information. People I'd worked with had been questioned. The media had a field day with my story when the charges became public. Reporters began camping out on my doorstep. I'd eventually sequestered myself at my uncle's house. Lana had flown in and just sat with me for hours on end. Peter claimed he had to work, so he stayed with his mom.

All it took was one lie, and my life had been destroyed. Why? Why had Zack made up the story? I hadn't talked to him since that day I'd dropped him off at home. Why someone would want to ruin another person's life was beyond me.

But ruin he had. My dreams had dried up. My career was ruined. My husband had walked out the door. Now I had a reputation that would always haunt me.

Where did that leave me?

Right now, it left me with red highlights, a spray-on tan, and a nose ring. Eventually I was going to have to figure out where I was going to live, what kind of job I might take. I was going to have to figure out who I really was. This transformation seemed like a start.

I turned off the computer.

Right now, I just needed to go to bed.

That night, the light from the street lamp outside slithered through my blinds and smeared itself across the wall in front of my bed. As the light filtered through the craggy limbs of the Bradford Pear tree in the front yard, the spots of illumination formed a scowl on the wall. Two eyes angled in, glaring at me. A crescent shaped frown burned into my mind. I could almost hear a *tsk tsk* coming from the face.

Even when I put my head under the covers, I still knew that scowl was there. It was like God materialized in those flashes of light and looked at me in disappointment. Hiding would do me no good, so I gave up and stared at the ceiling instead.

Of course I'd let God down. Though I'd only admitted it in the last couple of weeks, I'd begun to question His very existence. I wondered if my prayers were unheard. I wondered if I'd lived my life in vain, worshiping and serving a God who wasn't really there.

My very godly parents had taught me from a very young age that God had created the world in six days, that only Noah and his family had survived the flood, and that Christ died on the cross for my sins.

But what if I hadn't learned those things? What if I'd grown up with parents who weren't believers? Would I still have found my way to Christ? Would He have found His way to me?

I knew the answers. I could flip to John 3:16 in my sleep. I could name all the books of the Bible—the canon, mind you—from Genesis to Revelation—and that's Revelation, not Revelations. I could sing "Amazing Grace" in three different harmonies, in Spanish if need be, and even knew the sign language to boot. Yet all those things meant nothing to me now.

That scowl still eyeballed me. I wanted to apologize, but was it possible to apologize to a being who really didn't exist? I needed a burning bush, some writing on the wall—not a face glaring at me with disappointment.

I stared back at the scowl, wishing it would go away. It seemed to get brighter. No breeze danced outside, altering the lights. All was still. It was just me and the scowl.

I pulled the comforter over my head. I had to get some sleep if these delusional thoughts were ever going to go away.

13

The next morning, I sat at the computer and did an Internet search for the psychic from the article about Danielle Miller. Sure enough, she had...what did you call it? A practice? Business? Carnival booth? Regardless, she still worked in the area. Only a few blocks away, actually. I decided to pay her a visit. I programmed her address into the GPS on my cell phone and went to face the Hummer.

A few minutes later I stopped in front of a house that looked like a miniature version of a Palm Beach mansion. Neon signs advertising Psychic and Tarot Cards flashed in the windows. Fake palm trees were planted in the front lawn, and a circular driveway invited customers. Here, one could visit the exotic and all-knowing Miss Mystic.

I felt like I was in the middle of a bad Lifetime movie as I pulled into the driveway. Good Christian girls didn't visit psychics. If I were in Florida, I'd be looking around right now to see if anyone I knew was nearby. I couldn't be a stumbling block for those weaker in the faith. Nor did I want to be item number one on the church prayer list, a.k.a. the gossip chain.

I tossed my scruples like yesterday's leftovers. As long as my visit didn't get back to my mom, I'd be okay. I could already hear her telling me the story about King Saul visiting the witch and all the repercussions happening as a result. Then I remembered Bad Girls Rule #2, which lead me to Bad Girls Rule #3: Let people talk and hope it comes back to bite them in the bum.

My sandals thudded across the cement and up three steps to the wooden doorway. Did I knock? I wondered. After all, this was also a home. I raised my hand to tap it against the wood when the door swung open. A middle-aged Filipino woman with smoldering eyes stared at me. She had the hoop earrings and gypsy-like clothes I'd expected for Danielle Miller. Her dark hair stretched untamed halfway down her back.

Let me guess—she knew I was coming.

"Welcome to Miz Myztic," the woman said in broken English. Her whole body slinked with each word, as if she wanted to spontaneously begin belly dancing. Or maybe my imagination was just totally out of whack. "You like a palm reading?"

Before I could object, she grabbed my hand and began tracing the lines on my palm. I jerked back as if I'd touched the devil in the flesh.

So maybe I hadn't totally tossed those scruples.

"No, no palm reading," I started. Her face registered annoyance—pursed lips, raised eyebrow, one shoulder higher than the other. "I wanted to talk to you about Danielle Miller."

One shoulder relaxed. The wrinkles on her forehead ironed out. As quickly as they disappeared, they were back. "I have appointment."

I glanced behind me. "I'm the only car in the driveway."

Her scowl deepened. "They be here soon."

"But you have a few minutes until then." Another Bad Girls Rule. Be pushy, something I was so not good at. Which could easily lead into Bad Girls Rule #5: Don't play well with others.

Her eyes swept over me. "You a friend?"

"No."

Her eyes narrowed. "You the police?"

"No."

Her eyes were mere slits now. "How you know Danielle then?"

I swallowed. I probably shouldn't be here. I could mentally see my mother shaking her head at me, telling me not to flirt with darkness. "I'm living in Danielle's old house."

Miss Mystic's eyes lit up. "Are you?" She opened the door. "Come in."

I stepped onto the tiled entryway. Inside, the lights were dim. Incense, musky and strong, filled the air. Strange instruments played from speakers somewhere. Candles and beads and exotic scarves decorated every visible surface.

The sunlight disappeared as Miss Mystic shut the doors. I jumped, suddenly sick to my stomach. I shouldn't be here.

"What I do for you?"

I wiped my sweaty palms on my denim shorts. "Did you know Danielle?"

"We in same circle."

"How do you think she died?"

Her eyes lit, and she lowered her forehead in a know-it-all look. "The same way everyone else. Her husband."

"Did you know her husband? What was he like?"

"He not believer like Danielle. How you say? He *tolerate* Danielle."

I crossed my arms over my chest and tried to look relaxed and comfortable, although I was anything but. "Why would you say that?"

She shrugged and ran her fingers along the dusty frame holding the painting of a Native American. "He a church-goer. Not type to believe in crystal ball."

I could relate.

"But you think he was the type to kill her?"

She wiped the dust from her fingers and eyed me. I had the feeling she was trying to size me up. "Danielle visiting you, isn't she?"

Chills swept my arm. "I didn't say that. There have been some strange things happening lately, though. I...I don't know what to think of it."

She stepped closer and waved a finger at me. "You find things of spiritual realm hard to accept." Accusation tinged her voice.

I tried to step back but bumped into a table behind me. I glanced over my shoulder and saw a bunch of different herbs, all organized in small glass bowls. Did the woman also put curses on people? *She's a medium, Tara, not a witch.* I glanced back at the woman. "It depends on how you define 'spiritual realm.'"

Miss Mystic glowered at me. "Let me guess—God and Jesus easy to believe but ghost not?" Miss Mystic's finger still waved in the air. "Why one absurd and other not? Besides, you must be curious at least, since you come here."

"I just want some answers, an explanation for the things happening at my house. I don't even feel safe there."

She picked up a folded fan with an oriental design across it from the table behind me and waved it on her face. "I believe in God too, you know. Just because I psychic not mean I no believe."

My face flushed in surprise. "Do you believe Jesus Christ is God?"

"There no one god but many."

The doorbell rang, and she snapped her fan shut. "My client here. You leave." She jerked her thumb behind her in one big "get out" motion. She obviously hadn't learned the art of being subtle.

"About Danielle..."

Miss Mystic grabbed my arm and pulled me toward the door, her iron grip making my arm ache. "Ask her what happen yourself."

I slammed on brakes. "Ask her myself?"

"Come back and I ask Danielle what she want from you. For fifty bucks, that is."

I was out the door, passing a woman with short gray hair and wearing a business suit. And Miss Mystic had all but forgotten about me as she greeted a woman who'd actually pay her—I assumed. Gone was the woman's pushiness. I looked behind me and saw a bright, charming smile across her face.

Christians weren't the only ones who could be two-faced, I supposed.

14

On the way home, I pondered our conversation. How much difference was there between someone who believed in God and one who believed in ghosts? Both required a level of faith. But why was I so sure I was right? Or was I?

I pulled the Hummer up in front of Lana's and, instead of going inside, decided to go on a walk. The day was warm and some exercise sounded good—better than going into the house and keeping company with beings unseen.

As I paced the sidewalk, I couldn't help but note that the neighborhood was beautiful with sidewalks and massive trees that provided shade. All the streets were neatly laid out in blocks with strategically placed parks and ball fields. Lana was basically living the American dream. I, on the other hand, had woken up in the middle of a modern-day nightmare.

I shook my head and decided to replay my conversation with Miss Mystic instead of pondering how unfair life was.

Jeremy a churchgoer. Not type believe in crystal balls.

Would a churchgoer kill his wife? Christians had done worse.

Would Jeremy have been so humiliated by his wife's beliefs that he viewed killing her as the only solution? Sounded drastic to me. I supposed people had been murdered for lesser reasons, though.

Of course, for a fee, Miss Mystic could conjure up Danielle's spirit and find out for sure.

Uh-huh.

I closed my eyes and pictured it all unfolding. I could see Danielle's face blurred in the crystal ball while Miss Mystic spoke her broken English into the sphere. "What you have to say, Danielle?" she'd asked.

I'm still here.

I opened my eyes at the memory of the note I'd found when I arrived and swallowed hard. No, that just wasn't possible, no matter what people thought. Danielle was not trying to reach me from the grave.

The next thing I knew, I'd be finding out she played guitar. I chuckled, but the sound quickly died as a cold fear crept in. What if she *did* play the guitar? No, I couldn't think about that.

I looked up as a brisk wind fanned my face. A line of clouds was coming toward me. I didn't care. I kept walking, past homes in all shapes and sizes. The tree-lined street made me feel warm and cozy, despite all the craziness at Lana's. Ahead, I spotted an ice cream truck. Ice cream. That sounded like a good idea. I jumped in line, waiting amongst talkative kids still sweaty from playing in the park across the street.

I ordered a snow cone and then turned around, nearly colliding with someone with a broad, solid chest who smelled faintly of baby shampoo and spearmint. I looked up and saw piercing blue eyes squinting at me.

"Tara?"

I swallowed, my throat burning. "Cooper?"

He ordered two Popsicles. Austin stood beside him. Then he turned back to me, his eyes narrowing. "Your hair. It looks...good."

I shrugged and tugged a piece behind my ear. "I wanted to try something different." I looked down at his son and found the perfect topic for a subject change. "I thought Austin would be at the sitter's today."

"We're both playing hooky today." He rubbed the boy's head.

I smiled down at Austin and offered a wink. "It's nice to be at home with Daddy sometimes, isn't it?"

"I like your hair." Austin licked his Popsicle and looked up at me with those big blue eyes of his.

"Thanks."

The three of us escaped the crowd of children around the truck and began walking down the sidewalk toward the park together. Awkward silence fell.

Cooper was the first to speak. "Anything strange happening at the house lately?"

I took a bite of my rainbow-flavored snow cone, which lived up to its name because I could only taste the ice, and shrugged again. "Not really."

We paused by the playground. Austin ran off with some friends, leaving Cooper and me standing there. He shifted his weight from one foot to the other. "Look, Tara, about the other night..."

I waved my hand through the air, swatting away a fly in the process. "Don't worry about it."

He lowered his chin. Another chilly breeze swept through, ruffling his hair. "I offended you, and I didn't mean to."

"You did rub me the wrong way." Wow, it felt so good to be honest instead of covering up my true feelings in the interest of being polite. "But I'm a big girl. It's okay."

"I was out of line." He tossed his Popsicle wrapper into a nearby garbage can and shoved his hands into the pockets of his jeans.

"I've heard worse. Much worse." I sucked in a deep breath, my nose ring suddenly begging to be itched. I ignored it, wiggling my nose instead and trying to focus on the conversation. "To be honest, Cooper, I keep trying to shake off the old me, but I can't seem to do it. What you said reminded me of who I used to be."

"What was wrong with the old you?"

"The old me was all about rules." Of course, the new me was making up an entirely different set of rules. Bad Girls Rule #6: Neurotic thoughts will make people think you're more interesting.

"Being all about rules is bad?"

My nose twitched again. "You wouldn't understand."

"I'd like the chance to." His gaze was so earnest that for a moment

I wanted to pour out everything. But fear stopped me. He thought he'd understand if he knew the truth. But would he? Or would doubts about my innocence always linger in his mind?

I shook my head, glancing down at the cracked sidewalk at my feet before looking back up. The sun peeked through the approaching clouds for a moment and illuminated Cooper's hair, almost like a halo. "I'm a mess, Cooper. I'm like a house made of cards. I looked great for a while, but then the wind blew and everything fell down. I'm still picking up the pieces."

"I could help."

I shook my head. "I wish you could. I really wish you could. But sometimes I'm not even sure that picking up the pieces is possible."

"I hope you'll come to realize that it is."

I smiled, but it was a sad smile. "I hope you're right." I nodded toward the house. "I should go."

"Look, are you still interested in that security system?"

Maybe it was just the solution I was looking for. Besides, I was running out of options at this point—options short of Miss Mystic coming over and speaking to the spirits for me. I'd already borrowed Candy's gun, so I could be all *Lara Croft: Tomb Raider* when the bad guys showed up. But would I really be that brave? I doubted it. "I'd like that."

Cooper's gaze latched on to mine, making my heart beat double-time. "I'll stop by later then. Is that okay?"

I nodded, my throat burning with some kind of unwelcome emotion. "Thanks, Coop. That would be great."

With a wave, I turned and walked away.

A new rule came to mind. It wasn't a Good Girls Rule or a Bad Girls Rule. It was a protect-your-heart kind of rule. Maybe the most important kind of rule.

The rule's boundaries were clear: Stay away from Ben Cooper.

15

The first raindrop hit me when I was two blocks away from Lana's. I kept my slow, lazy pace and, by the time I reached the house, rain poured down in sheets. I started toward the front door but stopped in the middle of the yard.

I stood there, letting the rain fall over me. I lifted my head toward the drops. Moisture ran down my cheeks, my neck, my arms.

I wished rainwater could flow over my heart and wash it clean. Take away all of the bad stuff, all of the hurt that made me act and think in unappealing ways. Wasn't that what the blood of Jesus was for? Wasn't it supposed to wash me whiter than snow? Then why did my soul feel so stained and bruised?

A car door slammed. I looked over and saw Cooper and Austin running from the truck toward their house. Cooper paused and raised his hands up as if to say, *What are you doing?*

I waved him off. "Don't worry about me!"

He grinned, shook his head, and kept running.

I kept standing there. My clothes clung to my body. My hair clung to my face. And I didn't care. I let the rain saturate every part of me.

No one could see my tears as they mixed with the droplets from the sky—and mix they did. Rivers ran down my cheeks, but no one was wiser to my pain.

As quickly as the shower came, the rain faded. I stayed on my spot in the middle of the lawn until the spattering turned to random fat drops. When the rain stopped, I wiped my eyes with my hands and blinked at the world around me. I didn't even care if anyone had seen me or that my new hairdo was ruined. For the first time in a long time, I just didn't care.

A noise on the street drew my attention to a sedan parked in front of Cooper's. A younger woman jumped from the car, casserole dish in hand, and ran toward Cooper's place. Cooper opened the door a moment later and invited her inside.

Cooper had a girlfriend, I realized. Why did my heart feel heavy? He should be dating someone. He was a great guy. And I wasn't interested in dating, so the fact that a cute blonde was bringing him dinner should be endearing. My heart still sagged with unreasonable grief.

It was time to get cleaned up and dried off. I turned to go back inside when something made me pause. Eyes. Watching me.

I looked over my shoulder, just in time to see the strange man across the street staring out of his second-story window. Directly at me.

Unrest sloshed in my chest as I walked toward my front door. Why was that man watching me? Why did it bother me that a woman was at Cooper's, especially since I'd just vowed to stay away from him? And was I really living here alone, or was a dead woman still lingering between these four walls?

It was enough to give any girl a headache.

I deposited my keys on the table and started toward the bathroom for a shower when a knock pounded at the door. Who now? The creepy man from across the street? Or maybe the casserole fairy was making her rounds throughout the neighborhood and I was next on the list?

I pulled the door open, and on the other side stood two men

wearing golf shirts with "Safeguard Security" embroidered on them. Cooper certainly didn't waste any time sending them over.

They introduced themselves, told me it would take a couple of hours to install everything, and that they'd also be changing my locks and putting up new shades.

Why was I so disappointed that Cooper hadn't come himself?

I knew the answer. Cooper, in all of his kindness, had ignited that spark of hope in me—one that I hadn't felt in a long time. Since Peter, all my romantic aspirations had died. I didn't want to believe in love again. Cooper had somehow managed to break through that barrier, against all my wishes. And it appeared I was only setting myself up for more heartbreak. Yippee.

While the guys worked, I changed from my wet clothes and plopped on the couch, determined not to think about Cooper or the girl at his house or what they were doing. I refused to ponder whether he was as protective of her as of me or if Austin hugged her leg and looked up at her with those big eyes. I blocked out thoughts of her and Cooper sharing secret glances and having whispered conversations.

Yeah, right.

Jealousy...it did terrible things to your complexion. Good Girls Rule #9, but who cared? I was breaking all of the rules lately anyway. What would a bad girl do? They'd say, "Life is short so break the rules!"

I heard some commotion at the door and craned my neck to see what was happening. My eyes lit up at the familiar faces there. "Cooper. Austin. You're here."

I looked behind them, waiting to see the cute blonde. She appeared to be absent, however, which filled me with too much relief for comfort. My neighbors stepped inside, wiping their feet on the mat there.

Cooper's warm gaze met mine. "I hope you don't mind. I like to keep an eye on what's going on."

"You had this set up before you talked to me, didn't you?" I'd calculated how much time it should have taken to get a crew here, and either they were extremely under-worked or Cooper had arranged this without my permission. I knew I should care, but I didn't.

Cooper's guilty smile was all the answer I needed. I stood and approached them, winking at Austin as I got closer. The boy blushed and hugged his father's leg. I nodded toward the men working at my back door. "How am I ever going to pay for this? It looks like a seriously expensive system."

He stepped closer, his eyes sparkling with more clarity than the nighttime sky in Thailand. I'd seen that beautiful sight before—on a mission trip, to be exact.

His head tilted. "There is a way."

Please don't say I have to go on a date with you. I don't know that I'm strong enough to resist. It didn't matter how many times I told myself to throw caution to the wind—something habits were just hard to change. "What's that?"

"Go to church with me sometime."

I blinked several times, sure I hadn't heard him correctly. I hadn't pegged Cooper as a churchgoer, for some reason. "Church?"

He smiled, crinkles forming at his eyes. Crinkles that I'd imagined examining while on our date, which had merely been a pipe dream. "Why do you say it like it's a dirty word?"

I shook my head, trying to shake off his words in the process. "I didn't. Did I?"

"You kind of did." His expression was apologetic.

I had to buy some time and, to do that, I went with the truth. "I didn't know you were a Christian."

"I kind of thought you might be."

My throat burned as I wavered between my old life and my new life, between what I'd thought I'd known and the place of uncertainty where I remained now. "Why would you think that?"

"Just the vibe I got."

Interesting. I was still giving off that vibe, huh? I took a step back. "I don't know. I'm not really a big fan of church right now."

"Will you think about it?"

"Yeah, I'll think about it." I cleared my throat, deciding this was a good time for a subject change. "Cooper, you said that you had a mutual friend who knew the couple who lived in Lana's house?"

"Yeah, that's right. Why?"

"Do you think I could talk to him?"

He nodded slowly. "I could probably arrange something. Why?"

"I'm just trying to find out some more information. I know it probably sounds weird, but I wonder if everything going on here has something to do with her death."

He continued to bob his head in thought. "I'm actually going to stop at his place tomorrow after I drop Austin off at his grandparents. You want to tag along?"

"Would that be weird?"

His gaze pierced mine, questions dancing in his eyes. "Why would that be weird?"

"I don't want to put you in an awkward position with your girl-friend." As if him sleeping on my couch and having me over for a cookout hadn't already.

His head wobbled. "I don't have a girlfriend." He pointed outside, his gaze registering my assumptions. "You mean that girl that stopped by?"

I nodded.

He shook his head. "We're just friends."

"A friend who brings you dinner?" I couldn't stop the sparkle from glimmering in my eyes.

A smile stretched across his face. He'd been caught. "It's a long story. Maybe I'll tell you about it tomorrow on the ride up. You game?"

"Will that be awkward if I'm there when you drop off Austin?"

His hands went to his hips. "Do you always overthink things?"

"Yes, I do, actually." I didn't even have to overthink that answer.

"You're worrying too much. It's going to be fine. I'll tell them you're new in town and needed a ride. No big deal."

"I'm game then. Thanks. Again. I just can't seem to stop saying that to you."

"It's settled then. Now, let me go check on the work these guys are doing. With this alarm, you'll finally get a good night's rest."

I was fairly certain that I would never get a good night's rest again.

Even with the alarm—which Cooper had painfully explained to me, detain by detail, how to work—I wasn't sure anything would change.

As per my normal nightly routine, I lay in bed with the covers pulled up to my chin. My muscles were stiff and tense. My breathing was shallow, and my mind wouldn't turn off.

What would happen tonight? What would I hear and experience?

Gaga curled beside me in bed. I waited, aware of my every breath, my every heartbeat. The alarm clock beside the bed made a tiny purring noise with each minute that went past.

That's when I heard the first creak.

The house was just settling, I told myself. Old houses did that.

My heart continued to drum in my ears. But no other creaks.

My gaze went to the wall. I looked for that scowl again, a reminder of God's disappointment. Tonight, it was gone.

Instead of being relieved, the muscles between my shoulders tensed. I stared at the spot again. There was only one reason the scowl would be gone. The street lamp outside my bedroom window no longer let its light crawl through my shades. I had to wonder if it was poor timing or human manipulation that caused it, though.

I didn't have time to think about it as another creak sounded, causing my nerves to screech in fear. Was it the house settling? Or was it someone moving about on these floors?

Maybe I was hearing things. Yes, that was it. I'd built this up so big in my mind that I was beginning to imagine things. Creaky things. Spooky things.

I held my breath, waiting to imagine more things.

Another creak, this one closer.

Gaga sat up and growled at the door. Okay, maybe I wasn't hearing things.

The realization didn't comfort me. At all.

I grabbed Gaga and held her to my chest. She continued to growl. Was someone out there? Were they coming toward my door? Should I call the police?

Music floated into the room. Guitar music.

I couldn't move or breathe or halfway think.

Cooper's security system was supposed to prevent this. But someone had gotten inside anyway.

A ghost had gotten inside.

And I had no idea what to do.

So I prayed. Fast and furious. Any doubts about God seemed to disappear.

The music kept playing, some kind of enchanted-sounding melody that only managed to strike more fear into my heart.

Was it coming from inside the house? Could someone outside—like my creepy neighbor—be playing a guitar outside my window?

No, I decided. The music was definitely coming from the guest bedroom. But I'd moved that guitar to the basement just this morning.

My gaze focused on my door. I blinked. Was it my imagination or did the doorknob turn?

Gaga growled and then barked.

The doorknob went still.

Then something crashed.

16

I never thought I'd be so glad to get away from Elm Street. My initial impressions were incorrect. It was the street of nightmares and not the street of quaint American dreams. I could try to spin it any way I wanted, but the truth remained that something dark was going on inside Lana's house, and I had no idea what to do about it. At best, this seemed like a cheesy episode of *Scooby-Doo* and, at worst, like something that would one day end up on *Dateline NBC*.

I sat beside Cooper in the front seat of his truck while Austin played with some toys in the backseat. We went through a drive-through and got biscuits and coffee to enjoy on our two-and-a-half-hour journey up north.

I took a sip of my coffee and tried to erase the memories of last night, but the task was easier said than done. I'd remained chained to my bed by something invisible, unable to move. When daylight began lighting the windows, I managed to get out of bed. With bated breath, I'd opened my door, unsure what I might find.

In the living room, a clothes basket had either been knocked over or had fallen. Maybe I'd stacked my laundry more to one side, causing the basket to lose balance. I could justify that occurrence, if I had to. And that explained the crash I'd heard.

But the fact that I'd found the guitar in Lana's guest bedroom again was what really got to me. I'd moved the instrument down to the basement, but somehow it had ended up back in that closet. I had no explanation for that. Now, it was in the trashcan behind her house, which violated a Good Girls Rule on being a good houseguest and developed a new Bad Girls Rule: Stuff is just stuff, especially if it's not yours. For all I knew, the instrument might be worth hundreds of dollars. Right now I didn't care about money or value. Bad Girls Rule #8: Look out for yourself because no one else will. I had to care about my safety...and my sleep.

I sucked in a breath, determined to put last night out of my head, and glanced over at Cooper. I had to be careful not to let my gaze linger on him for too long because there was something about him that made me want to stare for hours on end. I quickly looked back out the window at the road in front of us. "So, you're dropping Austin off at your parents?"

"Sunni's parents, actually."

My eyebrows flickered up, and dread filled me. What had I gotten myself into? I was meeting his in-laws? Was it too late to ask him to turn around? "Oh. Wow."

"I take him up there for a week every summer. It's really important that they remain a part of his life. I hate to have him gone for so long, but he loves it up there."

What I wanted to say was, *Awkward*. Instead, I said, "That's great that he has grandparents so close who want to spend so much time with him."

He ran his hand over his chin before spreading his arm across the seat. "They took Sunni's death really hard. She was their only child. I would never keep Austin from them."

"So we're going to Duluth, huh? I've never seen any of the Great Lakes before."

"They have a house right on the lake. Gets mad cold in the wintertime, but in the summer it's perfect. We used to go waterskiing and camping up this way all the time." His voice took on a wistful tone, and I could tell he missed those days. My gaze went to his hand, to his wedding ring. It was still there, still a reminder of his unavailability.

"That sounds nice, Cooper. I've heard it's really beautiful up that way."

He glanced over at me. "You should spend some time up there while you're in town. It really is beautiful."

Get out of the ghost house for a while? That sounded fabulous. And impossible. "Maybe one day." *Once I figure out where I'm going to go and have my new start.* Maybe a small town on a lake would be nice. Or maybe I should go to a big city where I could virtually be invisible. So many choices, and I wasn't sure which one was the right one.

"You from up that way?"

"No. I'm from San Diego. I joined the Army after high school, became a Ranger, and then got out after serving for ten years. I got a job here and, about a month after I moved, I met Sunni in the produce section. I've been here ever since."

"Your parents still in California?"

"Retired down to Florida, actually. They live in one of those little retirement towns, and they love it."

Tension attacked my muscles. They lived in Florida? Then certainly they'd heard about me. Certainly they knew who I was and what I'd been accused of.

I didn't think there was any hope of a relationship between me and Cooper, but, just in case hope wanted to pop its head up, bullets of despair kept sending it ducking for cover.

"Tell me more about you, Tara. So far all you've said is that you're Lana's sister, you're dog-sitting, and you're divorced."

"That pretty much sums up my life." I forced a laugh out. "I'm in a weird place right now."

"How so?"

I looked out the window as the landscape blurred by. "Everything I thought I believed in has been turned upside down. Me along with it. I don't know which end is up anymore. I hardly know who I am."

"I can tell you who you are."

"But you don't know me."

He smiled. "I may not know all of the details of your life or your routines or the physical things that define you, but it's easy to sense your spirit, Tara."

Someone like you. I bristled. "And what do you sense?"

"In the short time I've been around you, I can tell that you have a sweet spirit, that you care about other people, that you're way too hard on yourself, and that you're struggling with a really big burden."

I nodded, speechless for a moment. "They teach you that in the Army?"

"Not exactly. I've always been pretty good at reading people."

"And you didn't run away from me?"

"Why would I do that?"

The sincerity of his voice nearly had me blushing. "Because lately I haven't liked myself. I'm not only disappointed in the circumstances around me, but I'm disappointed that I can't seem to let go of the hurts in my life. I thought I'd be so much farther along than this."

"You can't rush healing."

I was impressed. I really was. This man had more depth than most people I knew. He was kind but manly. Strong but gentle. Tough but compassionate. He was practically everything I'd ever dreamed about in a man. "You're pretty smart for a guy."

He grinned again. "You think?"

"Yeah, I do." I wrapped my arms over my chest. I couldn't remember the last time I'd felt this comfortable with someone or the last time I'd met someone who could see past my identity crisis and still like me, faults and all.

Not even Peter. On our second date, he'd pulled out a list of all the qualities he wanted in a woman. Thirty-one of them—an ode to Proverbs 31 perhaps? Right away, I'd felt even more pressure to be that perfect person, from the way I'd acted and dressed, to the words I said and the people I hung around. I'd been honored that I seemed to fit his expectations but, at the same time, his expectations had only fed the perfectionist beast inside me. The more I tried to conform into the person everyone wanted me to be, the more alone I felt.

I knew I had to stop feeling sorry for myself. But why did such a simple mission feel so impossible?

"Tara?"

I glanced over and realized that Cooper had said something. "I'm sorry, what was that?"

"Are you cold? I can turn the AC down." He reached toward the controls on the console.

"I'm fine." I stared out the window another moment, thoughts swimming around in my head. Finally one of them came up for air. Casserole Girl. "So you never did tell me about the girl at your house yesterday."

"I did tell you it was a story for another day, didn't I?" He glanced at me, a half grin on his face, and then shrugged. "There's not much to say really. She's a friend of a friend. I think she'd like to be more."

I wanted more information than that. I told myself it was just curiosity that drove my need for more details. "She was cute."

"She's young. Something about getting older and dealing with all of the setbacks in life helps you to build character, you know? I don't think she's there yet."

"You're in different phases of life. That makes sense." A man who admired character in a woman? I needed to pinch myself. When did that ever happen? "Have you dated a lot since...?" I couldn't even finish my question. I couldn't even say Sunni's name.

His jaw flexed as he stared ahead. "Here and there. It's hard to find time to date when you have a child. Plus there's the small issue of actually meeting women you want to date." His gaze flickered over to me. "You? You dated much since your divorce?"

If it wouldn't have been weird, I might have snorted in amusement. Instead, I shook my head. "No. Not at all, actually. Too many other things going on. My heart's just not in it, you know?" A few guys had asked. A couple had asked for the wrong reasons. None of them, not even one, had been a remote possibility.

"Yeah, I know what that can be like."

We pulled up to a large, well-kept cabin that had two layers of decks jutting out of the back with a direct view to Lake Superior. The blue of the lake rivaled the blue of Cooper's eyes. Cheerful flowers dotted the landscape, along with several whimsical flowerbed decorations—a tricycle with gardenias flowing from the basket at the front, some gnomes, and an iron stand with a blue and green ball at the top. The place looked welcoming and inviting.

Cooper stopped the truck and cut the ignition. "We're here. You ready, Austin?"

The little guy threw his hands in the air and let out a loud, "Yay! Grammy and Grandpa!"

Cooper opened the door, let Austin scramble out, and paused. "Aren't you coming?"

I hadn't moved. I hadn't even taken my seatbelt off. The word "awkward" continued to do a little dance in my mind, taunting me and reminding me that interacting with Sunni's parents would just be plain weird. "I should wait here. I don't want to be in the way."

"Tara, you won't be in the way. I promise." He stared at me with those intense, sincere eyes, leaned halfway in the truck.

His words were convincing, but I couldn't help but think that bringing another woman to your in-laws house was the worst idea ever. But maybe this would be a good step for me in not caring what other people thought. Besides, once my stay in Minnesota was over, I'd be leaving this place behind. How things played out today shouldn't matter to me—in theory.

I shrugged and climbed out of the truck. I tried to lag behind as we approached the front door, but Cooper waited for me while Austin skipped on ahead.

The door flew open and an older couple—whose faces absolutely beamed—stepped onto the porch and scooped down to give Austin hugs. The man was short with close-cropped white hair and a round face. The woman was plump with bobbed blondish-white hair and jellybean pink lipstick. A certain peacefulness exuded from them, and I instantly had the impression that these people were retired and loving a new laid-back lifestyle with each other in this dream location.

They straightened as Cooper approached and pulled him into a hug also. The picture twisted my gut with some foreign emotion. They just seemed to accept him so easily, as if he were the son they never had. Their fondness for him was evident by the tears rimming their eyes. What bittersweet memories must flood back to them at seeing Cooper.

Then they stepped back and looked at me with open curiosity. I suddenly wished I didn't have fire engine red highlights in my hair and a nose ring. I tensed, unsure of what to say, and settled for pulling a hair behind my ear and smiling with uncertainty.

"Gene and Margaret, this is Tara," Cooper started. His movements showed ease and not the slightest bit of discomfort. "She's from out of town and is along for the ride."

Gene reached his hand out to me, a welcoming smile across his face. "Pleasure to meet you, Tara. Why don't you both come inside? We've got lunch ready."

Margaret grinned. "It's your favorite, Cooper. Chicken pot pie."

"No one makes chicken pot pie like you, Margaret." Cooper slipped an arm around his former mother-in-law's shoulders as we walked inside.

As we ate, I watched everyone interact and slowly my unease faded. Sunni's parents seemed kind and loving. They gave me a glimpse into the person Sunni probably was also. Whomever Cooper eventually dated would have a lot to live up to. Dead spouses usually earned a sainthood medal. Sunni certainly had.

As the grandparents and Austin slipped outside to dip their toes in the lake, I decided to give them some time alone. I feigned needing some rest and stayed inside. As soon as everyone went out, I walked over to a bookshelf and stared at the pictures there. Pictures of Sunni were scattered throughout the house. She had a big smile, confident eyes, and sun-kissed skin and hair that made her look like the type who should be on the beach surfing. She probably looked perfect in a bikini too, for that matter.

"She was beautiful, wasn't she?"

I gasped and nearly threw the photo into the air. My hand covered my heart when Cooper came into focus. Not a ghost. Not a killer. Just Cooper.

"Didn't mean to scare you." His grin belied his words.

"I didn't even hear you come in." I tapped my heart, willing it to slow down. With Cooper this close, there wasn't a chance. I pointed to the picture. "She was beautiful. You guys looked very happy."

"We had some good years together." His gaze caught mine, and I realized how close he was standing. Close enough that, if I stood on my tiptoes, I could easily reach up and kiss him. Close enough that he could wrap his arms around my waist. Close enough that I was sure he could sense my heart beating out of control at his nearness.

"You're beautiful, too, you know." He said the words softly, so softly that I wondered if I imagined them.

Still, I found myself saying, "Thank you."

His gaze captured mine another moment. It had been a long time since I felt beautiful or desirable or even worthy of a relationship. All of the self-talk in the world hadn't changed anything. But a few words from Cooper seemed to begin the process of restoring something in me. I knew that change had to come from the inside out, but sometimes life and logic took on a mind of its own. Sometimes outside forces helped to start the inside process in motion. As Cooper stared at me now, I felt a connection between us as if it was a physical bond when, in fact, we weren't even touching.

The door flew open, and Cooper and I stepped away from each other. Gene paused in the entryway and grinned as if he knew he'd interrupted something. "Just grabbing some buckets so we can build a sandcastle."

Cooper shoved his hands down into his pockets. "We've got to get on the road anyway. I have to make a couple of stops on the way home."

I pointed behind me. "I just need to run to the bathroom first." I escaped quickly and doused my face with water. What had almost just happened? I looked around for a towel, but didn't see any. I let out a slow breath. Really? No towel? I seemed to remember Austin being charged with getting towels for the beach. I'd bet he'd grabbed every single one already in the bathroom.

I grabbed the next best thing—toilet paper—and blotted my face. At least it was dry now.

But when I looked in the mirror, I looked like an adolescent shaving for the first time. I pulled off white chunks of paper from my cheeks and chin. Great. Maybe I should go right to the loony bin where I could be known as Two Ply. Wouldn't Candy love that nickname?

After plucking off the gooey pieces of TP, I stepped outside. I'd tell them a quick good-bye and then I'd retreat to the truck to give them some privacy. I hoped Sunni's parents didn't resent me being here. My own former in-laws hadn't spoken to me in at least a year. I'd never truly felt accepted by them anyway, especially his mom. No one could ever be good enough for her little boy. Her last words to me were, "You should be ashamed of yourself." I'd held it together at the moment but as soon as I got into my car, I'd let the tears flow. Life could be so ugly sometimes.

My attention snapped back to the present. Sunni's mom smiled at me on the shoreline. I went to shake her hand and tell her thank you, when she pulled me into a hug. "You've got our approval," she whispered.

I stepped back, speechless. Did she mean what I thought she meant? She grinned and patted my arm.

What did I say to that? I didn't. I just stood there, my mouth open. But a fact settled in my heart. I didn't want her to like me or think highly of me because crashing down from a pedestal was one of the worst feelings in the whole world.

I offered an apologetic smile before trudging back to the truck.

Good Girls Rule #14,230,491: Never insult your hostess.

Apparently I wasn't very good at obeying my own rules, the good ones or the bad ones.

17

I slipped to the truck while Cooper told Austin good-bye. Austin tackled his father in the sand and Cooper pretended to fall back in defeat. The grandparents stood side by side, beaming down at their grandson. The scene warmed my heart. Here was a loving and kind family. Cooper obviously adored his son, and Austin looked up to his dad.

An ache of unfilled longing echoed in my chest as Cooper climbed into his truck, bringing with him the scent of fresh, lake-tinged air. He cranked the engine and the AC blew cool air through the vents. We waved to everyone as we started back down the road.

"That's got to be hard."

"It is, but it's easier because I know it's the right thing. I want him to know his grandparents. They're good people."

"It's great that you have a good relationship with them. That's important." Would I have been that gracious if I were in his shoes? I'd like to think so.

"They really have treated me like their son over the years. I couldn't have asked for better in-laws."

My in-laws had thought their son could do no wrong. But our problems went back farther than that. I'd always felt like I was simply the girl their son had married. Not the daughter they'd never had or a welcomed member of family. Maybe that was my doing just as much as it was theirs, though.

I decided to gracefully change the subject and move away from the topic of Sunni and the perfect marriage they'd had. "Do you know anything about the man who lives across the street from us? Next to Winnie?" Okay, maybe it wasn't all that graceful.

He sent me a side-glance. "Butch Mabry?"

"The one with eyes that look like they could freeze your blood and send you into cardiac arrest in five seconds flat." The way I described him, he might as well be a vampire.

Cooper chuckled and ran his hand over his face. "I don't know if I'd say it that way, but he's one strange cookie."

I leaned back into my seat and crossed my arms over my chest. "Is he married?"

"From all appearances. His wife is from Puerto Rico, I think. She doesn't speak much English, but she smiles when I see her across the street."

"What do you know about them?"

"Not much. I think he's a computer programmer. They're pretty quiet and to themselves. I don't think he's got very many social skills. He always seems a bit awkward...or like he'd like to freeze your blood with a mere glance and kill you." His wiggled his fingers in the air in an over-dramatic way that clearly poked fun at me.

I slapped his arm anyway. "He gives me the creeps."

"You talked to him?"

"I talked to a few neighbors to see if they'd seen anyone walk out with my blinds."

He cast a glance of approval as he nodded and raised his eyebrows. "Look at you. You're turning into a little detective, aren't you?"

"No, I'm not a detective, but I want answers."

"What did they say?"

"No one said anything, of course. Except Winnie, who saw Candy."

"Have you ever considered that Candy might be behind all of

this?" His voice sounded low and serious, as if he didn't want to ask the question.

"I've considered it. I mean, she likes attention, but I really don't think she's behind this. Nothing makes sense." Wasn't that the truth?

"I can't argue with that. It's almost like someone is trying to scare you out of the house. The question is why? Why now? Why you? Lana never had any of these issues, did she?"

I shook my head. "No. I mean, she had this stalker guy, but he's out of the country, and he never did anything like this. These recent issues didn't start until I came. And I don't know anyone in town, so I don't know why someone would want to scare me away."

Unless they wanted to get an accused pedophile out of the neighborhood. But there were other, more embarrassing and effective ways to do that.

"Let's think this through. What are some reasons that someone might want someone—not just you—out of a house?"

I'd thought of this a million times before and come up with the same lame answers. "There's something inside that they want?"

He shook his head with enough force that I could picture him sitting in on high-level meetings with his company, respectfully asserting his opinions. "But they've been getting into your house. If they can get inside, they should be able to get it."

"Maybe they can't find it."

"They don't want the person living inside to be around. They have something against them." He glanced at me. Watching my reaction maybe? "But it's like you said, no one around here should have a reason for wanting you gone. Unless they think you're Lana. You do look similar."

"Which brings us to the question of why would someone want Lana gone?"

"There could be a lot of reasons. She broke their heart and they want revenge. She took something that they felt was theirs—a TV role? A spokesperson gig? They just want to scare her to get their kicks?"

I shook my head. "You see—it's confusing. It doesn't make sense." I settled back in the seat and crossed my arms over my chest. My head was spinning with possibilities but no answers. I sucked in a calming breath, trying to gather my wits. "So tell me about this guy whose house you're stopping at."

"Steve's a fellow Ranger. We've had each other's back on more than one occasion. We stayed in touch after we got out. Jeremy was down in St. Paul looking for a house so I told him that there was one for sale beside me. He moved in, and the rest, as they say, is history."

"But even though you had mutual friends, you didn't really connect with the Millers, you said?"

"I gather that Jeremy Miller changed a lot after he got married. Steve will probably tell you the same thing." He pulled to a stop in front of an old white farmhouse surrounded by acres of nothing but open fields. "In fact, you can ask him now."

"That was fast."

Cooper hopped out and grabbed a fishing pole from the back of the truck. I joined him as we walked to the door. "We took a camping and fishing trip together a few weeks ago, and our poles got mixed up."

A stocky man with a buzz cut, a big smile, and sunburnt skin around the shoulders of his tank top threw the door open. "If it isn't Ben Cooper." He stepped back. "And who's this?"

Cooper stepped back. "This is my friend, Tara, who I told you about."

He grinned. "Pleasure to meet you, Tara. You two want to do some fishing while you're up here?"

"Wish we could. We'll plan another trip before the summer's up, though."

Steve waved his hand back. "Come and sit down for a minute. Let me grab you both a soda."

Cooper and I sat beside each other on a comfy, well-used beige couch. I looked around at the various deer heads adorning the walls, as well as a bobcat and bear. I shivered. I was definitely not the hunting type.

Steve set two cans of soda on the table in front of us before plopping into the recliner behind him. "What can I do for you, Tara?"

I popped the top of my drink and ran my hand along the rim. How did one approach difficult subjects like this without sounding off your rocker? "I know this might sound weird. I just want to say that upfront. But some strange things have been happening in the house, and I can't help but wonder if it's connected with the death of Danielle. I was hoping you could give me some more information on the couple, if I'm not being too intrusive."

The jovial man in front of me laughed and waved his hand in the air, taking a sip of his own diet soda. "Just ask Cooper about my gift of gab. I can talk for days about nothing, and for weeks about everything. What do you want to know?"

I swallowed hard before looking up and licking my lips. "Do you think he killed his wife?"

His smile disappeared. "No, I don't. He wouldn't hurt a flea, and he loved Danielle."

"Could you tell me about their relationship?" I leaned back with my drink in hand, ready to listen for a while.

Steve stared off in the distance for a moment. "Here's what I know. I know that they met at church, got married, and were like two bugs in a rug for a while. Then Danielle started experimenting with some weird stuff."

"What do you mean?" I took another sip of my drink, trying not to look too eager.

"Jeremy came home one evening. He thought Danielle was already asleep because the house was dark. He walked inside and found Danielle having a séance with some of her new friends in the living room."

"What did he do?"

"He demanded that everyone leave. He kicked them out. Same thing I would have done." Steve shook his head. "Danielle had dabbled with some tarot cards and crystals, but Jeremy thought it was just a passing phase. He'd prayed it was. That evening, it was clear that Danielle was all in."

"What happened next?" Tension built in my gut as I waited for him to finish.

"Jeremy didn't know what to do. He didn't want to break up his marriage. They went to counseling. The elders of the church came over to pray for them. He tried to give her space."

"It wasn't pretty." Cooper shook his head. "I could hear their arguments all the way over at my place."

Steve set his drink back onto the table beside him. "Jeremy still loved her. But some of the stuff she was doing really freaked him out.

Séances, tarot cards, crystals. It was like this dark cloud hung over their home, like she'd invited an unwelcomed guest in."

I was finally getting a clearer picture of the couple. "What caused the change?"

"Danielle grew up in a really great home with loving parents. They were always in church. Then Danielle's dad died. He had cancer, and the family had prayed and prayed for his healing and really believed it was going to happen. He ended up dying in this freak accident where he broke his neck and not from the disease. Danielle got mad at God. She wanted to talk to her dad, so that's how it all started. It spiraled out of control from there."

His words weren't lost on me. I didn't have time to ponder them now. "Did Jeremy ever mention how he thought she might have really died?"

"He's always thought it was one of her new friends she got mixed up with. But the murder weapon was never even found. The police have no evidence, just theories. It's the only reason he hasn't been arrested."

I stood. "Thanks for your help. I appreciate it."

He paused. "You think whoever killed her is still hanging around the house?"

"I'm wondering if the house was somehow the connection." I shook my head. "I know it doesn't make sense. I just know that something's going on, and I'm trying to get to the bottom of it. I have to. For my sanity."

A few minutes later, we were back in the truck headed home. The one thought from the conversation that stood out in my mind: *It was like she'd invited an unwelcome guest in.*

Chills raced through me at the thought. I knew the feeling all too well.

18

My utter exhaustion must have finally caught up with me on the ride home. The rhythm of the truck somehow lured me to sleep because, the next thing I knew, I was pulling my eyes open and un-suctioning my face from the window as the truck rumbled to a stop.

Only it didn't stop in front of my house.

I blinked, trying to gather my surroundings. Cooper's truck. On the way home. That was all I could remember. My heart rate quickened as confusion assaulted me. I looked over at Cooper, and, for just a moment, I wondered if he was the bad guy and this was part of his evil plot.

"Just one more stop," he promised.

Just hearing his voice made my doubts dissipate. I sat up and gazed out the window. We were parked in front of a stretch of businesses along a busy street. The buildings looked old and rundown with potato chip wrappers and fast food cups littering the sidewalk.

The sign in front of me read The Mercy House. The Mercy House? What was that exactly?

Cooper opened the door and climbed out. I could hear the cars zooming by on the busy street behind us, as well as a crowd of people somewhere singing a campy-sounding song. Cooper leaned into the truck. "Come in with me. There are some people I want you to meet."

I followed him into an older building that had once been a store but was now something called The Mercy House. Inside, people in dirty clothes crowded into a large room with old stained carpet, collapsible chairs, and a stage with a music stand. At the back of the room, behind some counters stocked with fruit and bottled water, were better-dressed folks ladling soup into bowls.

Was this a church? Church was the last place I wanted to be.

Suck it up, Buttercup.

Somehow I'd imagined Cooper going somewhere more polished and traditional. But this place...it was nothing like I imagined.

A middle-aged plump brunette broke from the crowds. She pulled Cooper into a hug. "I'm so glad you could stop by." She turned toward me. "I'm Wanda, the director for the homeless program. My husband Larry is the pastor here at The Mercy House."

"I'm Tara."

"Great to meet you."

I smiled. "Same here."

She turned to Cooper. "We fed fifty homeless today. Fifty. Our biggest turnout yet. But that's not all. Three of them are coming back to study with Larry tomorrow."

"From loaves and fishes to living bread. That's great." Cooper's big smile was gentle and genuine as he rested his hands at his waist and looked beyond Wanda to the crowds being fed. "It's good they can get out of this heat and get a little nourishment for the body and the soul. Did you have enough volunteers show up?"

"Just enough, as always. Isn't that the way God works?"

"It sure it." He handed her a folder. "Here's the estimate for a new sound system. I meant to drop them by earlier this week."

"We appreciate all your help, Cooper. We couldn't do everything we're doing here without our congregation being on board. God's moving in a big way through this church."

"Whatever you need, let me know. I'm always here."

Wanda grinned. "Nice to meet you, Tara. Come back and see us. Sundays at ten."

I'd rather stick my head in a toilet bowl than go to church, but I didn't say that.

We walked back outside to Cooper's truck and silently climbed inside.

With the door closed, I stared at the fading words on the church sign. "The Mercy House, huh? I like the name."

"It's a great place." He put the truck into reverse and pulled away.

"How long have you been going there?"

"Six years or so. I started off going to this church with a trendy preacher and flawless music. It should have been a perfect fit, but it didn't touch me here." He thumped his heart. "After stopping by The Mercy House on a whim, I knew God had stirred up something inside me. *I didn't want to look perfect while living a mediocre life. So I ended up here.*"

His words grabbed me. I didn't want to look perfect while living a mediocre life. I didn't have time to ponder the implications as Cooper continued.

"We just try to be the hands and feet of Jesus, and that means helping the poor and the hurting and the struggling. It's a great place. We're not polished. We may not fit the mold of the typical 'American Christian.' But that's okay."

"It sounds like it." The American Christian. Isn't that what I had been? All polished and clean on the outside, but lacking total abandon toward God. No, I may not have been like Lana, but I still treasured my nice clothes and house and taking vacations. I'd learned how to look and talk like a Christian, but never how to actually be a Christ-follower.

My parents had read the Bible and said prayers together and were at church every time the doors were open. For a while, I'd even wondered if I'd been born in the church's nursery. But sometimes I just felt like I was going through the motions, that I was just trying to follow in my parents' footsteps.

My parents had big footsteps to follow in, at that. My dad not only pastored a ten-thousand-member congregation, but he also had a radio show and had published three bestselling books on the Christian life and parenting. Almost anyone in the Christian community would recognize his name.

All of that just made everything that had happened that much more terrible. Disappointment bit down deep again.

If I were to be honest, I'd admit that I felt second-place to the church. My dad wasn't home often. When he was home, I'd felt a need to please him by acting perfectly. Maybe I'd get more attention that way.

No wonder I viewed God the same way as I'd viewed my father.

Don't get me wrong. I loved my dad. I just didn't feel like I could ever please him. He'd come to expect Lana to mess up and, instead, all of those expectations for her were placed two-fold on me. At least, in my mind they had been.

Cooper continued talking about The Mercy House. "It's full of people who aren't perfect. And I really mean not perfect. Former drug addicts and prostitutes. People who don't have things figured out and who don't pretend like they do."

I cast him a sideways glance. "You seem pretty perfect."

His eyes met mine. "I'm anything but perfect, Tara. Up until I got married, I lived a pretty wild life. I did a lot of things I regret. I hurt a lot of people. I wish I could go back and redo things, but I can't. Instead I just do the best with who I am today."

"Sometimes doing everything right still leaves you with regrets." I said the words so softly that I hardly recognized my own voice.

We shared a brief look. I didn't feel like he judged me, but that he understood.

We pulled up in front of our houses, and I smiled at Cooper as he sat in the driver's seat. "Thanks for everything today. I really appreciate it."

He nodded toward my house. "Is it okay if I walk you inside?"

My heart filled with relief. I hated that house and had dreaded going inside alone. "Of course."

We walked to the porch. At the front door, I saw a paper tucked in the brass handle. Who would be leaving me a note? I pulled it out and squinted at the scrawl there.

Danielle want to talk to you. Call me. Miss Mystic.

I stared at the letter. Didn't talking to the dead require a séance? I'd already considered having *Ghost Chasers* come to my place. When my life derailed, it seriously derailed, didn't it?

19

I stared at the note, at the eerie way the shadow of a tree branch splayed across it, at the spider-like scribble. The words blurred then came back into focus.

Danielle Miller—a dead woman—wanted to talk to me.

That or Miss Mystic was desperate for business. The prior was the most likely truth. Still, the idea intrigued me.

"Who's Miss Mystic?"

My cheeks heated as I realized that Cooper had read the note over my shoulder. It wasn't exactly like I'd been hiding it. Still, I licked my lips before answering, suddenly self-conscious. "The psychic who was friends with Danielle."

Cooper raised his eyebrows as he stood beside me, his surprise evident. "A psychic?"

I sighed, not in exasperation but in contemplation. "It's a long story." I punched in my alarm code and unlocked the front door.

Cooper followed me inside, shutting the door behind him. "I have time."

Of course he had time. My life would be way too easy if he didn't have time to give me a lecture on what was wrong with me.

I pointed to the couch, not slowing down in my efforts to escape his questions as I hurried toward the kitchen. "Why don't you sit down? Do you want some coffee?"

He lowered himself onto the couch, stretching his arm across the back. "I'd love some."

I started a pot and leaned with my palms against the counter as the liquid percolated. How was I going to explain this? What would he think of me when I did? I had no choice but to go and talk to Cooper while it brewed. There was so much that I didn't want to tell him. As much as I thought I'd been broken, there were still areas of pride in my life. Talking about a psychic and ghosts and my little-to-be-admired faith were not things he'd think highly of, and rightfully so. But they were true to where I was in my life right now, like it or not.

I sat down across from him and pulled my feet under me. He said nothing, waiting patiently for me to begin. The words didn't want to dislodge themselves from my throat. Finally, I licked my lips. "I've told you about the weird stuff going on here."

Cooper nodded. "You have."

"I went to talk to Miss Mystic this week—not talk as in consult with her, but just to ask her a few questions."

"You think a psychic has the answers?"

I shook my head, probably a little too hard. "No. I asked her about her friendship with Danielle. I thought she would have those kinds of answers."

His shoulders seemed to relax some at my statement. "Did she?"

That was the question of the hour. I shrugged. "It's confusing. I don't know. I just know that something weird is happening." I would tell him about the guitar, but then I'd sound crazy. I knew I would. And, I had to admit, I was starting to like Cooper, so the thought of him thinking of me as loony didn't have much appeal.

He leaned closer, no signs of teasing on his face. "I just feel like you're on the verge of getting pulled into something dark and dangerous."

The concern in his voice was enough to twist my heart. "I'm not trying to get pulled into anything. I'm just trying to find answers."

He leaned back again, his gaze strained. "I'm not trying to quote Scripture to you here or to preach or to judge, Tara, but light and darkness don't mix."

Irritation ground away at the good feelings I was having toward Cooper. I felt judged, and I was so tired of feeling judged. "I know that. Believe me, I know that."

"Then why do you keep teasing it?"

"How am I teasing the darkness?" My voice rose in pitch with each word.

"By considering jumping into it!"

"I'm not considering it." My voice had risen beyond what I intended. I just realized that my legs were no longer pulled underneath me, but were now on the ground as if I was ready to lunge. "And even if I was, what difference would it make?"

Cooper leaned toward me. "What do you mean what difference would it make? It would make all the difference in the world." His voice sounded surprisingly even.

I stared at him. Was he talking about a difference in life or in our budding friendship? Maybe both? I shook my head again. "You wouldn't understand."

"I just expected more from you."

"Don't expect anything from me. Please." I rubbed my temples, which were beginning to throb. "You know, I'm getting a headache. We should have that coffee another day."

"Tara..."

"Excuse me." I stood and went to my bedroom, shutting the door behind me. I was breaking every rule I'd ever created about not being rude and how to be a good hostess and not make others feel self-conscious. I was just so tired of disappointing people. I was tired of being burdened with being good. Tired of not living up to expectations. I'd tried so hard for so long. All of those efforts had failed, so why keep up the effort?

A few minutes later, I heard the front door open and shut. Tears burned at my eyes. Yet another person I'd let down. I thought it would hurt less with time, but it didn't.

I curled up on the bed and closed my eyes.

The doorbell caused my eyes to flutter open. Gaga stood in bed beside me, growling toward the other room.

Had I fallen asleep? I rubbed my eyes and looked at the clock. Nine p.m. I rubbed my eyes again. Who would be coming over at this hour? Against my better instincts, I climbed out of bed and crept toward the door.

My gaze skittered across the floor, looking for a sign that something was wrong. Everything appeared in place.

Cooper. It was probably Cooper. Coming over to apologize? Our conversation replayed in my mind, and my heart plunged in hurt. I just couldn't bare the thought of disappointing one more person. For that reason, maybe I shouldn't form any more relationships ever. Wasn't that the only way I'd truly ever avoid letting someone down?

I peered through the peephole and stepped back when I saw the figure there. She wore big hoop earrings, a fancy scarf around her head and a gypsy skirt. I pulled the door open and scowled. "Miss Mystic. What are you doing here?"

She leered at me, her tiny chin rising. "Danielle have a lot to tell you. You ready to listen yet?"

I started to shut the door. "I don't have anything to say to Danielle."

The strong little woman jammed her foot on the threshold. "You not hear me? I said *Danielle* has stuff to say to *you*. You no talk. Just listen."

"You can't talk to the dead. It's impossible. Even if it is possible, it's wrong, and I don't want anything to do with it."

"I know where murder weapon is. She tell me and want me to tell you."

I paused against my better judgment. "Murder weapon?"

"Her husband stab her with a knife."

The newspaper had reporter that there had been a lot of blood found at the house. But, with no body, stabbing hadn't been confirmed. Couldn't a gunshot cause a person major blood loss? Why did Miss Mystic think she'd been stabbed? "How do you know that?"

Her chin jutted out. "Danielle tell me."

My throat was as dry as Elisha's bones. "You're making that up."

Her chin rose. "No, I not."

"Then where is it?"

"It hidden inside house. Danielle trying show you where, if you let her. I only want friend to find peace." She drew out the word "peace," her breath spraying into my face and halitosis threatening to knock me flat on my back.

I couldn't handle this conversation anymore. It was going to cause nightmares tonight. "You don't know what you're talking about." I tried to push the door shut, but that foot was still there, blocking the action.

"I see great deal of pain in you past. It tear you apart inside. You must deal with it, Miss Lancaster. You must open yourself up again."

How did she know about my past pain? I closed my eyes, refusing to believe she knew anything. She was just a good guesser. "Good-bye, Miss Mystic." I managed to shut the door before I melted against its wood with my eyes closed and my heart racing.

Bad Girls Rule #9: Don't stay within the lines. I really liked boundaries, though, for everything to be neat and ordered.

But the even bigger question was this: If a supposed psychic was going to come to my house, why couldn't they look like Simon Baker from *The Mentalist*?

Again, I hadn't gotten any sleep the night before. There were no crashes or guitar music, but I had heard some creaks. Maybe my lack of sleep was a part of my problem. Not getting enough rest could play with you mentally and cause all sorts of problems like hypersensitivity, hallucinations, premature aging.

I woke with a new resolve. I wouldn't get answers from Miss Mystic. But I would try to find answers somewhere else. I'd hunt for answers the way Cooper's friend Steve hunted for deer.

I called the *St. Paul Star* and found out that reporter Bryce Stephens still worked for the newspaper. I figured if I was ever going to get any sleep, I had to have some answers. Besides, figuring out this mystery was a better option than sitting around thinking about myself all day.

Suck it up, Buttercup, I repeated mentally. It was my new goal, and I was determined to do just that. Even I was sick of my whining.

A receptionist put me through to the reporter, and a gravely voice came on the other line.

"Mr. Stephens? My name is Tara Lancaster. I have a question about the supposed murder of Danielle Miller and wondered if we could meet for coffee sometime."

No response. I wished I had a phone cord to twirl as I waited. Anything was better than the baited breath I held. "Miz...Lancaster, you said? I'm afraid I'm a very busy man. I just don't have time to chat."

"I live in the house where the supposed crime occurred."

Silence. A tapping sound in the background. I pictured him clicking a pen on his desk, trying to think of an excuse to get off the phone. "Do you have information on the crime?"

"Some weird things have been going on at the house. I'm trying to find some answers, and I was hoping you could help me." I crossed my fingers, hoping he might change his mind.

"You live in the house, you say?" Silence. More tapping in the background. "Where would you like to meet?"

I closed my eyes and uttered a mental *yes*. As I used to say in junior high, *cha-ching*!

We arranged to meet at Java the Hut, a nearby coffeehouse, in an hour. That meant I had to get ready now. I shuffled into the bathroom and frowned at my reflection.

Huge circles haunted my eyes, evidence of my sleepless night. I'd stayed awake, under the covers, just waiting to hear another sound, to have someone rip my comforter off. Nothing had happened, nor did anything look strange or out-of-place this morning—except me, paranoid Tara looking like a zombie.

I smoothed my hair into a ponytail and pulled on some jeans and a button-up blue shirt. I hardly recognized myself in the mirror still, not with my new fake tan, edgy hair color and nose ring. I ran a hand under my eyes. "Who are you, Tara Lancaster?" I mumbled.

No ghostly voice answered back.

Within the hour, I was sitting at a corner table at Java the Hut, sipping on a non-fat, sugar-free vanilla latte. I inhaled the scent of coffee and cinnamon and chocolate. I listened to the grind of the coffeepot, to the squeal of whip cream being slathered atop a warm, sugary drink. I closed my eyes, absorbing every sensory detail. I loved this place, from its warm, chocolate-colored walls to its chunky wooden chairs and tables.

Each time the glass door at the front of the store opened, my head jerked up and I expected to see someone who looked like a Bryce Stephens. In my mind, the reporter was a cranky old man who wore horn-rimmed glasses and had elbow patches on his blazer. The truth was I had no idea who I was looking for.

I took another sip of my drink and mentally reviewed my questions. I had to find some answers. Despite my overblown imagination, I refused to think that a ghost lived in Lana's house. I couldn't believe that. It put everything I valued in jeopardy. I probably shouldn't have been so hard on Cooper. I mean, he was right. I'd been defensive and immature. If he didn't speak to me again before I left, I couldn't blame him. My heart twisted with surprising sadness, though.

Tara Lancaster had ruined something else great. It was becoming one of my many talents.

"Tara Lancaster?"

A man in his forties with square shoulders, a fading hairline, and rimless glasses stood at my table. His face was pale and his clothes wrinkled as if he spent too much time inside. "I'm Tara. You must be Bryce."

He pulled out the seat across from me and sat down slowly. His steadfast gaze made me squirm. This was a man with a mission, not someone who wanted to sit down and casually chat. I didn't dare ask him if he wanted a drink. "How can I help you, Tara?"

I swallowed and pushed my latte away. "I was hoping you could tell me about the murder—the supposed murder—of Danielle Miller."

His gaze remained on me, unblinking. "You said strange things have been happening at the house?"

I shrugged and stared at my paper cup for a moment. "Strange is one way to say it." I explained about the missing shades, the threatening note, and my visit with Miss Mystic. Bryce snorted when I said her name, and I raised a brow. "You have an opinion about St. Paul's local psychic, I take it."

"Lots of opinions." He rolled his eyes.

"Like?"

He crossed his arms and sat up even straighter than before. "She's tried to lead the police to a body that wasn't there."

"I hadn't heard that."

"She doesn't know anything. She's just blowing off steam, hoping something she says will be true and she'll get credit for solving the crime one day. That's how they all do it."

"Who's 'they'?"

"Psychic detectives. They make random guesses. Until a body shows up. Then they take the credit. Sometimes they prey on innocent families who have missing children, giving them hope. The families are so desperate to find their kid that they'll pay huge amounts of money for any crumb of insight a psychic might have into where their child is. They're all frauds."

"Are you saying Miss Mystic is preying on innocent people?"

"I'm saying she tries to butt into police investigations all the time."

"Has she said anything else about this case, other than Danielle needs closure before she can cross over?"

"Oh yeah. She apparently gave the police the location of Danielle's body—a shallow grave. In the woods. By a body of water. That didn't get their attention. So then apparently she had a clearer vision. She told them the section of town even. The police went there and there was nothing. Nada. Zilch."

"I heard she and Danielle were friends. I guess she just wants to help."

He shrugged. "She tried to give more clues later. Something about the murder weapon being underfoot. No one took her seriously this time. Thankfully."

"In other words, I shouldn't believe anything she says?"

He pulled his lips back in a scowl. "You need me to tell you that?"

My eyes went back to my cup. "Not really. I'm just confused. I don't understand what's going on, but I do know that Danielle Miller keeps coming up every time I try and find out anything."

"Have you ever considered it could be something unrelated?" His brows hung suspended.

"I've considered it."

He leaned forward and sighed. I thought I saw pity in his eyes.

"Listen, I've been following this case since the beginning. A year ago next Tuesday, Danielle's husband killed her."

"A year ago next Tuesday? You mean, the anniversary of her death is coming up?" I shivered as I said the words.

"That's right. It looks like it will turn out a cold case."

"Who do you think did it?"

"Her husband. He makes the most sense. He had motive, means, and opportunity. The police will find their evidence one day."

"What's her husband say?"

"Keeps claiming he's innocent. He's trying to track down who 'really' did it, apparently. I think it's just for show."

I leaned forward now. "Why are you so sure he's guilty?"

"Because there are so many holes in his story. Besides, I know a guilty man when I see him. Jeremy Miller is guilty as sin. He killed his wife and got away with it. It's enough to make anyone—alive or dead—want vengeance."

His words made me shiver. I took another sip of my now lukewarm latte. "Are there any other suspects?"

Bryce shrugged and leaned back stiffly. "The police checked out a couple of leads, but nothing came of them. Some people think it was a random crime. Nothing was stolen from the house, though."

"But it could have been random. Sick people do sick things all the time. Random things. I hear about them every day on the news. Serial killers. Psychos. Loonies."

"Some people think that maybe it was a client of Danielle's, someone who'd received a vision into their future that they didn't like."

"But you say it's Jeremy."

He shrugged. "He had motive, means, and opportunity. You tell me who else has all three of those?"

20

I stared at Cooper's house as I pulled the Hummer up to the curb between our houses. Was he inside working? Did he hate me? Was he still reeling from his revelation last night that I was even more messed up than he'd given me credit for?

I tried to pretend like I didn't care, but I did.

I stepped out of the car, and my skin pricked. My gaze swung upward. My neighbor stood at his window, binoculars in hand. He ducked when he spotted me. Chills crept over me. Not again. Just what was that man up to?

It was already six o'clock when I walked inside. It was hard to believe I'd spent the whole day as an amateur sleuth. And again I had to face this awful house alone. The thought of the neighbor across the street keeping an eye on me sent another army of imaginary spiders crawling over my skin.

I let Gaga out into the backyard, careful to stay inside just in case Cooper was outside. I didn't want to face him. I seemed destined to ruin anything good in my life, and I had no one to blame but myself. I stayed at the back window, staring at the backyard where darkness was beginning its entrance into the sky. That meant the Creepy Hours were getting closer. Already anxiety began to set in. What would happen tonight, and how would I handle it?

My doorbell rang. Apparently, no one in St. Paul believed in calling before stopping by. That had been my experience so far, at least. For a brief moment, my heart fluttered with the hope that it might be Cooper. Maybe we could talk and make things right.

When I jerked the door open, Candy and Mark stood on the other side. "Hey Maui!" Candy barged inside, Mark behind her. "We're taking you out tonight. You've been cooped up in this house alone for too long."

If she only knew about where I'd been and what I'd discovered...

"We want to show you a little bit of the Twin Cities." Mark winked.

I shook my head, knowing exactly where this was going. "I'm not going to a rave."

"It's not a rave. It's a social gathering, and it's going to be a blast." Candy looked me up and down. Was that a sneer? I thought we'd come farther in our friendship. "Go on. Get dressed."

"I am dressed." Black shorts and a T-shirt.

Candy grabbed my arm and pulled me toward the hallway. "Let's go raid Lana's closet."

Fifteen minutes later, I was wearing a skirt and a burgundy shirt that hugged my skin a little more than I was used to. Candy had wanted me to wear a skin-tight shirt with a plunging V in the front, but I'd refused. I looked in the mirror, and the result wasn't too bad. A little edgier than I usually liked, but the outfit was still modest enough.

"Tell me about this party," I said as we walked back into the living room.

I had a feeling today Candy was more of chocolate-covered grasshopper—something some people would consider a delicacy but that most would consider crazy. "It's going to be a blast. You'll see."

I also had a feeling that Candy's idea of a blast and mine were totally different.

Bad Girls Rule #10: Seize the party.

Mark let out a low whistle when we walked into the room. "You look hot."

My cheeks heated. "Thanks...I think."

"Don't tell your sister I told you this, but you might even be prettier than she is."

I'd never heard that one before. I knew I looked decent, but Lana had always been the strikingly gorgeous one. Her looks had gotten her in trouble on more than one occasion, but they'd also opened up some amazing opportunities.

We climbed into Mark's lime-green Jeep. The first thing I noticed were the crystals hanging from the rearview mirror. Crystals? I hadn't taken Mark as the type.

Immediately my muscles tightened. Did he know Miss Mystic? I mentally shook my head. No, I was reading too much into things. Mark had no connection to any of the craziness around me. Still, I felt shaken and trapped as we pulled away from the curb.

I glanced back at Cooper's place and saw him step out of the front door. For some reason, my heart panged with unexpected sadness. Spending time with Cooper seemed much more appealing than partying.

I was just one big mess. I didn't know what I wanted or who I was, and, for that reason, I was enough to drive myself crazy. At moments, I thought I wanted love. But not love like Peter's love. He'd fled like a frightened cat at the first sign of danger.

I thought I'd loved that man. He'd made my heart race and made me feel like I was the most special woman in the world. Then the going had gotten tough and he'd skedaddled from my life. When love was wonderful, it was wonderful. But when it was awful, it was awful. Would I ever be ready to take the good with the bad again? I didn't know.

Candy rambled in the front seat, all while looking at her phone and reading Facebook status updates aloud. I found myself liking Candy more and more as I got to know her better. Sure, our worldviews were entirely different, but her total disregard for the opinion of others was like a breath of fresh air.

I caught Mark looking at me from the front seat, and heat rushed to my cheeks. He laughed and looked back at the road. Why would someone like Mark be interested in me? It just didn't make sense. It was both flattering and unnerving.

If I were to truly do the opposite of whatever I would normally do, then I'd let my hair down. I'd give Mark a chance. I'd try to actually have fun.

We pulled up to a large house located on what had to be ten acres on the banks of the Mississippi. Forget *Jersey Shore*. This was *Mississippi River Shore*. As we stepped out of the car, I could hear the music and crowd inside the house. My muscles tightened, and my heart pumped harder. I shouldn't be here.

I should have driven. That way I could turn around right now and go back home, just as everything inside me screamed to do.

I couldn't move from my spot on the grass. Instead, I watched as adults acted like teenagers and chased one another around the house. Whenever the door opened, music poured out. I could only imagine what was going on inside.

Mark's hand went to my back. His presence was overwhelming. So why didn't I feel safe like I did with Cooper? "Let's go."

"I..." I put on brakes.

Candy did her head tilt. "It's going to be fun. Live a little. No one's going to make you do anything you don't want to do."

A moment of temporary relief came over me. Right. I could still make choices.

But, at once, I imagined being with Cooper, running errands and chatting. Most people would consider it boring. But I found comfort in the thought. I wasn't a party kind of girl, and I had to face the fact that I never would be.

Sometimes you could take a girl out of the church, but you couldn't take the church out of the girl.

I was swept inside the massive house and immediately stopped in my tracks. The overhead lights were off and flashing lights were in their place, electronic music blared, people danced and drank and made-out. The place reeked of body odor and alcohol.

I looked back at Candy and shouted, "This isn't a rave?"

"Not officially." She grinned and grabbed my hand. "Come on. Mark and I will show you the ropes."

She pulled me into a sea of people and turned toward me. "Let's dance." She threw her hands in the air and began moving with the music.

I stood there and stared at her. I really was a party pooper, wasn't I?

"Dance!" She grabbed my arms and waved them in the air, all while my hands hung limply at my wrists. What had I gotten myself into? This was not my thing, and I couldn't even pretend like it was. I guess if I was a cool Christian, I could come here, blend in and witness. But I wasn't. Likely, I'd never be.

"I don't really dance." Well, sometimes I danced when no one was looking, but it was never pretty when I did. Mostly I did jazz hands and the two-step. Occasionally I might throw in the sprinkler, but only when I wanted to feel like a complete dork.

She continued to flop my hands in the air. "Just move a little."

"No thanks."

"Come on."

She wasn't going to give up, was she? I rolled my eyes and bounced a little.

Candy did her head tilt again. "That's pathetic, Tara."

I nodded, not in the least bit ashamed of my lack of coordination. "I know."

At least she dropped my hands. Two women came up to talk to her. I tapped her on the shoulder. "I'm going to mingle."

Candy's eyes widened, but she nodded. I stepped away, overwhelmed by the crowds around me. What had I gotten myself into? This might be how the other half lived, but it wasn't how I lived. My faith in God or lack of faith didn't matter. This just wasn't me.

I pushed my way through the crowd, the music so loud that I could hardly think. The music was doing more than make my head spin—it was starting to give me a headache, and I'd only been here for ten minutes so far. This was going to be a long evening. I thought of calling Cooper to come get me despite not seeing eye to eye. Except I had no idea where I was.

I found a place against the wall, away from some of the crowds that flooded the interior. I'd bet the place looked nice minus the party scene. I felt like a high schooler who'd snuck off to a party at my friend's house while her parents were out of town. Weren't these people a little too old for that?

This was totally Lana's scene, wasn't it? She'd fit right in, dancing and drinking with the best of them. She had no regrets while all I seemed to have was regrets. I'd have an easier time trying to make sense of the book of Revelation than I would making sense of myself.

I was determined to make changes in my life but finding those changes much harder to come by, especially since my conscience was involved.

"Not your scene?"

I looked up and saw Mark staring at me. He was good looking. Way good looking, and he obviously knew it. For some reason, he seemed to have his sights set on me. I didn't seem like his type unless he liked women who were hard to get. His attention was flattering, but that was all. I shook my head and shouted, "Not my scene."

He nodded toward the crowd. "It can be fun. You just gotta let down your guard."

"I'm not good at letting down my guard."

"I could show you." Blue and red lights from the disco ball on the ceiling flashed on his face while a techno dance version of "Call Me Maybe" played overhead.

I shook my head. "I'm going to pass on that one. Thanks, though."

"How about if I get you a drink then? We can go outside and talk. Get away from some of this noise."

Mark? Go outside and talk? Surprisingly sensitive, but maybe I'd misread the man. "I'd like that. I just want a soda, though."

He winked. "You got it."

I drew in a deep breath. Maybe this wouldn't be so bad if I could just get away from this pulsating music and the sea of people inside the home. Mark appeared a moment later and handed me a plastic cup. His hand wrapped around my elbow, and he led me out the door and onto a massive paved patio, complete with lighted fountains and a pool—which was also crowded with people.

We kept walking until we were past the crowds there. Instead, we perched on a ledge with a bird's eye view of the river. I could still hear the music behind me, but my heart beat much slower out here. Crickets sang their nighttime song and calmed my racing heart some.

"So you're nothing like your sister, are you?" Mark took a sip of his drink. His watch slipped down, and a tattoo on his wrist became visible. I thought they were called a "third eye," the mystical symbol associated with New Age.

Crystals and a third eye? What did that mean?

I snapped back to our conversation. "No, Lana and I are nothing alike."

"Lana...she's hard to keep up with. She's one crazy chick."

I smiled, thinking about my sister. "Yeah, she is."

"You guys get along?"

"Surprisingly, yes. We disagree on most lifestyle issues, but we're still sisters. We're there for each other when no one else is." She'd been there for me after the Peter fiasco, and I'd been there for her during hangovers, breakups, and after foolish things she'd done on camera. Lana had a tendency to grieve and then be done with it. I, on the other hand, had a hard time shaking things off. No amount of praying or self-help books had changed that, so I'd simply accepted that trait for what it was—a trait that I needed to make the best of.

I took a sip of my drink and nearly spit the liquid out. "What is this?"

"Diet Pepsi."

"Is that all?"

He smiled, a telltale sign. "Maybe."

"I said no alcohol."

"Just a little won't hurt."

Was he right? Why did I always fall to the extremes? And, even if drinking alcohol wasn't wrong in itself, was it wrong to go against my conscience, which screamed, "Don't do it!"? I didn't know. Living with black and white answers was much easier than living with the unknowns. I took another sip.

"Isn't it weird being here and not knowing anyone?"

It was the number one reason I liked it here, actually. "No, not really."

"Sometimes it's good to be anonymous, huh?"

I nodded. "It sure is. You don't seem like the type who would understand that." I wasn't sure why Cooper had told me to stay away from Mark. He seemed like nothing but a gentleman. I took another sip of my drink, trying to follow my new rules. Bad Girls Rule #10: Being sensible does not translate into being fun.

"I have my moments of understanding." He ran his finger across my cheek. "You're really beautiful, you know."

His touch seemed so foreign...and so forward. I didn't quite know how to react, so I took another sip of my drink. "Thank you."

"You're like one of those women who's a trophy wife."

I'd been called a lot of things before but never a trophy wife. I wasn't sure what to think about that. I'd been up on a pedestal before, but I didn't like it. I'd much rather be at someone's level. Even the mention of being a trophy made tension build in me. Sometimes I just didn't want people to have expectations of me.

My thoughts drifted back to Cooper. I wondered what he was doing. Why was I thinking about him when I was here with a handsome man who seemed to be enjoying my company? I didn't feel judged around Mark. Could it be because he had no standards?

I resisted a sigh, frustrated at myself and my inability to stop thinking. Instead, I took another sip of my drink. My head was beginning to feel fuzzy and warm. What had he put in it?

Mark leaned over until I looked him in the eye. "Listen, I know this isn't your thing, Tara. If you want, I'll drive you home."

Home? I could go home? That sounded lovely. As my head spun some more, it sounded even more than lovely. I put the cup on the ledge, needing to stop drinking, but I was afraid the damage had already been done. I hadn't been sure how my body would handle alcohol but now I knew—not well. "I'd love to go home. Thanks Mark. What about Candy?"

"I'll text her. She'll find a way home. Believe me."

I nodded. "Okay then. Thank you. I appreciate it."

Maybe my impressions of people were totally wrong. When would I ever learn?

21

Mark pulled up in front of my house and walked me to the front door. I supposed that tonight hadn't been too bad. I mean, sure, I'd felt like a fish out of water. I'd had one too many drinks—only one drink for that matter, but I had no tolerance for alcohol. I'd listened to music that glorified activities I'd at one time been adamantly against. I embraced a hedonist lifestyle that I'd told people would only leave them empty.

But what if I was wrong? What if we only get one chance at happiness and had to make the best of it? *You only live once*, wasn't that the saying?

On second thought, maybe I should wait until this alcohol was out of my system before I made any big life decisions like that.

Mark stopped by the front door, the light from the porch illuminating his hair. Not like it had Cooper's, though. Cooper had appeared to have a halo while Mark...I wasn't sure what the light did for him. I was surprised he'd even been gentleman enough to walk me to the door, but maybe I'd pegged him wrong. He'd been nothing but considerate.

"It was fun tonight." He stepped closer, and his hands went around my waist.

My throat felt dry. Maybe walking me to the door wasn't so much the act of a gentleman as it was the act of someone who wanted something.

"Thanks for driving me home."

His eyes had a smoldering look about them as he leaned into me. "Aren't you going to invite me in?"

Invite him in? Was he crazy? Not with the way my head was spinning. What had he put in my drink exactly? I'd assumed it had been a shot of some kind of alcohol. Now I didn't know. "It's a mess inside."

He kissed my neck, and his hands began traveling places where they were unwelcome. "I don't care."

I tried to take a step back but couldn't. He was too close, and I was too pressed up against the door. "I do."

"Come on, Tara. Don't be a prude."

A prude? Like I'd never been called that before.

That may have been the lifestyle I was trying to forget, but one couldn't shrug off their conscious like a winter coat. Some things took time, and everything in me said no.

Before I could answer, his lips covered mine. His kiss was hungry, wanting more—more than I wanted to give.

I pressed both of my hands against his chest and pushed him back. Fear burned in my throat and shot warning flares into my brain. "No. What do you think you're doing?"

"Don't play all innocent with me, Tara. I know who you are."

The warning flares stopped firing long enough for numbness to spread through me. "What does that mean?"

"I know about you. About Florida. I like it."

I shook my head, my raging emotions—and the alcohol—making my brain spin. Making nausea roil in my gut. Making tears wet my eyes. "You don't know anything."

"I won't tell anyone." He looked behind me. "If you let me come in for a little while."

"Don't try to blackmail me."

"Come on, Tara. Drop the act." His lips covered mine again, even more aggressive than last time.

I tried to push away, but couldn't. He had me pinned where I was, and he kissed me like it was his right. Panic clawed at my stomach. Why did I get myself in this situation? How was I going to get myself out of it?

All of the sudden, Mark jerked backward.

"What do you think you're doing? I think the woman said back off."

My gaze cleared until Cooper came into focus. Cooper who held Mark by his shirt collar.

"Mind your own business, Cooper." Mark growled the words. I prayed a fight wouldn't break out, for more than one reason. Mostly because if I tried to break it up, I'd most likely fall limply on the ground with the inability to hold myself up.

Cooper shoved Mark back. "I can't mind my own business when you're over here being a jerk."

"What Tara and I do is between the two of us. She doesn't need you acting like a knight in shining armor."

I held up a finger, but I saw two of them. Man, my head was messed up. "Actually, I do need a knight in shining armor. Not some...some... someone like you."

Mark stared at me a moment, anger simmering in his eyes. Finally, he jerked out of Cooper's clutch and stomped toward his car, throwing another scowl back toward us before he climbed in. He jerked his door open. As soon as he drove away, my pittering heart slowed.

If Cooper hadn't shown up, I wasn't sure what would have happened. I only knew that I was an idiot and that I was scared. My hands trembled. My cheeks were wet. My heart pounded in my ears.

I remembered the crystals on Mark's rearview mirror. His tattoo. His desperation to get inside my house. Was he connected to all of the craziness going on at Lana's place? Nothing made sense.

Cooper was on the porch in two strides. The look in his eyes held concern and uncertainty, almost like he wanted to hold me but couldn't. He seemed to settle for cupping my elbow to steady me instead. "Are you okay?"

I didn't know what to say. So I let my tears fall freely.

I shouldn't have had that drink. Shouldn't have let Candy convince me to go out tonight. Shouldn't have ignored Cooper's advice earlier.

His grip tightened. "I think we need to get you some coffee. Can I see you inside?"

Could he see me inside? Said like such a gentleman. I nodded, not sure if I'd make it inside by myself the way my head was spinning and my muscles turned to Jell-o.

His arm clamped around my waist. He helped me through a maze of blurred surroundings and deposited me on the couch. He disappeared into the kitchen and clanked around as he made coffee.

Images of Mark flashed into my mind. My muscles seemed to tighten with each memory. That could have been bad. Really bad. Mark was aggressive and could have easily overpowered me.

How had my life turned into such a circus?

Tears began pouring down my cheeks again.

I've made such a mess of things.

And without God in my life, where did I find hope?

I grabbed a tissue and blew my nose, all too aware that I was a blathering, sobbing mess. Not put together. Not in control. I had no answers.

And I didn't know what to do with myself.

Cooper sat a mug of coffee on the table in front of me. No way would I be able to drink it in my current state. I'd end up spilling the hot liquid all over me.

"Mark's a first-class jerk."

I sniffled. "How do you know?"

"He has a reputation."

Would Mark tell everyone who I was? Would he make good on his threat? An unflattering sob escaped again.

"Do you want to talk about it?" He leaned toward me, reminding me a bit of a counselor.

I opened my mouth, but another sob escaped instead of words.

Humiliating. Letting someone else see me like this was out of my comfort zone. But there was nothing I could do about it.

I sucked in a shaky breath. "I built my whole life around a lie."

"You mean with your marriage?"

I shook my head. "No, with God. I dedicated everything to him. I followed all the rules. I did everything I was supposed to. I was such a fool to believe that there was a higher power out there who cared about me. I believed in a fairy tale."

"God disappointed you?"

"Someone who doesn't exist can't disappoint me." I hadn't been able to say it, but I thought it enough times. I wasn't sure I was ready to take that step. Was I an atheist? The word sounded so foreign beside my name. "I was determined to forget about who I used to be. But it's not that easy, is it?"

"No, it's not that easy." His voice sounded soft, just above a whisper. "Don't mistake your hurt for a change of heart."

I shook my head, grabbing another tissue. I felt my heart softening, so I stood and began to pace. How did Cooper always get to me like that? How did he read me so well? "You should consider a career in counseling. You're always there when I need you, even when I've been horrible. I don't know how you do it."

He appeared behind me, his hands rested on my shoulders, and I wanted more than anything to step back into his embrace. "I just treat people the way I'd want to be treated, Tara. I want to be treated with grace and forgiveness and understanding."

Would I test the limits of his grace and forgiveness and understanding if I told him about Florida? I couldn't do it. The thought pressed in on me, but the words couldn't leave my mouth. Cooper was my only true friend here in St. Paul, and I couldn't stand the thought of turning him against me.

I remembered when I told Peter what had happened. He'd come home, and I'd been curled in a corner on the floor, released on bond. He'd been out of town, and I'd waited until he returned to share what had happened. Miraculously, his mother hadn't gotten to him first.

He'd walked into our home. It was obvious I'd been crying. My entire face was blotchy and red. I'd prodded myself up off the floor and managed to sit at the kitchen table with some water. Between sobs, I told him that a student had made accusations against me.

Peter's face had gone stark white. He'd remained expressionless as I told him the rest.

There wasn't enough evidence to charge me. They were going to keep investigating. I couldn't leave the area and I should probably get a lawyer.

I don't know what he'd been expecting to hear. That I had cancer? He would have taken that news better.

I'd desperately hoped that he would tell me that he believed in me, that he knew I'd never done anything like that. Instead, he'd stood and told me he needed some time alone. That night, he slept in the guest bedroom. I'd cried myself to sleep, rehashing in my mind every encounter I'd ever had with the student.

Eventually, Peter seemed to come back to his senses. He finally said the words I'd wanted to hear, but he said it with less than enough conviction. Our relationship had its first fracture. It continued to fracture until finally one day, he announced he was leaving. He couldn't take the pressure anymore.

Those months were torture.

Once I'd even stared at a bottle of pain medicine and wondered what it would be like to take it. I wondered if it would put an end to my pain and humiliation.

"Why do you dislike church so much, Tara? What happened?"

I came back down to reality and shook my head. "I can't."

"Why?"

I shook my head harder. "It's a long story."

"I've got time."

"You wouldn't understand."

"I'd understand more than you probably think."

"I doubt it."

He shifted. "My wife had an affair with one of the deacons at our church after we'd been married for two years."

My heart seemed to stop. I soaked in his words as they settled over me like the aftershock of a nuclear bomb. In my mind, he and Sunni had the perfect marriage. This... this wasn't even close to being on my radar. "Wow. I had no idea."

"It's true. It happened. It was devastating. The whole church knew what had happened. They asked us to leave." Lines formed around his eyes, and his words sounded heavy.

I had no right to ask my next question, but I did anyway. "What happened after that? You...you stayed together?"

He nodded.

I shook my head. "You are..." *More of a man than almost anyone else I've ever met. You're a hundred times the man that Peter was.* The words remained in my brain, though.

He leaned closer. "I'm what?"

"You're amazing, Cooper. Not many people would have handled the situation like you did."

"It would have been easy to walk away. Really easy. I almost did, for that matter. But instead I chose to honor my commitment. It took months and months of counseling for things between us to even feel halfway normal. It took years to truly feel happy again."

"And then she passed away..." The words caused an enormous lump to form in my throat.

"I'm so glad things were right between us, and that Sunni was right with God."

I ran my hands over my face, the emotional strain of everything making me feel as if I'd aged ten years. "I'll tell you my story sometime, Cooper. I wish mine had a happy ending, but it doesn't."

"It still can."

I smiled as his words settled on me. "You're right. It still can."

And for the first time in a long time, a tinge of hope fluttered in my heart.

Cooper stood. "You going to be okay here tonight?"

The last thing I wanted was to be alone. But I knew I had to be. No way was I asking Cooper to stay over on my couch again. So I nodded. "Yeah, I'll be okay." I wouldn't be totally alone. I had Casper here with me, soothing me to sleep with some beautiful guitar music.

A shiver crept up my spine.

Cooper stared at me a moment. Tension stretched between us. Did he feel it too? I'd bet he did. There was a part of me that wanted to reach up and kiss his cheek good night. At the very least, to give him a hug. Instead, I stepped back and jammed my hands into my pockets. "I'll see you around."

He nodded. "Yeah, I'll see you around."

22

Today was Friday. I'd been in St. Paul all of a week, but at moments it felt like I'd been here a lifetime.

Last night had been surprisingly quiet. No guitar music or creaking gates or anything. Not that I'd slept, but still.

For some reason, I felt more grounded today as I sat at the breakfast table with my coffee and cereal. I'd already been up, gotten some work done, and made a few phone calls.

Was it my talk with Cooper that had me feeling steadier? Was it my glimpse into what life was like on the other side—and my total desire to have nothing to do with it? I wasn't sure.

I decided right then and there that I had to decide if Jesus was real and then live with abandon for him, or decide if he wasn't real and walk away from everything I'd built my life around. I didn't want to be in between. I didn't want to be mediocre. I either wanted to give my life to Jesus 100% or I had to find a new path to walk. I could find gobs of people on both sides of the issue to give me solid reasoning. I had to combine my own faith and reasoning, though.

For the time being, I was going to forget about my crazy rules—I was going to try to forget, at least. My self-imposed sanctions were doing me no good. Maybe there was no black and white.

My cell phone buzzed. Finally—was someone actually calling instead of stopping by? I recognized the number from one of the calls I'd made this morning. Lindsey Buchanan, a friend of Danielle's, had called me back and agreed to meet with me. Surprisingly, she said Bryce Stephens, the reporter, had called her also, and he would be there.

As soon as I hung up with him, my cell buzzed again. It was Candy.

"Hey Bahama Mama. You disappeared last night and left me alone."

"I left you? You left me with that jerk Mark." I couldn't keep the irritation from my voice.

"I would have never suggested that you two go off alone. But you didn't ask me. You left me."

"Mark offered to take me home early, and he said he'd text you."

"Yeah, well he didn't." I was guessing from her tone of voice that Mark hadn't shared his discovery about me with her. Would he?

"Why are you the one upset? I'm the one who almost had my face mauled off at the front door." I shivered just thinking about it. Thank goodness Cooper had been around. He had a knack for being close by just when I needed him.

"Friends look out for each other. I can't look out for you if you do stupid stuff like go off alone with Mark."

My mouth dropped open as I wiped spilt milk off the table. "You're his friend, Candy. If he's so terrible, why do you hang out? Why did you suggest I get to know him?"

"He's fine as a friend. He's got mad connections in the area with different promoters and stuff. But I'd never suggest you date him. Well, officially I did, but that was before I knew you."

"Lana did." Did my own sister give me the Judas kiss? That didn't seem like Lana.

"Lana doesn't know him like I do. He gets his sights set on one person, and failure isn't an option. He likes getting his way. He legally changed his last name from Spitzfarger to Champion, for goodness sake."

I shook my head. I still couldn't shake the notion that maybe Mark was involved somehow in the haunting at this house. "Well, it's done. It's over. And I'm okay."

Silence stretched for a moment. "What are you doing today?"

"I have a meeting."

"I just so happen to be in the neighborhood..."

A motorcycle revved outside my house. So much for people not showing up unannounced. I pressed the "end" button, and, a moment later, Candy strode up the cracked sidewalk to my front door. I grabbed my keys from the table and met her outside. "You up for doing some sleuthing with me today?"

Her thin eyebrows reached toward the ceiling. "Sleuthing? Yeah, baby. What are you doing?"

I waited a beat, just for the dramatic effect of it. "Talking to a friend of Danielle's."

Her expression remained curious but didn't register the name. "Who's Danielle?"

"The woman who was murdered in Lana's house." I waited, watching her expression morph from curiosity to total intrigue.

"We're going to investigate?" A wide smile cracked her face. "We're going to take a stab at it." I moaned. Bad, bad choice of words.

"Awesome. We can be like Kyra Sedgwick on *The Closer*. Only we're not real detectives. Or blonde. Can I use my worst southern accent?"

"Please don't."

"I've been practicing, though. Listen to this." She sucked in her cheeks and made her eyes look smoldering. "Frankly, my dear, I don't give a—"

"Candy! We should get going."

She laughed and looped her arm through mine. "I do like you, Tara Lancaster. You're like...you're like the bomb-diggity."

The bomb-diggity? I shook my head. Candy was a Pixie-stick today—pure sugar.

Two hours later, we were sitting in the Hummer outside of a new coffee shop, this one aptly named The Bean Scene. I was seriously going to give St. Paul an award for having the cutest and most clever coffeehouse names ever.

When we walked in, I spotted Bryce Stephens seated at a table, tapping his foot impatiently. A woman sat next to him. She was probably my age with long, reddish hair and nervous eyes. Lindsey, I realized.

Bryce looked up and scowled. Weren't reporters supposed to be friendly as a means of getting information?

I introduced him and Candy as we sat down across from him. His scowl deepened, the expression clearly aimed at Candy this time. "I know you. You're the girl who can never get enough attention."

Candy smiled without a care in the world. "Pleasure to see you, also. Charmed, I'm sure."

I introduced myself to Lindsey. She licked her lips as if nervous. I'd found Lindsey because Bryce had interviewed her for one of his articles. She'd been Danielle's best friend from childhood on.

"Bryce has been wanting to meet with me also, so when you called, I figured it was a sign and that I'd get it all over with at once," she started. "I don't really know what I can offer."

Did Bryce Stephens have a change of heart? He seemed to have no interest in revisiting this story when I spoke with him a couple of days ago. I put that thought aside and leaned toward Lindsey. "It's like I told you on the phone. Someone's desperate to make me believe that Danielle's spirit is haunting the house. I'm trying to figure out what happened, so I can put an end to this craziness."

"I'll do whatever I can to help," Lindsey said.

"Could you tell me about Danielle, Lindsey?"

"I used to know her back when she went to church. We used to sing in the youth band together."

"She sang?" I asked.

"And played the guitar."

Candy and I exchanged a glance. The guitar? This just kept getting creepier and creepier.

"Then she changed. Said she started having visions. She thought they were a way of helping people. She had the desire to help people be better, to make sure they got justice."

"She considered her abilities a gift." Candy sounded convincing and compassionate.

Lindsey nodded solemnly. "Even as a child, Danielle was always standing up for people. Getting into fights when people picked on her friends. Helping people who no one else wanted to help."

I remembered Cooper saying that the family had been churchgoers. How did someone go from loving God to being involved with the occult? Maybe it wasn't unusual. Maybe Danielle had an interest in all things spiritual—both good and evil. I broached the subject carefully. "I heard she grew up going to church."

Lindsey nodded again. "When her father died, her belief system crashed like an old computer. She started dabbling with other things. She researched Islam and Buddhism, and talked some about Scientology. Then she went and had a palm reading, just to see what it was like. Apparently, she was told that she had great psychic energy or something like that. Maybe that's what she needed to hear. Maybe she needed some encouragement and that's where she found it."

Sadness again pressed in on me. Maybe Danielle and I weren't that different. There are a lot of forks in the road of life. Danielle had veered onto a different course. If I wasn't careful, what route would I end up taking? The dry and shriveled-up Christian path? The one where I went to church, but had no life left in me?

"And her interest just grew from there?" Candy asked.

"No one could pull her away. She got involved with tarot cards and Ouija boards. Things of the darkness. But she said she was going to use them for good." Lindsey shook her head. "I'm not sure how."

God had strong words on that.

What fellowship can light have with darkness? 2 Corinthians 6:14.

Avoid every kind of evil. 1 Thessalonians 5:22.

Anyone who does these things is detestable to the Lord. Deuteronomy 18:12.

I cleared my throat again. "Then she started doing readings in her home?"

"Yes, she did. Jeremy freaked out. He didn't want to leave her but didn't want to live with her either."

I leaned even closer. "Did her readings ever get her in any scrapes?"

"There was one incident that shook her up." Lindsey looked beyond us, as if reliving some past conversation. "I really think this guy had some type of mental problem. Apparently, he had awful mood swings.

I know he scared Danielle sometimes. He wouldn't leave her alone. He said he had a curse on him, and he wanted her to remove it."

Could this be the killer? I rubbed my hand against my jeans. "Did she tell the police, Lindsey?"

"She mentioned him." She shook her head and sighed. "Apparently, he was questioned and released. He had no record. There was no evidence linking him to the crime."

There wasn't evidence of anything, was there? No body, no murder weapon. All the police were going on was blood. Which was enough, I supposed. Still, why hadn't the police taken this man seriously?

"What was his name?" I asked.

Lindsey looked at the ceiling. Tilted her head. Closed her eyes. "Philip something? Philip...Philip Whitehurst, I think."

"What else did Danielle say about him?" Candy asked.

"Just that he was off his rocker. He honestly thought he had a curse on him, and he was desperate to have it removed. Thought Danielle was the only one who could help. He was pretty aggressive."

I pictured Danielle letting the man into her home for a reading or consultation. Maybe she'd said something he didn't like. Maybe he'd flown off the handle, grabbed a knife..."Did Danielle try to help him?"

"She tried, I guess. But she told him he wasn't cursed, he just needed help. Therapy. He needed a shrink, not a psychic. He didn't understand. He kept offering to pay her a lot of money to remove whatever spell had been placed on him. Eventually, Danielle told him to stay away, that she couldn't help anymore."

This had to be the man! "Did Philip ever threaten her?"

Lindsey shook her head. "Threaten? No, not directly."

What did that mean? "Did he threaten her indirectly?"

Lindsey looked me straight in the eye again. "He used to wait outside the house for Danielle. At night. Scared her to death. He just wouldn't leave her alone."

23

Candy and I were quiet as we rode down the road. The interstate blurred by, and my mind drifted from Philip Whitehurst to Danielle's involvement in church. What did it all mean? I didn't know. I needed more time to ponder what we'd learned.

Candy cleared her throat beside me. "Which is crazier to get mixed up in—the church or the occult?"

"I'd say the occult. For sure." I glanced over at her. "You really don't know?"

She half-shrugged. "I went to church for a while in high school."

Surprise registered in me, which I realized was awfully judgmental. "Did you? And?"

"It started off okay. I thought I'd really found a place where people were different and where I could be accepted." She clicked her nails together and stared out the window. "I'd never really been accepted in high school. I was kind of nerdy and annoying and hyper."

"What happened?"

"The Queen Bee—the unofficial leader of the youth group—decided she didn't like me. Like really didn't like me. She didn't want me

158

there, didn't want me as a part of the youth group, and she didn't care how I felt about any of it. Suddenly no one else did either."

I kept my eyes on the road ahead, curious to learn more about the woman beside me. I knew there was more to her than love of fame and blue hair. "What happened?"

"We were on this bus trip to a youth convention. I was asking some questions about the Bible. I honestly wanted to know. I wasn't trying to be provocative or anything. The Queen Bee walked over to me and announced to everyone that she thought I was weird. For the rest of the weekend, I was the outcast. Only the youth leaders would talk to me."

"I'm sorry, Candy. That's terrible." But not surprising. Lots of ugly stuff happened in church, partially because the church was filled with imperfect people.

"I never went back. Ever. And I never will again."

"People think social dynamics change after high school but, the truth is that wherever you have groups of people, it feels like high school again. The church...well, it's not always much different than that." No, you had the leadership clique, the churchgoers who liked to party, the jocks who played on the church softball league, the Sunday onlys, and the list could go on. "I'm sorry. The church is full of imperfect people."

"Where do you stand on the whole church issue? I know your dad's a pastor, but I'm getting mixed vibes from you."

I nodded. "Yeah. He's at one of the largest churches in Florida."

"So you're a Christian?"

I shrugged, my heart feeling unusually heavy. "I don't know."

"Why?"

I sucked in a deep breath. There was no way to get out of this conversation. I was driving and we still had a good ten miles until we got back home. "I just want to be authentic. But I'm not sure how to do that right now. If I believe in God, I want it to be because I believe it with my whole heart."

"You're different, Tara."

"Different how?"

"I'm still trying to figure it out. But I like you. You surprise me."

"The one thing about facing disappointments in life is that those hard times deepen your character. I know that firsthand."

"From what Lana said about you, you were handed a golden platter."

"That's funny because I think that life sends all of its kisses Lana's way." Did my sister really feel that way? My parents—my dad especially—had always given Lana so much attention. Even with all of her craziness, my dad's eyes still lit up whenever he saw my sister. I'd always felt second best.

"She says you're a saint."

Of course, my sister had broken the rules and earned favoritism with my dad. Was God the same way? Did I need to break some rules to get his attention? I shook my head. "I'm anything but a saint. Anything."

"You could have fooled me."

My heart dropped, heavy with sorrow. "The last thing I want to do is fool anyone, Candy."

I sighed. Wasn't that exactly what I was doing?

Back at Lana's, I Googled Philip Whitehurst. Thousands of entries popped up on the screen so I added "St. Paul," which drastically curtailed the matches.

I scrolled through several listings. On the second page, one caught my eye. It was a blog called "Expose."

"Click on it," Candy mumbled beside me.

Please don't let this be a porn site.

I clicked on it. To my relief, no pictures popped up on the site. Just a black background and white spaces where the blog entries were.

I clicked the first one, the one that dated back the earliest.

March 11.

She said I was cursed. Told me to take an egg, wrap it in a white T-shirt and rub it over my body. This is supposed to take away the bad energy in my life. I feel hopeful for the first time... ever.

"What is this?" Candy's eyes widened. "I mean, I like weird things, but that's super weird."

"You'll get no argument from me there." I kept reading.

March 12.
I brought the egg to her. She rubbed it against my face, then cracked it open. Black mucus gushed out. It's my curse. It's gone! I have to light a candle to keep the spirits from coming back to me. I told her I'd pay as much as I had to in order to keep the curse away.

This guy actually believed this stuff worked? He must have been desperate. Lindsey had said Danielle wanted to help people. Had Danielle helped Philip Whitehurst get rid of a supposed curse?

Curiosity filled me. I had to know what happened next.

March 20.
If I pay her money from my savings, she said the money will come back to me triple. That the curse will stay away, as long as I keep burning the candle. I asked if a five-dollar candle would do the same trick. She said no.

"Danielle was draining the poor man's bank accounts." Candy shook her head. "Now that's a motive for murder."

For some reason, I was disappointed in the woman. I thought she was misdirected, but not a con artist. How deep was she into this scam?

April 3.
I'm burning the candle, but the curse is back. The voices haunt me. I think bad thoughts. Bad, bad thoughts. Thoughts I can't write. But they're watching me. I know they are. They'll take me away, and I can't let that happen. I rubbed another egg on my head. Then I cracked the egg. The inside wasn't black this time, so the curse is still with me. I don't know what to do.

April 4.

The voices are still there. I can't get rid of them. Soon the men will get me. They'll feed me to the rats and no one will be the wiser.

April 5.
She won't give my money back. It hasn't come back to me triple. And I have bills to pay. The shadows are getting closer, and the blackness grows inside me. The voices are telling me bad things. Dark things. It's eating me alive.

Did the police know about this blog? The voices obviously told Philip Whitehurst to kill Danielle Miller! It was plain to see.
I continued reading, more quickly now.

April 6.
I told the police. They won't do anything. They think I'm crazy. I am. But I'm not crazy when I tell them she took my money. She's a fraud. The darkness grows inside me more and more each day.

April 9.
She stole my money. I want it back. I'll die before I let those varmints eat me again.

April 12.
She thinks she'll get away with this. She won't. I'll make sure of it. I even flushed my meds so I could hear the voices more clearly.

May 1.
I've found a solution. It's brilliant. The darkness is fading.

May 16.
I think I'm in love. The men aren't shadowing me. Is the curse finally broken?

May 21.
I'll love you forever.

"So...Philip got distracted because he fell in love with someone?" I tried to sort my thoughts aloud. "He let the whole 'curse' thing drop? Is that what that last blog meant?"

Candy shrugged. "Don't ask me."

There were no more entries after that last one. Had he realized how crazy the whole scenario was? I mean, really, using an egg to transmit a curse through osmosis? Get real. But maybe he had some type of mental illness. He'd mentioned meds and men chasing after him. Was Danielle preying on the weak?

These were the ramblings of someone who was desperate and needed help.

They were also the ramblings of someone who waited outside Danielle's home for her.

I sighed and leaned back. What did all of this mean? Should I mention it to the police? Lindsey said they'd already investigated the man. The police were competent. If they thought the man was clear, he was clear.

Right?

Candy leaned over my shoulder. "Don't forget who's coming tonight."

"Someone's coming tonight?"

"Yeah, my friend with *Ghost Chasers*."

I shook my head, that topic long forgotten. The verses I'd quoted earlier while thinking about Danielle dabbling in the occult came back to me. "I don't know."

"What can it hurt?" Candy's wide eyes held the promise of adventure.

Before I could respond, I glanced over her. I screamed as I saw a man's face smeared against the window there.

24

A beat-up turquoise-colored minivan void of hubcaps pulled up to my house at seven o'clock. As I stepped outside, the man's face at my window continued to stain my memory.

After remaining frozen for a couple of minutes, Candy and I had eventually come to our senses and went outside. By that time, the man was long gone. But who was he? I had no idea. All I had now was one more creepy puzzle piece that didn't seem to fit anywhere.

As I helped haul things inside, Cooper stepped outside. My heart sank as Ms. I-Avoid-Conflict-at-All-Cost came face to face with my worst reality. How was I going to explain this?

"Find a new roommate?" He crossed the lawn and grabbed a blue bin from the stack I carried inside. The air felt thick with humidity and mosquitoes tonight, reminding me more of Miami than St. Paul.

I shook my head, using my knee to nudge another bin up higher in my arms. "Not quite."

"What's all of this stuff then?" He walked beside me.

"It's a long story." I didn't have the energy to get into it.

"We're ghost hunting tonight," Candy called from across the lawn.

My cheeks heated as Cooper's gaze fell on me. I could always count on Candy.

Cooper stopped, his lips parting in dumfounded surprise. "You have a ghost hunter coming over? You're not serious."

"It was Candy's idea." I cringed, wishing I could take the words back and take responsibility for this little foray into the dark side. After all, I'd given the go-ahead...kind of. "Look, I know it sounds crazy, but I keep hearing noises and finding things moved in my house for no explainable reason. I have new locks. I have a security system. It doesn't matter. Strange things are still happening."

"But a ghost hunter?"

I wanted to keep my chin raised, but I just couldn't. My gaze fell to the ground, and I sucked in a deep breath. His intense gaze met mine when I looked up, interrupted only when Candy breezed past me with a box full of wires and gadgets.

"I know I should stay away from stuff like this. But I've followed all the rules for my entire life and it's gotten me nowhere. I've gotta have some answers. About ghosts. About God. About how I should live and what I should believe."

"Let's go then." He nodded toward my front door.

I raised my eyebrows, surprise rushing through me. "You're coming too?"

"Yeah, I'm coming too. Why wouldn't I?"

"Something about staying away from anything that hints of evil...I don't want to pull you into this mess."

He shrugged. "Tara, I'm going to be there so I can watch an exercise in futility. I don't believe in ghosts. I don't think your house is haunted, and I want to see how this guy tries to make the evidence look like it is. As far as I'm concerned, this is no different than watching someone search for leprechauns or the Loch Ness monster. Nor do I want you to be taken advantage of by some thrill-seeking con artist."

"I'm perfectly capable of discerning for myself when I'm going to be taken advantage of. But you can still stay." Something about knowing that Cooper would be there made everything seem better, safer, less shifty.

Cooper helped us carry the rest of the equipment inside, and then Candy's friend Mickey called us together in my living room. I wasn't exactly sure what a "Mickey" was supposed to look like, but this guy fit the bill. Thick dark hair that was messy, trendy oversized glasses, skinny jeans that accentuated his slight build, and a Bon Jovi T-shirt. Plus his ears kind of stuck out.

Cooper and I sat on the couch while Candy and Mickey sat in the two chairs across from us. Everyone looked tight and tense—except Cooper, who looked amused. I needed that.

But if Cooper was the picture of logic and steadfastness, Candy was the picture of chaos and excitement.

"Ghosts are creatures of the night." Mickey pushed his oversized glasses up on his nose and continued to twiddle with his machine on the coffee table between us. "This is a highly sophisticated electronic voice recorder. It will capture any sounds that the human ear may not pick up on. Your ghost may be trying to communicate with us. You might be surprised at the results. Most people are."

I pointed to another hard-sided case. "What's that?"

"It's a thermal heat monitor that will show us thermal imaging— again, something that's not visible to the human eye." Mickey rose and set up his equipment while a torrid stream of questions ran through my mind. I chose one.

"So you work for that TV show?"

He glanced up. "I used to."

"What did you do for them exactly?"

"I was a technician. I'm hoping to break out on my own."

I stored away that information. Someone who wanted to break out on their own just might be desperate enough for success to interpret results in a certain way.

"If he's picked up for his own show, I'm going to be one of the investigators with him." Candy pulled on some headphones and dramatically pursed her lips. "It's going to be rad."

Cooper looked at me, and I could tell his thoughts were the same as mine. What had I gotten myself into?

Mickey turned off the lights, and a creepy darkness fell over the room. Shadows loomed all around us, and everything seemed eerily still. I inched a little closer to Cooper, not liking the way a cold sweat had popped over my forehead.

I turned toward Mickey, trying to ignore that shivers had claimed my muscles. "Is that really necessary?"

"More than necessary. We're not going to see or hear anything with the lights on." He barely glanced at me as he said the words. He was too focused on the ghost hunt.

Thunder clapped outside, and I nearly jumped out of my skin.

Great. Just what we needed. A spooky storm in the midst of a paranormal investigation. What would my dad say if he knew about this? Hopefully I wouldn't become a chapter in his next parenting book. Of course, thanks to me, he probably wouldn't be getting any more book offers for a while.

Candy grinned. "This is perfect."

"Where does most of the ghostly activity seem to take place?" Mickey pushed his glasses up again. He looked me in the eyes this time.

"My bedroom." At least, that's how it seemed to me. "But the living room, also. This is where the shades disappeared. It's where I hear the floor creaking. But the spare bedroom is where I've heard the guitar music."

Cooper snapped his head toward me. "Guitar music?"

"Yeah, I haven't even told you everything. I thought I'd sound crazy if I did." Yet here I was with an alleged ghost hunter in my living room. What was crazier? I couldn't even think about it anymore.

Lightning lit the room, and I nearly jumped into Cooper's arms.

Instead, I rubbed my sleeves, ready to get down to business. "Okay, so what are we doing?"

"I need everyone to stay still while I get some initial readings on the house. Candy's going to help me. Remember that negative thoughts can drive away spirits." He looked at me and Cooper as he said the words.

"This guy's a fruit," Cooper whispered as Mickey disappeared down the hallway. I could feel his breath on my ear, which caused a whole new set of shivers to jiggle down my arms.

I didn't turn to look at him because I knew we'd be face to face if I did. Instead, I kept my gaze on the equipment in front of me and shrugged. Every cell in my body seemed alive and aware. "I'm out of ideas."

I was. I had no explanation for what had been happening. At least after tonight I could rule one more thing out...right? I felt Cooper shift beside me, and felt some distance separate us. I missed his closeness, but I knew the space was needed.

"Tell me about the guitar music, Tara."

I shifted also, pulling my leg under me as I looked his way. Lightning flashed again, outlining his figure in pale blue light. *The perfect man*, I thought. Then I reminded myself about the wedding ring he still wore. Any rush of infatuation I felt dissolved. Instead, I filled him in, trying to just stick to the facts.

"Have you looked for any logical explanations?"

I swallowed, my throat burning. "Such as?"

"A hidden music player, maybe remote controlled?"

"I hadn't even thought about that." But I should have. Why hadn't I thought about that? If someone was trying to scare me, that would be one way of doing it. One very effective way. "If we check now, we'll get fussed at."

"You should have told me. I would have checked it out for you, Tara."

My cheeks burned. Of course he would have. He was that kind of guy. But, of course I hadn't told him, because I was that kind of girl. Too proud to ask for help? Maybe.

Mickey and Candy came back into the room, chatting about drafts and the AC and how that could affect some of their tests. They joined us in the living room in a little circle. All of the equipment was placed in the center.

Thunder boomed again, and the shadows seemed even deeper. My imagination was obviously working overtime, because the air just felt heavier to me. It was almost like I could feel a presence around me, even though I knew there was no one there.

Mickey cleared his throat and grabbed the tape recorder. "I think we're ready. Let's start with some questions. We'll introduce ourselves to any ghosts in the room." We sat in a circle with the lights out. "Spirits who are dwelling nearby, we come in peace."

I tried not to roll my eyes as Mickey continued. His voice sounded so serious, and his expression was so solemn.

"If you're here, will you give us a sign?"

Nothing. Just lightning flashing again, followed by the rumble of thunder.

"What's your name?"

Nothing except a smattering of rain against the roof. So why did my throat feel so dry and achy?

"Are you a kind spirit?"

Again, silence followed. This was a waste of time. The only thing speaking to us was the storm.

"Is there anything you'd like to tell us?"

I just couldn't keep my mouth shut any more. "Shouldn't we take the hint that no one's talking?"

"Shh!" Mickey eyebrows formed a V as he scowled at me. "Negative energy will ruin all of this. And we may not hear anything now, but the electronic voice recorder may pick up something."

I clamped my mouth shut and finally muttered, "Got it."

Mickey's face drew into serious lines again. He sat as if posed to do yoga, slowly sucking in deep breaths. "Are you the spirit of Danielle Miller?"

The only sound I heard was Gaga tippity-tapping across the wood floor.

"Are you trying to tell us who killed you?"

I was certain a cold breeze swept across the room. Just the AC, I told myself. Just the AC.

"Who killed you, Danielle? Was it your husband?"

Eerie silence.

"Was it Philip Whitehurst?" Candy added.

Mickey's gaze roamed the room. "We need a sign. Any kind of sign that you're here."

Thunder clapped outside. The timing had me wound tighter than a spring. I exchanged a glance with Cooper who still looked rather amused by the whole process. This stuff was playing with my head.

Something crashed downstairs.

I screamed and grabbed Cooper's arm. Mickey screamed and grabbed Candy's arm. Then their eyes lit up and they rushed to their feet. I composed myself and dropped Cooper's arm, but that didn't stop my heart from racing—racing because of the crash, not because I'd touched Cooper, of course.

"We've got to go check it out," Candy muttered. She grabbed Mickey's hand. "Come on."

I didn't go anywhere. I just stared straight ahead, trying to expel the heebie-jeebies that fell over me. "That was just a coincidence."

Cooper nodded. "The power of suggestion. You're just associating the crash with the ghost hunt."

Logical explanation, but... "The timing was impeccable."

"The thunder could have knocked something down."

I nodded, fear still freezing me. "Right. The thunder."

"This really has you freaked out, doesn't it?" His arm slipped around me, and he rubbed my shoulders with smoothing precision.

I couldn't lie, even though I was tempted. "Yeah, it does. I'm trying to be levelheaded. It's just not working."

Before he could respond, Mickey and Candy came back into the room and held up a picture frame. Mickey grinned as if he'd struck gold. "Fell off the wall. There's definitely something going on here." He sat back down, shaking his head in what appeared to be delight. "I think we're finished with our questions. Now let's listen to the recording and see if we can hear anything."

"Can we turn the lights on for this?" *Please say yes. Please say yes.*

Mickey scowled at me again. "I suppose."

I rushed to my feet and fumbled with the light switch. Finally, light filled the room. My heart immediately slowed. Everything looked the same. Candy picked up the video camera again but then pulled it away.

"Actually, will you tape this, Cooper? It might be good if I'm seen on screen."

He took the camera. "And I would love not to be seen on screen, so sure."

Mickey rewound his recording. "Are you guys ready for this?" Any minute now I expected him to rub his hands together and cackle like a witch out of Macbeth.

Just then, lightning flashed, electrifying the air. It electrified my nerves, which were already charged with adrenaline. "Ready as I'll ever be," I mumbled.

He hit play and his voice came over the recording, filling the room.

"Spirits who are dwelling nearby, we come in peace. If you're here, will you give us a sign? What's your name? Are you a kind spirit? Is there anything you'd like to tell us?"

He hit stop and breathlessly looked up at us. "Did you hear that?"

My eyes widened as I wondered what I was missing. "Hear what?"

"The spirit spoke." There was enough conviction in his voice to nearly convince me.

"I didn't hear anything." Cooper still held the camera, looking more than happy to escape the mess around him.

Mickey rewound the recording. "Listen again."

His recorded voice filled the room again. "Is there anything you'd like to tell us?"

Candy straightened. Lightning illuminated her face again. "I heard it! It sounded like 'I'm still here.'"

"Candy, you're just saying that because that's what the note said!" My voice rose in accusation, and I tried to bring its pitch down.

She pointed to the recorder. "Play it again! You'll hear it too!"

I heard static. It could be the recording. It could have been Gaga walking around in the background. It could have been anything.

The fourth time Mickey played, I almost convinced myself I did hear *I'm still here*. The power of suggestion, I told myself. It's just the power of suggestion.

Mickey shook his head. "Let's keep going."

He pressed play again. "Are you the spirit of Danielle Miller? Are you trying to tell us who killed you? Who killed you, Danielle? Was it your husband? Was it Philip Whitehurst?"

Static rang out through the speaker again.

"Did you hear that? Did you hear it?" Mickey practically jumped on my couch in a moment to rival Tom Cruise. Yep, he was crazy all right.

I shook my head. "I didn't hear anything."

Mickey bounced up and down like a kid at in a toy store. "It was a clear 'yes'! It was there. She was speaking to us! Danielle Miller is speaking to us!"

"Come on. That could have been anything. We could have been picking up a frequency from somewhere else, from one of the neighbor's houses." Cooper started to lower the camera when Candy waved her hands in the air as if nudging the device back up.

"It was a yes. I can't believe you can argue with that." Mickey's nostrils flared as he stared at us. I wasn't sure if he was passionate or desperate in his pursuit, nor was I one-hundred-percent sure I'd heard a yes.

He wiped his brow with the tail of his shirt. "Let me show you this. It will convince you." He plugged his video camera into the TV. A moment later, fluorescent images of Lana's house came on the screen. He pointed to an orange blur in the center of the scene, on the wall in the basement. "This is called a heat image. This means that there's some kind of life form right there. We can rule out any animals or people. That just leaves a spirit."

Again, I shivered. I didn't want to. I didn't want to believe any of this. But was the evidence telling me otherwise?

Cooper cast me a sideways glance, his skepticism apparent and serving to ward away some of my fears for a moment.

Mickey turned the TV off and stared at me.

I cleared my throat, ready to wrap this evening up. "So what are your conclusions?" I dared to ask the question.

Mickey looked me dead in the eye. "My conclusion is that you have a spirit inhabiting this house, waiting to ascend into the afterworld. From what you've told me, I believe this spirit wants something and that her haunting will only escalate until she gets whatever that something is."

25

Mickey left at one a.m., but Candy didn't seem to be in a hurry to go anywhere. I had to admit that my adrenaline was pumping, and I was sure sleep wouldn't find me any time soon—if at all—tonight. Between the experiments and the suggestions that a spirit did live here, it would be another restless night.

I began turning on as many lights as I could, anxious to ward away some of my tense muscles and my jumpy reflexes. Ghost or no ghost, that was just plain spooky. Cooper didn't seem at all frazzled as he leaned back on the couch, the slight tilt of his lips almost making him look amused. Candy, on the other hand, paced the room as if trying to keep up with her thoughts.

"That was one of the coolest things ever. I can totally see myself being on a TV show like this. I was working on my expressions." She widened her eyes, parted her lips and held her hands up by her face. "What do you think? Surprised? Too over the top?"

I chuckled as I sat on the couch next to Cooper—not right next to him, mind you. A respectable distance away. "You're over the top, Candy. But I love you anyway."

Candy paused by the front door. "Something is definitely going on here. The question is: What kind of secret does this house have? What is it trying to tell us?"

Even hearing her question made me tense. "Why do you think this house is hiding something?"

She shrugged. "Everyone has a secret."

I cringed. "Everyone?"

Candy's eyebrow shot up and half of her lip curled in a smile. She plopped down on the chair across from us. "Yeah, everyone. Even you, Tara. What's your secret?"

I shrugged, suddenly uncomfortable and trying to think of an excuse to hide under the couch. Going into the basement with my ghost even seemed a better option. Instead, I choose redirection. "If you're so certain, what's your secret, Candy?"

Her smile slipped, and then she reached for her hairline. The next thing I knew, she pulled her hair off. Or, her wig off, I supposed. Underneath the blue was a smooth, totally hairless head. I blinked in surprise, not sure what to say.

"No, I don't have cancer. That's always everyone's first question. I have an autoimmune disease called alopecia. I don't have a strand of hair on my body. Anywhere." The normal playfulness in her voice disappeared.

"Wow. I had no idea."

"Most people don't. Most people haven't even heard of the disease. But it's out there, and it's real. I've got it. I'm officially a hairdresser without hair."

I stared at her head. She actually looked quite lovely with no hair. She had the even, balanced features to make it work. "When were you diagnosed?"

"When I was nineteen. I had clumps of hair falling out, and we didn't know what was going on. At first, I tried everything I could think of to cover up my bald spots. I felt so ashamed and ugly and embarrassed. Finally, I shaved the remainder of my hair off and decided to wear some funky wigs instead. I'm not ashamed anymore, but I do like my blue hair."

I was liking Candy more and more as the real parts of her became apparent. I couldn't say she was someone I would have ever hung out with in Miami. No, I'd hung out with people who were like me. But Candy didn't pull any punches. She didn't try to be someone she wasn't. She was just herself, like it or hate it.

Candy looked at Cooper. "How about you? What are you hiding?"

He leaned back against the couch and shrugged. "I don't know."

"Oh, come on," Candy prodded.

He was silent for a moment before nodding and leaning forward. "Okay, okay. I do have a secret. I don't tell very many people about a hobby I have."

My curiosity was pricked. "Do tell."

His gaze bounced from Candy to me and then back again. "I actually have a collection of animatronics animals in my basement." He moved his arms in a robotic motion, ending with a stiff wave.

I blinked, unsure what to say. I knew Ben Cooper was too good to be true. I knew he had to have some kind of terrible secret. Animatronics animals fit the bill.

I pictured his basement, filled with little moving and dancing stuffed animals. I pictured him downstairs, delighting in each of them. A wiggle of disbelief traveled down my spine and into my stomach. That was a terrible, terrible secret. Almost as terrible as mine. Well, not really, but still.

I looked up and saw him staring at me. Slowly, a smile cracked his face. "Just kidding."

A laugh began in my throat and turned into an all-out, hold-your-belly bellow. He was joking. Thank goodness he was joking.

"Very funny, Ben Cooper." Candy wiped under her eyes where tears had escaped with her laughter. After one last chuckle, she forced a scowl. "Now tell us a real secret."

He shifted, still leaning forward on his elbows with that familiar sparkle in his eyes. "Okay, for real this time. I used to be a B-Boy."

I shifted. "A B-Boy?"

He shrugged again, smiling slightly. "You know, a break boy. Some people like to call it break dancing." He moved his arms in a little worm motion.

Candy slapped his arm. "Shut up! No you weren't. You're just trying to get one over on us again."

His eyes twinkled. "Oh, but I was. We lived in San Diego for a while. Some kids at my high school were into it, so I decided to learn some moves. Turned out I was pretty good at it."

"Prove it." Candy already had her phone out.

He shook his head. "It's been a long time. I haven't done some of those moves since I was in high school."

Candy clapped her hands together. "Show us, show us, show us," she chanted.

Cooper glanced at me, and I shrugged. "I have no objections."

"Just one move." He moved the coffee table out of the way. "This is called a freeze. An airchair to be precise." He raised himself up into a handstand then lowered his body into a horizontal position. He bent one arm until his body weight rested entirely there and raised his legs and other arm into the air.

I blinked in shock. The strength a person had to have to do this perplexed me. This man was strong. I had no doubts. And he had personality and character. He was practically the eighth wonder of the world.

Candy cheered, and I joined her. Cooper held the move for a moment and then, in controlled motions, lowered himself back to his feet and held his hands in the air. "A B-Boy. We used to show off our moves downtown and get a crowd around us. Those were some fun times."

"I'm way impressed," Candy said, putting her phone down. Then she looked at me. "Okay, Tara. Fess up. What's your secret? We shared ours."

My face burned. *Tell them, tell them.* This would be the perfect opportunity to open up about my past.

But I couldn't.

What would they do if I dropped that bombshell?

My name almost ended up listed on a sex offender's registry.

I could have written a book called *How to Lose Friends and De-fluence People.*

I sucked in a deep breath. "Not sure what's to tell. I'm divorced." *Lame, Tara. Lame.*

Her head tilted again. "I know. What else? Something good."

I licked my lips. What could I say? The words were on the tip of my tongue, but they couldn't seem to get past the barrier that was my conscience...or was it my pride? I didn't know.

Instead I blurted, "In college, I won a mud-wrestling tournament one time."

"You mud wrestled." Candy stared at me.

"Only once."

"And you won?" She continued to stare.

"I think it was mostly because I simply wanted to get it over with." I'd attended a Christian university, and they'd staged a fundraiser to help starving kids in Africa. One person from each dorm hallway was chosen by their peers to participate. Guess who everyone on my floor picked? Me, of course. I was the resident assistant on my hallway and, as a generally prissy girl, I was the natural choice.

Candy's eyes sparkled with more gleam than a Ring Pop. "So if I staged a mud-wrestling tournament, would you participate?"

I shook my head. "No way. Once was enough for me."

"What do you have to lose?" she challenged.

My self-respect? No, I'd already lost that. "Nothing," I admitted.

She nodded, a suspicious twinkle in her eyes. "Good to know. I'm glad you shared that, Tahiti. See, sharing secrets can be fun." She yawned and stretched. "All this ghost hunting has me tired. Is it okay if I crash here tonight?"

I had to admit, the thought of someone else being here with me brought an immense sense of relief. I couldn't let her know that, though. "I guess."

She nodded toward the hallway. "Spare bedroom's mine. I'll catch you in the morning."

As she disappeared, Cooper stood and we faced each other. "I guess I should run too."

I looked up at him, my breath quickening as I realized we were standing just a little too close to claim "friends only" status. Still, I didn't step back. "A B-Boy, huh? That one surprised me."

Cooper's gaze tantalized me as he looked down at me. "I'm more than a dad, you know." His voice sounded low, serious. Dare I say... sexy?

"I hadn't noticed." I winced. I hadn't noticed? *Really, Tara?*

Some of the sparkle left his eyes, and he brushed his finger across my cheek. "You're a tough nut to crack, Tara."

"Nut is probably appropriate."

He laughed and hooked his arm around my neck, pulling me toward him in a friendly hug. Except were friendly hugs supposed to make tingles surge through you? To make your heart rate speed? Definitely not.

We stepped back and were face to face. I wondered what it would be like to have the freedom to reach up and kiss him. I wondered what it would be like to feel his lips against mine, to experience that intimacy again.

His gaze captured mine and seemed to draw me into the depths of his soul. Our faces inched closer.

At once, the heartache of Peter flooded back to me. The burden of disappointing people lassoed my heart, pulling it downward. The crush of rejection hit me with more force than a slap.

I stepped back, hooking a hair behind my ear before looking up apologetically at Cooper. "Thanks for everything." My voice sounded hoarse, strained.

He stared at me another moment, layers of depth in his eyes. Finally, he nodded and stepped back, his hands shoved into his pockets. "Yeah. I'll catch you later."

He left, and I covered my face with my hands. Had I just ruined something that could have been beautiful? Or was I already ruined for life? Hope and despair collided inside me. Despair won.

As always.

26

I'd just lain down in bed when I heard the door handle to my room jiggle. Fear—an emotion that was becoming all-too familiar—seized me, gripping each of my muscles.

Then Candy appeared through the crack in the doorway, a big grin on her face as she strode across the room and plopped in bed beside me. A bag crinkled in her hands and orange powder covered her fingers. When had she brought her stuff inside? With the ghost hunting equipment maybe? That would have meant that she had intentions of spending the night from the start. I wouldn't complain, not given the circumstances.

"So you and Cooper. When did that happen?"

I pulled myself up to sitting position. "When did what happen?"

"When did you guys become an item?" She popped a cheeseball into her mouth. Where had those come from? And how could she eat those and stay so skinny?

"We're not."

"Could have fooled me."

I sat up straighter, honestly curious. "Why would you say that?"

"Oh, come on. I saw you guys. You can't keep your eyes off of each other. You shared these secret looks all night, that whole communicating-without-saying-a-word thing. If you're not a couple, you should be." She licked her fingers, but the orange wouldn't go away.

I looked down at my hands, laced together in my lap. "I haven't dated since my divorce. Cooper's the first person who's even ever stirred up any interest."

"Playing it safe never won anybody any awards."

"I don't want any awards. I've got those, and they mean nothing." I did have them. Teen of the Year for the entire state of Florida. Young Leader to Look Out For. Teens Making a Difference.

"This has got to be about more than your divorce, Tara. I know divorce is terrible, but it happens to a lot of people. They get over it."

"You wouldn't understand." People didn't understand what it was like to be in my shoes. They couldn't.

"Try me."

I stared at her a moment. What would she say? She seemed like one of those people who accepted everyone...but was she? "Someone spread some lies about me."

"And?"

"And it was terrible. People believed them."

"Your reputation is really important to you, isn't it? But your reputation isn't everything. There's more to life, you know. You just have to be right with yourself."

"When you're supposed to be an example to other people then your reputation is everything. I don't do things for shock value. I don't even like attention. But I did like being looked up to, and that all disappeared. Everything I worked for was gone, just like that."

"I think it's time you stop feeling sorry for yourself and get on with life."

I opened my mouth but shut it again. I couldn't argue with Candy. I really couldn't. She was right. I did need to get over everything and move on. But my failures had consumed my thoughts so deeply that they became a part of me—an inescapable part of me. How did I change that?

"Are you kicking me out of the house now for offending you?"

I shook my head. "No. I want you to tell the truth around me, even if it's not what I want to hear."

She stood and patted my shoulder. I didn't bother to look to see if orange fingerprints now stained the white fabric. "You're a pretty cool girl, Tara. Thanks for the talk."

"No, thank you for the talk."

"I'm going to go to bed now." She froze as a creak sounded in the hallway. With wide eyes, she looked back at me. "Did you hear that?"

I nodded, my breathing shallow. "Yeah, I heard that."

"What was it?"

"The house settling?"

Another creak sent shivers over my skin. I hated this house. I truly did. Everything happening here was pushing me to the edge. Of all the things I thought might do me in, a haunted house wasn't one of them.

Suddenly, everything went quiet. I glanced at the alarm clock and blinked. Where were the numbers?

"What's going on?" Candy whispered. She scrambled back in bed beside me. I didn't even care about the chain of evidence she left, convicting her of crimes against health food.

"I think we just lost electricity."

That's when we heard glass shatter. And shatter. And shatter some more. Gaga began barking frantically, her little body taut and on high alert.

"Is someone breaking in?" Candy's eyes widened even more. I never thought I'd see her look frightened of anything, but seeing her fear only increased mine.

Were those windows breaking? Was someone inside the home? And what about the power? Had the entire neighborhood lost electricity or just us?

Candy pulled the covers up to her chin. I realized I was doing the same thing.

"Call Cooper," she whispered.

"Not the police?"

"Cooper can get here faster."

I was about to argue when Gaga went eerily still, like she was afraid, too.

I didn't argue. I grabbed my cellphone and dialed his number. I had no idea what time it was. I knew I'd be waking him up. As Gaga continued to growl, any guilt evaporated. There was a time for manners, and a time to fight for your life. Right now, as my throat thickened with fear, I had to fight to survive.

"Hello?" Cooper's voice was sharp, no-nonsense.

"Cooper—"

"What's wrong?"

"The power is out and something's going on out in the living room."

He didn't hesitate. "I'll be right there. Meet me at the front door."

The mere thought of leaving this room caused me to tremble, to cower like a scared puppy dog. "I don't know if I can."

"Take Candy with you and meet me there. You can do that, Tara." His voice didn't hold any doubt, only strength and confidence.

I could do it. Cooper said so. "Okay."

I hung up. Cool and collected Candy stared at me, her fear putting her into a stupor. "Well?" she asked.

"He said to meet him at the front door."

Her eyes widened even more, if that was possible. Any thought I had of Candy being behind all of this as either a practical joke or as a publicity stunt disappeared. "That means we have to get out of bed. We have to go out there with...with...whatever it is that made that noise."

Ghosts. Spirits. Demons. Intruders. Serial killers. All of those possibilities raced through my mind. "I know." We stared at each other, each perfectly understanding the other's thoughts. The bed felt safe. Getting out of bed, leaving this room, might mean confronting something or someone we were unprepared to face.

Gaga barked, her tiny body rigid. What was wrong with this house? Why did every night feel like a bad horror movie was about to take place? I didn't want to be the stupid heroine who went upstairs when a madman was chasing her. I didn't want to be that person, but I had a feeling I was.

Pounding sounded outside.

Cooper. He was fast, and I wasn't complaining.

"We have to let him in," I whispered. I grabbed the gun from my nightstand and then Candy's wrist. "Come on."

Together we scrambled to the door like Tweedle-Dee and Tweedle-Dumb. We were both stumbling and tripping and breathless. My hand shook as I undid the locks. My heart raced. My breathing was shallow.

"Hurry!" Candy whispered behind me.

"I'm trying." Why wouldn't my fingers do what I wanted them to do as fast as I wanted them to do it?

"Tara?" Cooper's concerned voice drifted through the wood door.

"One minute." The deadbolt finally unlatched, and I jerked the door open. Cooper pulled me into a hug. Even as his arms went around me, I felt his gaze looking beyond me to this house of horrors.

"Are you okay?" he asked.

I nodded into his chest. "We're fine. Just scared."

I stepped back, and Candy raised her arms in the air. "Don't I get a hug too?"

Without flinching, he pulled her into a side hug. He didn't look awkward or uncomfortable—just compassionate and concerned. He rubbed her arm before stepping forward, his eyes serious. Then he saw my gun and stepped back. "Whoa, where did you get that?"

"I filed an application to carry it."

He eased it out of my hands, which was probably a good thing since I was trembling uncontrollably. "Why don't you let me hold that for a moment?"

I nodded, almost relieved.

"You two stay here. I'm going to check out the house for you."

"Be careful," I mumbled.

He walked toward the kitchen and stopped in his tracks. "What...?"

"What is it?" Ectoplasma? Butcher knives? A dead body?

He looked down at the floor. "All of your glasses have been shattered, Tara. There are pieces of them all over the kitchen floor. It looks like someone was angry."

My fear squeezed harder. Why would someone do that?

"Maybe we upset the spirits on our ghost hunt," Candy mumbled.

My thoughts bounced back and forth. What if she was right? No, that was crazy. Honestly, I didn't know what to think.

Cooper paused in the doorway, his gaze stern on both of us. "Let me check out things outside. Stay there."

As he disappeared, Candy and I clung to each other and huddled in the corner. In the midst of our distress, Candy blurted, "You two are *so* a couple."

I ignored her. "I hope Cooper's okay."

"He's a former Army Ranger."

I held my breath, waiting to hear a sudden movement, a moan, some signal that something had happened to Cooper. I waited to see Philip Whitehurst appear from the basement, holding the missing murder weapon or a supernatural being streak through the walls and into the living room. "I hate this, Candy. I hate living in fear."

"Fear is a body's natural defense mechanism. It signals that we may need to defend ourselves, get out of danger's way."

I cast a skeptical glance at my friend for her textbook answer. "Okay, Freud."

"It's true, though."

"But we're not supposed to have spirits of fear, but of power and love and discipline." I don't know why I was talking Bible to Candy. It was my default mode, I supposed.

"Fear is a part of our basic human existence." Candy's shaky voice belied her bravado. "It's normal, especially when danger lurks."

Silence fell again, heavy and electrified.

"Do you think Cooper is okay?" I whispered.

As soon as the question left my mouth, the lights begin blinking on the DVD player. I let out a sigh of relief.

The backdoor opened again and Cooper emerged from the kitchen, scowling. Glass crunched beneath his feet. "Something's wrong with the power meter outside. I found some screws on the ground."

Shivers raced up my spine. "So, some*one* did this?"

"Given the broken glasses in the kitchen, I'd say yes." Cooper's firm gaze confirmed I was right. "The power meter is fixed now, and I've reset the alarm."

I looked at the wood floor. That creaky wooden floor that's given me a thousand nightmares. I crossed my arms over my chest, trying to get a grip. I had to say something, because I could feel Cooper's gaze on me.

"Thanks for your help," was all I could manage.

He squeezed my arm, and I could feel warmth at his closeness. But I still couldn't look up. I was afraid he'd see my fear.

"Look, I don't usually do this, but why don't the two of you stay at my place tonight? Just to be safe," Cooper said. "You can have my bed. I'll camp out in Austin's room."

Candy and I glanced at each other. I could see from the bright look in her eyes that she was feeling what I was—total relief. We'd be able to get out of this house. Maybe get some sleep.

"Okay," we answered at the same time.

It took every ounce of my being not to dart as quickly as possible to Cooper's house. To not sprint as if the grass beneath my feet was on fire. To hide my terror in knowing that someone was bent on tormenting me.

But first I'd waited until the police left. Cooper had insisted we call them. The crew had come out and dusted for prints and promised to get back with us. As soon as they left, I herded everyone out of the house and over to Cooper's place. Just being out of that house brought me a certain sense of relief.

Cooper unlocked the door to his place and ushered us inside. "I'll put some fresh sheets on."

He grabbed a bundle of linens from the hall closet, and I followed him into his bedroom, depositing my overnight bag on the floor. Somehow, I felt like I shouldn't be in this room with him. I was sure there was a rule somewhere I was breaking. Guilt tried to push to the surface, but I swallowed it. I had nothing to feel guilty about. I was simply helping him put sheets on the bed.

"What are you thinking about?" Cooper asked.

How much I enjoy everyday, mundane things with you, and I could imagine myself doing this with you for the rest of my life. I swallowed, desperately hoping he couldn't read my thoughts. Finally, I croaked out, "Ghosts. Ghosts, of course."

He flapped the sheet several times, and I grabbed the other end. "My aunt used to think her house was haunted."

"Was it?"

"She was actually a little crazy."

I licked my lips. "Like me?"

"You're not crazy."

"Then what am I?" I hardly wanted to ask the question because I wasn't sure I wanted to know the answer.

"I think you're being haunted—but not by a ghost."

Relief flushed through my heart. Maybe there was hope for me. "So it's good that I have a gun."

"Not if you don't know how to use it."

"You just pull a trigger, right?"

"How about if I show you sometime?"

I nodded. "Yeah, that would be good." He hadn't given the gun back, probably for fear of his own life. Maybe it was better that way. I'd gotten the gun from Candy spontaneously, and I didn't have any idea what to do with it.

I finished tucking in the sheets and stuffing pillows into fresh cases. Then I slipped into the hallway and spotted Candy falling asleep on the couch. I ushered her into the bedroom. I was ready to go to bed also, but I needed to thank Cooper first.

I closed the door behind me so Candy could go to sleep, then turned around and took a step. I gasped when I realized that Cooper was waiting in front of me. I was close enough to feel his breath on my cheek. To smell spearmint and baby shampoo. To feel electricity zig-zagging up my spine.

I forced myself to swallow. Something almost magnetic seemed to connect our gazes. I wanted to break the invisible hold, to look away. But I couldn't.

"Thanks. For everything. For being there. For being...Cooper." I smiled weakly, mentally chiding myself for losing my ability to speak properly. For feeling like I wanted to melt.

"You're welcome, Tara."

Something about the way he said the words made my face flush. He sounded husky, like his tone was reserved especially for me. He looked at me another moment, and I wondered what he was thinking. Finally, he pointed behind me. "I just need to grab a couple of things from my dresser."

My cheeks heated. Of course. He needed to get something before

Candy and I settled in for the night. What did I think? That he wanted to kiss me?

He slipped inside, grabbed some clothes, and stepped into the hallway. For some reason, I still remained standing where I was, frozen to the spot. Cooper smiled down at me again. The sparkle in his eyes made my throat burn with emotion and desire.

I pointed behind me, still not breaking eye contact. "I'm going to bed now." I swallowed, fast and hard.

His smile went soft. "Good night," he said. Was it my imagination or was his face getting closer? Were his eyes becoming more mesmerizing?

I realized I wasn't breathing, and I needed to breathe. Otherwise, I'd faint. Which would only give Cooper another chance to save me.

Goodness knows he'd had enough chances to do that already, without my initiating any more.

With an arm behind me, I twisted the latch and leaned back into the bedroom door as it opened. "Good night," I mumbled.

I quickly shut the door and stood beside it, waiting for my breathing to even out. What was wrong with me? I'd been married. It wasn't like I was an amateur in the men department. Yet I felt jittery, like a sixteen-year-old on her first date.

Candy was tucked in bed, her eyes closed. I climbed in beside her, trying to be quiet so that I didn't wake my friend.

Silence filled the room.

My thoughts quickly filled the space.

Had I almost kissed Ben Cooper? Had he almost kissed me?

Was I losing my mind? Had I not learned anything from the fiasco with Peter?

Despite my thoughts, I smiled.

I liked Ben Cooper. I liked him a lot.

"You two are *so* a couple," Candy said beside me.

I hit my friend with my pillow, realizing she'd been awake this whole time.

27

I woke up with a start the next morning. My hand reached for the empty space in the bed beside me. Peter wasn't there. He hadn't been there in a long time.

I shook my head. No, Candy had slept there last night. We'd been like two little girls at a slumber party, whispering and giggling and experiencing a real-life ghost story.

Who would have thought that I'd come to consider a fame-hungry party girl as one of my closest friends? Or that I thought I might be falling in love with a B-Boy? Or that I was actually considering the reality that a ghost was living in my house?

I lay there for a moment, absorbed in my thoughts about my past, my present, and my future. Maybe closing the book on my past was the best thing that could have happened to me. I would have never wished my experiences on anyone, and I didn't promote divorce or think that God smiled on it. But Candy was right. I had to buck up and put everything behind me. If I could do that, I'd be a better person for it.

I could hear Cooper talking in the living room. He seemed so grounded and stable, like he didn't pull any punches. Peter...well our relationship had just been one, big punch in the gut. Nothing that I thought it would be. He'd left me, which made him more of a boy than a man.

Already, in the short time I'd known Cooper, I felt like what we had was real.

At least Cooper and I could disagree. At least we could come at things from different angles without holding a grudge. In the short time since I'd known Cooper, our friendship felt more real than my relationship with Peter ever did. Of course, I wouldn't have thought that back then, back when I met Peter and fell in love. Back then things felt perfect.

Peter and I had never argued. Ever. Even when we got divorced, we didn't argue. We simply stopped speaking. Maybe in order to truly love someone you had to learn to disagree with them. Wasn't disagreeing a part of being real? Because disagreements were bound to happen sooner or later, and you had to learn to deal with conflict effectively in order to move past it.

I sighed, my heavy thoughts already settling in for the day. The scent of bacon teased my stomach. I threw my clothes back on and walked into the kitchen to find Candy and Cooper chatting at the kitchen table over coffee. Candy's hair—her wig—was on, and she'd already done her makeup. She wore flannel pants and a black tank top. Cooper, on the other hand, wore jeans and a white T-shirt.

Having someone to wake up with made me aware of the empty ache in my heart. I'd been separated from other people for too long, only I hadn't realized it.

"Morning. Pull up a seat and dig in." Cooper pulled a chair out for me.

"I've got to have coffee before I sit down." I grabbed an empty mug from the counter and decided to drink it black. As I did that, Cooper put together a plate of food for me and set it at the table. My mouth watered as I breathed in the scent of toast, eggs, and bacon. The breakfast of champions. Big, fat champions.

"We were just talking about the broken glasses," Cooper started.

"Did you draw any conclusions?" I took a bite of egg.

"Not a single one. It doesn't make sense. I checked the alarm stats, and it was on all night. No one could have gotten in or out of the house without it registering."

"Even with the power cut?"

"Even with the power cut."

"So you think it was a ghost?" I nearly choked on my coffee as I asked the question.

"No, not a ghost. I'm sure there's a logical explanation. I just don't know what it is. I'm going to install some cameras, if that's okay with you. I want to see what's going on while these things happen."

"Anything to get some answers."

"Just don't put the cameras anywhere naughty." Candy's eyes twinkled, and I kicked her under the table.

Cooper shook his head. "Don't worry. Your privacy will be intact."

"Can I talk something through with you guys?"

"Only if I can interject my opinion whenever possible," Candy muttered.

I leaned back, the stiff chair fitting for my rigid thoughts. "Okay, let's assume this isn't a ghost."

"Even though it could be," Candy insisted.

"But assuming it's not, who would have motive for doing these things?"

"Maybe someone wants you to move out so they can buy your house," Candy suggested.

"But the house next door is for sale. Why would someone want this specific house?"

Cooper shook his head. "I have no idea."

"If this is connected to Danielle's death somehow, then there are some people who could be persons of interest. There's Philip Whitehurst. Maybe he would have something to gain by letting us think there's a ghost in the house?"

"Who's Philip Whitehurst?" Cooper asked.

We filled him in. Cooper listened carefully, his eyes registering each new detail. "What would he have to gain?"

I shook my head. "I have no idea. I'm no good at this detective thing. There's also Miss Mystic. She seems desperate to communicate with Danielle in the house."

"Maybe she just wants fame?" Cooper suggested.

That's what reporter Bryce Stephens had indicated. "I did hear that she's always wanted to be famous. But she was friends with Danielle. What if she really thinks she can communicate with her? What's if she's just...misled?"

"There's always Lana's stalker," Candy reminded.

I shook my head. "Lana said he's in India now." I nodded toward the street. "There's the strange man across the street. He gives me the creeps."

Cooper took another sip of his coffee. Even seeing him drink coffee made my heart race. I had it, and I had it bad. His crystal blue eyes turned serious. "You find a killer when you find someone who has the motive, means, and opportunity. Do any of those people have all three?"

I shook my head. "I have no idea. I think this is all making less sense with time instead of more sense." I finished my breakfast and pushed my plate away. "Speaking of which, I've got to get back to the house and clean up the mess there."

"We went over and did it this morning," Cooper said.

"You did?"

He nodded. "I figured you wouldn't want to see it."

"But I took some video just in case you do," Candy added with a wink.

My gaze bounced back and forth between them. "You guys are the best."

Candy pulled a cheeseball out from the bag on the table and popped it in her mouth. "I know." She chewed and swallowed. "So what's next?"

"What's next is I'm installing security cameras. I should have done it from the start, I supposed, but I had no idea things would escalate like this." He looked at me. "Is it okay if I come over in an hour?"

I smiled, wanting to say he was welcome over whenever he wanted. Instead, I nodded. "An hour will be fine."

As soon as I stepped into Lana's house, chills swept over my skin. Something wasn't right about this place. I didn't know what, but something creepy was definitely going on. I just didn't know if it centered on the house, Lana, or me. I'd taken my gun back from Cooper and slipped it into the nightstand drawer again. Just in case, you know?

Candy—since she didn't have to do her hair—was ready in fifteen minutes. I'd just finished drying mine when she waltzed into my room and began rummaging around Lana's jewelry box.

"What are you doing?"

"I'm borrowing some jewelry. Lana lets me do it all the time." She slipped on a ring and held her hand out. "I like this one."

I looked closer. "That's the ring my dad gave her when she turned sixteen." And it was worth thousands of dollars. Would Lana really be okay with Candy wearing it? I didn't feel okay with it.

"He has good taste."

It was supposed to be a purity ring. Things hadn't quite worked out that way, however. "Maybe you shouldn't wear that one."

"Yeah, maybe not." She tried to pull it off, but the ring remained at her joint. "Oh no."

"Oh no what?" The words nearly stuck in my throat.

She tugged again. "The ring. It won't come off."

"You're joking."

"No, I'm really not."

"How can it be stuck?"

"I don't know, but it is." She tugged at it some more. The ring didn't budge.

"Here, let me try." I grabbed the jewelry and pulled it toward me. It was stuck all right. How was I going to break this news to Lana? Even though she hadn't kept the vow associated with the ring, I still knew it meant a lot to her. "I'm going to get some cooking spray."

I grabbed some from the kitchen, ignoring the heebie-jeebies that filled me when I stepped onto the linoleum. The shelves where the glasses used to rest were now empty, and I still had no idea how that had happened.

I raced back to my bedroom and sprayed Candy's finger. Then I tugged at the ring. It remained glued where it was. I pulled harder.

All of the sudden, the ring slipped off. But I'd pulled so hard that the momentum caused my hand to fly back, the ring with it. The sapphire-studded band flew through the air, as if in slow motion, and then clinked on the ground behind the nightstand.

"Gracious," I muttered.

"Did you say 'gracious'?" Candy asked.

My cheeks heated. I liked to work on crossword puzzles, go to bed early, and I said gracious. I was basically turning into my grandmother. "Yes, I did. Why?"

"That sounds so old-fashioned."

"Is that a problem?"

Candy shrugged. "Of course not." She moved the nightstand. I expected to see the ring there, waiting to be put back on its throne in Lana's jewelry box. Instead, I saw dust balls.

"It went back here, didn't it?"

I nodded. "That's what it looked like to me." I got on my knees. "Maybe it ricocheted off the wall and went under the bed instead."

We pulled out the boxes under the bed but still didn't find anything but dustballs. Then we searched under the dresser and anywhere else it might have gone. Nothing.

"Rings just don't disappear," I muttered.

"Maybe the ghost got it." She waved her fingers in the air while making ghostly sounds before snickering.

"Very funny."

She dropped her hands. "What else could have happened to it?"

My gaze roamed the floor and stopped at the vent by the window. "Do you think it could fit between those slats?"

Candy knelt on the floor and inspected them. "It's a possibility."

Side by side, we took the cover off. A tube waited there, like an endless, dark abyss. No way did I want to stick my hand down there. I stared at Candy instead. "You pulled out the ring. You reach down there and see if you can find it."

"Do I have to?"

"Someone does." I sure didn't want to stick my hand into the unknown, not after everything else that had happened.

She sighed and lowered her hand down. "I don't feel anything."

"Reach farther."

"Easy for you to say." She sunk farther into the floor. "My arm doesn't bend like this."

"It's got to be down there. Where else would it be?"

"I don't know, but you're going to have to try. Your arms are all tiny and petite. You can probably reach farther than I can."

I imagined Lana's reaction if we told her we'd lost that ring. We had to find it, because I didn't want to face the consequences if we didn't. "Fine."

I walked my fingers into the AC vent, much like a spider going down the waterspout. The tunnel turned, so I twisted my body until my entire arm was plunged into the floor, all the way to my shoulder.

"Anything?"

I shook my head. "I don't think." I reached my fingers a little farther. That ring had to be down here. It had to be.

Something connected with my fingertips. What...? I reached farther, my shoulder aching as it pressed against the opening. Finally, my fingers wrapped around something. But...it was too big to be a ring.

Slowly, I pulled my arm out. I screamed when I saw a bloody knife in my hands.

The police swarmed the house again. I was beginning to know each of them on a first name basis, which was never a good sign.

From all indications, I'd found the murder weapon used to kill Danielle Miller. Authorities had to test the blood to be sure, but the detective made it sound like a done deal. They'd gone into the basement, lifted some ceiling tiles and cut out the rest of the vent where the knife had been found. Sure enough, Lana's ring was there, too.

Cooper showed up right about the time the police arrived, and we'd filled him in on what happened. As soon as the police left, Cooper began installing the cameras in the kitchen and living room. Candy and I sat stiffly on the couch. I didn't know about Candy, but I couldn't shake the chills that swept over me.

"That's what Danielle's spirit wanted you to find," Candy muttered. "That's why she's been hanging around. I can't wait to tell Mickey."

I wanted to argue with her. I really did. But how could I? What other explanation was there? The blood on that knife was obviously old, so someone couldn't have planted it recently...I didn't think.

Cooper came back into the living room, screwdriver and wires in hand. "Where did you say you heard that guitar music, Tara?"

"Coming from the guitar in Lana's closet. I threw the guitar away, though, and I haven't heard it since then."

"When did you throw it away?" Candy asked, her voice strangely brittle.

"A couple of days ago. Why?"

She shook her head. "Because I saw that guitar in the closet last night."

28

I stared at the guitar as it rested like a corpse on the coffee table. Sure enough, somehow the instrument had ended up back in the closet of the spare bedroom. Cooper inspected it now as my chills deepened.

"This looks like a starter guitar. Probably cost a hundred or so." He looked up at me. "What do you think about me destroying it?"

Would that stop the guitar music or the ghost?

My confusion must have registered on my face because Cooper explained, "I want to see if there's a music player somewhere in the body. I have to take it a part to check, though. Even with a flashlight, I can't see anything."

That explanation sounded more like Cooper. I nodded, not having any special fondness for the instrument. "Of course. Feel free."

He went outside and, a moment later, returned shaking his head. "There's nothing inside."

Why did that not surprise me?

Candy patted my shoulder. "I think you need to get out of this house and relax some. Unfortunately, I have to go to work." She looked at Cooper. "Someone else needs to be charged with that task."

Cooper's hands were on his hips as he looked over at me. His eyes held...what was it? Fondness? Concern? "I'm sure I can think of something to distract you."

"I don't want to be a burden." I meant it. Cooper had gone out of his way time and time again. When would that get old?

"Friends are never burdens."

Cooper's comment made me feel both warm and secure—because he thought of me as a friend—but also rejected in the romance department. Why did I do this to myself? Why did I let my heart go to unwelcome places?

We ended up helping Winnie with some yard projects. I found out that Cooper cut her grass every week and helped her whenever she needed a handyman. It felt so good to get out of the house, to feel like a normal human for once. Out here there was no worrying about creaky houses.

As I pulled a weed from her flowerbed, I looked toward the sky where the sun began to set. That's when I noticed the broken streetlight. I remembered the scowl I'd seen on the wall, the one that had mysteriously disappeared. I had a feeling that streetlight hadn't broken on its own or even by accident. I had a feeling that someone had broken it.

I shuddered and continued to work. The sun began setting, and Winnie offered to bring us some lemonade. As we waited, both Cooper and I plopped onto the grass and stretched out our legs.

"You making out okay without Austin?" I brushed some grass from my leg.

Cooper's muscles rippled as he leaned back on his palms. The edge of his eagle tattoo peeked out, and the fading sunlight bathed his face in an orange glow.

"I'm ready for him to be home. He's been my whole world for the past five years."

"You're doing a great job with him, you know." In the short amount of time since I'd known Cooper, I'd realized what a good father he was. Firm but patient. Kind but assertive. That described Cooper as a person, as well.

"I call every day like some neurotic father. I know he's okay and that his grandparents are taking good care of him. It's just hard to be so far away."

My heart ached for a moment. That was really all I'd wanted as a teenager when I thought about growing up. I imagined myself married to a wonderful man who provided for the family while I stayed home and cooked dinner and had play dates at the park and chased my kids. Occasionally, I'd like my husband to chase me around, too.

What if my life continued on this path it was on now? What if I remained single until well beyond my childbearing years? Could I even adopt or were the allegations against me enough to have me rejected?

"I think it's sweet."

I imagined myself for a moment with a daughter. I imagined meeting someone, falling in love, and then discovering that the man I was with had been accused of being a child molester. It didn't matter how much he claimed his innocence or how much I loved him. I'd probably never trust him with my daughter alone.

Cooper was probably the same way, and I couldn't blame him. The moment I told him the truth, he'd run far away. Isn't that what a good father would do?

The thought weighed heavy on my heart.

"Everything okay?" Cooper asked.

I nodded. What would it be like to shake my head and tell him the truth instead? I'd pondered that question a million times, but I couldn't bring myself to actually take action. Here in Minnesota, no one knew who I was, and that felt nice. I didn't want people to know who I was. I wanted a new beginning. But were new beginnings even possible? Fear seemed the predominate emotion in my life.

There was a difference between *feeling* fear and having a *spirit* of fear. I'd developed a spirit of fear—about living in Lana's house, about falling in love, about letting people down. I had to figure out how to change that into having a spirit of power and love and self-control.

Cooper's voice pulled me from my thoughts. "You're going to church with me tomorrow still?"

Church. I'd forgotten. Going one Sunday wouldn't hurt anything. Besides, I was feeling better about God. I wasn't ready to jump into anything, but my gut told me that he was real. Even if I felt like I'd failed him and he failed me, I still couldn't shake my belief that he existed. I simply had to come to terms with how I felt about his work in my life. I had to accept that following the rules could ultimately just lead to heartache. Ask Jesus. He'd followed the rules and ended up dying on the cross.

"Yeah."

Winnie brought some lemonade outside. We chatted with her for a few minutes until she yawned and we realized we should leave. As we stepped onto the porch, Cooper stopped me. "Hey, Tara."

I looked up, absorbing the glorious features called Cooper's face. All perfect lines and melt-worthy eyes and...my gaze stopped at his lips. Kissable lips. Why bother denying it?

All of those realizations collided with my earlier realizations that something long-term between us wouldn't work.

"That day we ran into each other at the ice cream truck—"

"After I got mad at you?" I remembered my immaturity clearly.

He smiled. "After you got mad at me. The first time."

"That's a big step for me, you know."

"Getting mad?"

"I usually stuff those negative emotions down deep inside me instead of addressing them." Pretty much I'd done that all of my life.

"I'm flattered, then."

Our gazes locked. What was he getting at exactly? I raised my face. "You were saying?"

"When I got home and I saw you standing in the rain—"

A car horn sounded, and I jerked my head toward the street. As I did so, I glanced at Lana's house and realized I'd left the lights on. My windows lit up like eyes, like the house had taken on a mind of its own.

Crazy thoughts. Houses didn't take on minds of their own.

But a ghostly looking woman wearing all white and staring at me out my window might.

29

Cooper took off across the lawn just as the wispy woman disappeared from the window.

A ghost? My hand remained over my mouth in shock and horror. Had I been seeing things? I had to have been. What other explanation was there?

Except that Cooper had seen her too.

I snapped back to my senses and crossed the street. With trembling fingers, I opened the front door and slipped inside. Cooper was nowhere to be found. I remained in the entryway, waiting to hear something, to see something.

Finally Cooper emerged from the kitchen. He paused in the doorway, his hands resting on his hips and a new heaviness in his eyes. "Nothing."

My lips parted in surprise. "You saw her, too, didn't you?"

He nodded. "Yeah, I saw her." He stormed toward the computer. "Time to use those security cameras I had installed."

He sat at the desk and pulled up a website. A moment later, video feed filled the screen. I pulled up a chair, afraid I might not be able to stand. My hands trembled as the image of the woman haunted my mind. She'd looked so eerie, so still.

So ghostly.

A woman appeared on the camera in the basement. I gasped in disbelief. There she was. In my basement. Where had she come from? No one could fit into the basement windows. They were too narrow.

The woman looked like a ghost. She walked like a ghost.

I could hardly breathe as I watched her climb the steps. Her steps were light. She wore all white and even her face was pasty.

Was that Danielle Miller? I couldn't be sure. Aspects seemed the same, but the feed was too fuzzy for me to get a handle on the woman's age.

The woman in the video appeared in the kitchen. She nearly floated across the floor and into the living room.

It was like she knew I was across the street and she'd purposely gone to the window so I'd see her.

"I've never seen anything like this before, Tara." Cooper's voice held disbelief.

The woman on screen turned and moved quickly back toward the basement. That must have been when Cooper started toward the house.

"People can't walk through walls," I mumbled. "Where did she go?"

Cooper shook his head, still staring at the screen and rewinding the video. "I have no idea, Tara. Not a single clue."

"Should we call the police?"

"At this point, I'm not sure it would do much good, to be honest."

His words caused a chill to breeze over me. Just what was going on here?

Candy had shown up at Cooper's place last night, heard about the ghost, and asked if she could crash at Cooper's. I was glad that she was there because guilt pounded at me at the thought of staying at Cooper's alone. I knew I was overthinking things, but me staying there looked so bad. At least with Candy present...well, it still seemed weird, but a little more excusable.

I hadn't been able to get the ghost out of my mind all night. The next morning, Candy and I went back to Lana's place to get dressed, and I shuddered as I stepped inside. I was never going to stay here again, and that was all there was to it.

Nothing seemed disturbed, so we let Gaga outside and got dressed for church.

"I don't have anything to wear," Candy moaned.

I could tell she didn't want to go. I didn't want to go either, so I understood completely. However, I decided to be an adult about it and, instead of whining, I'd try and convince her that going would be fun. "It's more of a come as you are type of place. What you have on is fine." Skinny jeans, black boots, and a black T-shirt.

I, on the other hand, had white linen pants and a turquoise top.

Cooper picked me up. Candy decided to ride her motorcycle, and I wondered if she would actually show up at church or use this as an excuse to run the opposite way. Surprisingly enough, she pulled in beside us, pulled off her helmet, and stared at the building.

"Fancy," she mumbled.

Sweat covered my brow as we started toward the door. I didn't care how laid back this place was. Church was no longer a place where I felt loved and accepted. Flashes from my last several Sundays back in Miami began assaulting my brain. The stares, the whispers, the head shakes. Some people had actually jerked their children away from me as I walked toward my seat.

I rubbed my neck and took a deep breath as we stepped inside. I didn't stop to talk to anyone but went straight to the back row of seats. At least I could make a quick getaway here. Candy sat on one side of me and Cooper on the other.

I soaked in the crowds of people. There were more than I'd imagined. Cooper had explained earlier that there was a core group of around twenty people, and everyone else looked what might be considered "rough." There were bikers and homeless and women who dressed more provocatively than Candy.

Candy seemed to approve. If Candy was going to go to church, this seemed like a good one to visit.

A college-aged girl stopped by our chairs and extended her hand. "I'm Tonya."

Cooper introduced us but the girl's gaze remained on me until I squirmed.

"Tara? You look familiar." She tapped her chin, and I realized that in the brief moments since we began chatting that Tonya reminded me an awful lot of me. Clean cut, preppy, innocent.

I shrugged, trying took casual. "I'm new in town, so I'm not sure why."

"Tara Lancaster. Your name is even familiar." She squinted.

Panic began to lace itself up my spine. "Must just be the name."

She snapped her fingers. "Oh my goodness! You're Tara Lancaster. The Tara Lancaster. I used to read your blog religiously! I loved it. The Good Girl Chronicles? You're practically my hero."

Her voice rose with each sentence until several people stared at me. I wanted to sink and continue sinking until I was under the chairs. I couldn't deny her claim. But how much else did she know?

"And your father is Henry Lancaster. He wrote all of those parenting books. He's a pastor, right?"

My throat burned as I nodded. Yeah, he'd written the books on parenting back when Lana and I had been sweet and innocent. Then Lana hit puberty and went wild. He wrote *The Wayward Daughter*, and that was his last book. My fiasco had further called into question his parenting skills. He'd never told me he resented me for it, but I always wondered.

"I wish I'd have known you were going to be in town. I would have totally had you come out to my college ministry group and speak. Your posts on purity were some of the best I'd ever read." She held up her hand and wiggled her fingers. "Purity ring!"

I'd talked about waiting for the right one. And I had waited, and I'd waxed on and on about how glad I was that I had. I was glad, but, despite my efforts, things had still turned rotten.

"Is your husband here?" She glanced around. "Peter, right?"

My cheeks burned. Here was the moment of truth...at least, some truth. I thought about skirting the issue, but I couldn't. "I'm divorced, actually."

The smile slipped from her face. "Divorced? No." Her hand went over her heart.

I guessed she hadn't read the "Saint Turned Sinner" headlines. I could hear the disappointment in her voice nonetheless. I'd heard it so much before that I'd become an expert at identifying the fallen look in people's eyes.

"It's a long story. It didn't end the way I wanted it to. Your story can have a happier ending, Tonya. You should follow your heart and stick to your guns. Despite my marriage, I still believe that you'll never regret holding firm to your standards." Had I just said that? Did I really mean it? I wasn't sure, which wasn't surprising lately.

"Thanks, Tara. I'm...I'm sorry to hear things didn't work out for you."

"They didn't. But they will." Again, where did the confidence in my voice come from? I'd been in denial for months, but suddenly I sounded really convincing, like I believed those words myself.

Thankfully, the music started. Candy gave me a quick glance, wagging her eyebrows up and down. "I'm impressed. You're practically a celebrity yourself."

I ignored her. I ignored Cooper's gaze. What was he thinking? I'd told him parts of my story, but never about The Good Girl Chronicles.

I could barely pay attention to either the music or the sermon. I heard the preacher talking about making a difference with our time here on earth and not living just to meet our own selfish ambitions.

At some point, Cooper's arm had slipped around my shoulders, and he squeezed my bicep. I couldn't even imagine what he was thinking. He knew some of my story, but he didn't know all of that. He didn't know that some people had classified me as some kind of superstar Christian and modeled their lives after mine.

Church ended, and I prepared myself to face questions from Cooper and Candy. Instead, Candy turned to me with wide, dancing eyes. "I have the perfect idea."

I blinked, having no idea where to expect this conversation to go. "Okay."

"That pastor was right. Everything I do is for me. I want to do something that really makes an impact."

Satisfaction spread through me. Good. Life-changing realizations weren't overrated. Even with everything I'd been through and this weird place I was in, a small part of me still clung to hope. "That's great, Candy. You should do that."

"I'm going to start a new program."

"What kind of program?" I braced myself for her response.

She clapped her hands. "I'm going to call it 'Hugs for the Homeless.' Did you know that in order to maintain a healthy life, people need an average of five hugs a day? I bet homeless people don't even get one. I'm going to start a campaign to help them feel some love."

A million scenarios raced through my mind. Most of what I pictured ended with Candy being hurt. In the very least, it ended with her getting lice. Hugs for the Homeless was not a good idea. I didn't want to dim her enthusiasm, though.

"How about 'Haircuts for the Homeless,' since that's your thing and all? Even the homeless need haircuts." But that still didn't eliminate the lice problem...I'd think about that later. Better alive with lice than dead.

Her eyes got bigger. "That will be step two of my plan. Then I'll do H2O for the Homeless. Hummus for the Homeless? So many ideas are floating around in my head right now." Her hands flew through the air with each word.

"Candy—"

She turned toward me, and I almost stepped back when I saw the moisture in her eyes. "Seriously, Tara. Something about that sermon struck a nerve. I felt so rejected by the church when I was a teen. What if I could help other people to never feel like that? What if I could use my experiences and be a part of the solution?"

I couldn't argue. "I think that would be wonderful."

"The past few years, I've been living for myself. What would it be like to not always have my number one priority be me and my happiness? It's like the pastor said...it's an empty pursuit."

I nodded, not one to try and douse someone else's passion, even if I did have my reservations. Candy seemed really sincere, and the best I could do would be to pick her up and give *her* a hug if anything went wrong. "Okay then. You should do it. I'll go with you."

Cooper stepped forward. "Me too."

She grinned. "I'll meet you back here in two hours. Does that work?"

"Sure."

Candy's Hugs for the Homeless outreach had gone so well that Wanda opened up the church building as a cooling station afterward. I was really proud of Candy. Though her idea had been crazy, she'd completed the task as she completed everything in life—with enthusiasm.

She'd donned sandwich board signs proclaiming her mission and made her rounds. Would it be a non-Christian who taught me how to truly live as a Christian? Life was full of irony. There was one thing I'd realized today, though. I'd realized that as much as I tried to fight it or over-analyze it, I believed in God. I truly did. And it was time to stop making excuses and to realize that, no matter how hard life felt, God was still good. Peace fell over me at the realization.

We were back now at The Mercy House, and Cooper and I helped to hand out water and Popsicles while Candy mingled. Wanda worked beside us.

Her gaze fixated on someone in the distance, a man standing beside a table packed with brochures and tracts. "Many of the homeless are on the street because of mental illness. Some days you just never know what's going to transpire here at the church as a result." She nodded to the man she was watching. "That man over there...he's been coming here for a couple of years now. He used to be an engineer, but then something caused him to have a mental break of some sort. I can't be sure, but I think he has some form of schizophrenia."

She continued. "He has this obsession with eggs. He's always asking for them and then rubbing them against his head."

Eggs? Connections began forming in my mind but not nearly quickly enough.

He approached an artificial bowl of fruit and picked up a piece, bringing it toward his mouth. Wanda took off toward him. "Philip! Philip Whitehurst, that's not a real apple!"

I froze. Had she just said Philip Whitehurst? Eggs? Everything suddenly made sense. I rounded the counter, feeling like some other force was driving me toward the man. He was the man I'd seen staring in my window that day. He was short and chubby with a ruddy complexion and a receding hairline. His brown eyes darted about uncertainly as Wanda took the plastic apple from his hands.

I stopped and stared. Homeless. Possibly schizophrenic. Believed he was cursed. Angry with Danielle. Was this man a killer?

Lord, give me the right words.

"Excuse me, are you Philip Whitehurst?" I tried to soften my tone.

The man flinched and backed up. His eyes darted from person to person, and sweat poured down his face. I had to do something before this man took off like a scared rabbit.

"I live in Danielle Miller's house."

His Adam's apple bobbed up and down as he swallowed. He paused. "Danielle?" His eyes lit up as he said her name.

I nodded. "That's right. Danielle. She was your friend, wasn't she?"

His eyes began twitching again. Was this man a murderer? Had he gone off the deep end when Danielle took his money?

"I didn't kill Danielle! I loved her!" He backed up and hit the table.

I soaked in his features, the way his hands shook, how I could see the white around his pupils. This was a man on edge. But why? "Why have you been following me?"

His hands began flying through the air, swinging wildly with his words. "People think I killed her. I just wanted to talk. To talk."

"What did you want to talk about?"

"Danielle."

I made sure my words sounded even. "What about Danielle?"

"I just want to talk to her." His voice took on the strain of a desperate man. His eyes pleaded with me. But desperation led to funny things sometimes, things like murder.

"She's dead, Philip. You know that."

He rubbed his head, the movement becoming more vigorous with each second. "I heard that she's been trying to talk to you. Her spirit. I want her to talk to me, too."

"She's not trying to talk. Someone's just trying to scare me." Even as I said the words, I heard the doubt in my voice.

"You're wrong," he whispered. "You're wrong."

Before I could say anything else, he darted toward the exit, and he was gone.

30

I returned to the Little House of Horrors, a strange satisfaction fully settled in my gut. Maybe a church like The Mercy House was just what I needed to wash myself of the legalism staining my life. Maybe Minnesota really could be my new start.

Cooper was behind me as I unlocked my door, and I was all too aware of his every movement. It was like he didn't even have to touch me, but I was profoundly aware that he was there. The electricity that flashed between us was stronger than any thunderstorm, yet it was grounded also. Really, it was the perfect mix. Really, we were the perfect mix.

I pushed the door open, wondering what this evening might hold. Would Cooper and I continue on this path as friends? Or would something change?

As soon as I stepped inside, I skidded to a halt. My gaze latched on to the wall in front of me. I gasped in horror. Words were slashed across the wall as if Satan himself had risen from the depths of hell and threatened me, using his own blood as ink.

Don't suffer the same fate as my father.

I turned around, and Cooper wrapped his arms around me. He covered my head, as if he wanted to shield me from the bone-shattering fear that coursed through my body. I felt him staring at the words, his ever-analytical mind processing and trying to find solutions.

He stepped away, his hands still at my shoulders, gently massaging my rock hard back muscles. "It's going to be okay," he soothed.

The words stained my memory, though. Whoever was doing this just wasn't going to stop, were they? They were going to keep going and going until...until what? Until I left? Until I went crazy? Until I did a Brittany Spears and shaved my hair off? "I don't see how things are going to get better. Things have gone from bad to Zombie Apocalypse type of bad."

"We're going to find out who did this."

I pulled back so I could see his eyes. "What do you mean?"

"The cameras I had set up." He walked toward the wall and touched a red letter then examined his finger. "It's still wet."

"Blood?" My throat felt dry as I said the word. This had to be a nightmare.

He shook his head. "Some kind of paint, I think. Maybe one that's been mixed with a stain to give it the color and tint of blood. It's not blood, though."

Some of the tension that had knotted itself over my heart loosened.

But there were still other things to worry about. "What does that message mean?"

"I have no idea."

I leaned against the wall for a moment. "Wasn't it the death of Danielle's dad that triggered all of this psychic stuff in Danielle? What is someone saying? Don't trigger someone else's disbelief? It just doesn't make sense."

He went to the computer. "Come on. I can check out things and maybe find some answers for you." He sat in the chair and pulled up a website. A few minutes later, the video feed from Lana's house came on to the screen.

Cooper tapped a few more buttons. I could sense from how he forcefully hit the keyboard that his frustration was rising. "This doesn't make sense."

"What?" I leaned toward the screen, which had gone black.

209

"The video feed is only an hour long, and it's from yesterday. That's impossible. I set up these cameras myself." He stood. "Unless..."

"Where are you going?"

He went over to the bookshelf and moved aside a few things on the top shelf. "You've got to be kidding me..."

"What?" I sounded like a parrot, repeating the same word over and over again.

"It's gone."

I stopped and put my hand on the couch to brace myself. "What do you mean gone?"

"I mean the camera's not there anymore." He started toward the kitchen. "I'm going to check the one in the basement."

I didn't want to stay up here with that eerie warning and the missing cameras, so I scrambled behind him. He took the first step into the basement when there was a crack, followed by a crash. He tumbled downward.

I screamed.

Finally, I came to my senses and ran down the stairs. I alternated my gaze between Cooper's body at the bottom and the steps themselves. Had someone tampered with them?

Just as I reached the bottom, Cooper sat up and rubbed his head. A gash ran down the side of his face. I knelt beside him. "Are you okay?"

He nodded, still rubbing his head and scowling. "Yeah, I'm fine."

"What happened?"

"My guess is that someone knocked the first board on that step loose."

Don't suffer the same fate as my father. How exactly had Danielle's father died? Steve had said something about a tragic accident. Did I really want to know?

I started to touch Cooper's wound, but stopped myself. "We've got to get that cleaned up."

I helped him to his feet.

"I don't think you should stay in this house anymore, Tara. I think that accident was intended for you."

Getting the chills was becoming about as common for me as sneezing or coughing or eating and breathing. The "ghost" had never really tried to harm me before. Were things changing? I knew one thing: I didn't want to be here anymore. Ever.

The lead detective called me on Monday to see if I could come down to the station and talk. Candy and I had crashed at Cooper's again. Cooper had put in a call to his friend Steve, who'd confirmed that Danielle's father had died in a tragic accident where he'd fallen down the stairs.

My soul was beginning to feel comatose from all of the insinuations and creepy revelations. Enough was enough. Either a real ghost haunted the house or someone was doing a great job emulating one.

Cooper graciously said he'd come with me to the police station, and I didn't refuse. I didn't know what this meeting would hold, but I could use some support, someone to hold up my arms for me while the battle raged. Cooper was just that person.

We walked into the precinct and were immediately ushered into a plain office. The lead detective—Hensley was his name—sat behind the desk, looking as weary and exhausted as my soul felt. He instructed us to sit in the chairs across from him. I braced myself, feeling like I was boarding a roller coaster and about to take off on the ride of my life. Bad news had a way of doing that to you.

Hensley laced his hands on top of his desk calendar and stared at us, his eyelids sagging with both age and wariness. "Thanks for coming down here, Ms. Lancaster. We have good news and bad news."

I stared at the detective, wondering if I really wanted to know. Of course, I did, especially if the news meant I was closer to getting some answers. "Okay, go ahead."

He picked up a paper at the left of his desk and his gaze lingered on it a moment. "The good news is that the lab results came back on the slime we found on your bathroom mirror. The substance wasn't otherworldly, as other threats may have alluded. It was actually just slime you could find at any toy store or online."

A strange relief settled on me. "That is good news." The relief only lasted a moment. My mental roller coaster was merely creeping up the large hill and about to plunge downward and scare the snot out of me. "That bad news?"

The detective shifted, as if he didn't want to say what he had to say. "We dusted the note found underneath the butcher knife for prints. We found a useable print there that we were able to trace."

I sat ramrod straight. "And?"

He looked away. "The print belongs to Danielle Miller."

Any relief I'd felt dissipated, and I leaned back in my chair—hard. What sense did that make? How was that even possible? "I see. What does this mean for me?"

"We'll continue our investigation and make sure to report anything else that happens."

Why did I not feel any assurance at his words? They were about as likely to find the person behind this as I was likely to find a ghost.

We went out to Cooper's truck. I wanted to talk through things with him on the ride home but, before I had the chance, my cell phone rang. It was Candy. She greeted me with a high-pitched squeal. It was a Pop Rocks Candy kind of day.

"You'll never believe this."

"Believe what?" I glanced at Cooper and shrugged. Even he'd heard her squeal.

"I posted that video online last night—the one about Hugs for the Homeless."

"That was fast."

"Yeah, but that's not the point. The point is that it went viral overnight. Like *viral* viral. It's had a million hits already. I got a call from *Entertainment Hourly*, and they want to do a feature on me. A feature on *me*. This could be what I've been dreaming about, Tara!"

"That's great, Candy. Very exciting." I knew she'd been trying to catch her big break for a long time.

"And get this—they want to come out tomorrow. They want to know if they can interview me at The Mercy House and maybe get some people to be there with me. That's even better because not only would my video be featured, but so would the church. What do you think? Could you talk to Cooper about it?"

"Of course. I'll see if he can call Wanda."

"I'm so excited, Tara. And not just for myself. I mean, sure, I'm all into marketing and trying to promote by work. But I just feel like there's something bigger at work here, Tara. Do you know what I mean?"

I smiled. "Yeah, I know what you mean."

"I'll call you later."

I filled Cooper in on the conversation. "That's pretty amazing. There's more to Candy than I gave her credit for. I really think that something in the sermon yesterday changed her. "

"God can change hearts." Cooper glanced at me. "Is he working on yours?"

I slowly drew in a breath. "Yeah, he is. He's showing me some sides of myself that I don't really like."

"If your life was perfect then you wouldn't have a need for a Savior."

"Amen," I whispered. Wasn't that the truth? My heavy heart had nearly become a hardened heart.

We stopped in front of Lana's place in time to see someone outside the neighbor's house, the one that was for sale. I got out of Cooper's truck and paused on the sidewalk, watching as the woman shoved a sign into the grass reading Open House.

Why did the woman look familiar? She saw me and smiled. Before I lost courage, I charged across the lawn. Cooper caught up quickly. "What are you doing?" he asked.

"I'm not sure."

The woman—an older lady with gray hair, minimal wrinkles and a pressed suit—smiled broadly as we approached. "Good afternoon. Know anyone who's looking for a house?"

"I would love to see the inside of this place." I wondered if the owner would be interested in renting it? Maybe I'd leave my life in Miami totally behind and come here. I shook my head. No, that was a crazy thought. I would have to make some decisions soon, though. Lana was due back at the end of the week, and what would I do then?

But that wasn't the real reason I wanted to go inside. I wanted to figure out where I'd seen this woman before. A tour of the house might give me the time I needed to do just that.

She glanced back at us as we climbed the steps to the porch. "Are the two of you looking for your first home?"

I looked up at Cooper and my cheeks heated at the woman's assumption. "Oh no. We're not. No. It's not like that."

Cooper's lips curled in that amused grin again. What would it be like to look for a house with Cooper? The thought caused a rush of excitement to travel up my spine and end with fireworks in my brain.

His arm slipped around my waist. "We'd just like to see what's out there."

She opened the front door and spread her arms to showcase the living room. "Well, this is really quite a lovely place. A perfect starter home."

I blinked at what I saw. The house was nearly an exact replica of Lana's place. In newer neighborhoods, this wouldn't surprise me. But this neighborhood had houses in all shapes and sizes, each as unique as a fingerprint. I supposed I should have noticed the similarities in the houses from the outside, but I hadn't. I'd had other things to think about since I'd been here. Namely, my own house and the nightmares that had transpired there.

I was speechless as I saw the rest of the house. Even the basement was a perfect match for Lana's.

We paused in the living room. "How long has this place been vacant?" I asked.

She clasped her hands in front of her, appearing prim and proper. "About a year. The previous owners left rather quickly. They were anxious for a move."

"Why was that?" I shifted my weight, curiosity pressing in on me.

"I'm not sure. I assumed it was because of their growing family. The place is bank-owned right now, however."

I stared at the woman another moment. Did she just have one of those faces? I didn't think so. We thanked her for showing us the place and then hurried back to Lana's. Cooper kept a hand on my back as if he feared I might pass out as we trotted across the grass.

Back at Lana's, I hesitated by the front door, fearing what might wait for me on the other side. Cooper took the key from me and unlocked the door.

"I'll check things out first."

I nodded, grateful. "Thank you."

He slipped inside, and I waited just beyond the front door until he appeared again a moment later. "All clear."

I crossed my arms over my chest and leaned against the front door. He'd have to get past me first to get to work. I knew he had to get back to work, and I didn't plan on keeping him long, but I needed to talk through a few things. "Okay, so how did Danielle's fingerprint get on that paper?"

Cooper leaned on the back of the couch, bracing his hands on either side of him. "Maybe someone had an old sheet of paper that she'd touched."

"Do fingerprints last that long?"

He shrugged. "I don't know. They could."

"Someone used that slime to make it look like a ghost." This ghost was anything but. I didn't have all the answers, but someone was desperate to scare me away from this house. Why? How could that benefit someone?

He leaned closer. "Listen, I'd love to stick around all day and hang out, but I've got to get some work done. You're welcome to hang out at my place."

I shook my head. "No, I'll be okay. Will you call Wanda for Candy?"

"Sure." He paused. "Maybe we could have dinner together tonight?"

Warmth spread through my blood like honey over toast. "That would be nice."

He grinned. "Okay. Tonight then."

I watched him walk away and realized I was grinning also. Could God actually be giving me a second chance? Not only at love, but at happiness? The thought had been unfathomable just a month ago. But somehow being here in St. Paul had changed something inside me.

31

I plopped down on the couch when my cell phone rang—again. I fully expected to see Candy's number on the screen. My heart skipped a beat when I saw...my dad's. Any sticky sweet warmth that I'd felt only moments earlier disappeared.

I licked my lips before answering. "Hi, Dad."

"Hey, honey. How's it going for you out there?"

I nodded, as if he could see me. "It's going." No need to mention ghosts, threats, or anything else that had happened.

"Listen, there are a couple of things I need to tell you. Do you want to hear the good or the bad first?"

Panic sent off flashes in my brain. What could have possibly happened? Were the charges against me being reinstated? Did the police find some evidence that wasn't there? Did the church suffer more harm, even without me there?

"The bad." My voice sounded strained, even to my own ears. The way I was clutching the arm of the couch made me feel like I was in a nose-diving airplane. Emotionally it felt like I was.

"Peter got remarried this weekend."

216

I blinked. He'd been dating? Engaged? How had I missed that? Did I really care? "Wow," I mumbled. "I had no idea."

"He married Gretchen Eubanks."

I blinked again, slowly processing his words. Gretchen Eubanks was the principal at the school where I'd taught. She'd resigned a few months into the so-called scandal, and she'd been one of the main people who'd pointed a finger at me throughout the whole process. And now she'd married Peter? Really? How appropriate that two of the people who'd ended up hurting me the most were now married.

"You still there?"

"I'm here. I...I don't know what to say."

"You know I'm a big fan of marriage. I always think a husband and wife should work things out if possible. But I'm glad he's out of your life, Tara. We were all shocked by how quickly he turned on you and walked away. If I'd thought you two could still reconcile, I would never say this. But since he's out of your life, I just want to let you know that there's someone better for you out there."

My throat ached with emotion. "Thanks, Dad. I know your ministry took a big hit with all of this. I'm sorry." I don't think I'd said that to him yet. I'd thought it, but really I'd been so wrapped up in my problems that I didn't give a second thought to anyone else's.

"The split wasn't your fault, Tara. What happened just brought out some ugly things in the congregation, things that had been simmering for a while. We're doing okay now. Our numbers are growing. People's hearts are changing. We're going to be okay."

"I just feel like it's my fault. I feel like I brought so much disgrace to the family and caused so many problems. I didn't do it, Dad. I didn't do anything." I'd always held on to the fear that some part of him didn't believe me, just like Peter hadn't believed me. On the outside he acted supportive, but he had to act supportive. He was my father. It would be natural for anyone in his position to feel resentful, though.

"I know you didn't, Tara. There will always be people who like you or don't like you, who agree with you or don't agree with you. You just have to be right with yourself. I think that's been the biggest thing holding you back." His deep, booming voice reached all the way to my heart.

Tears burned my eyes. "You're probably right."

"That brings me to my good news. The attorney called this morning."

I straightened. "Okay."

"Before Zack Morris lived in Miami, he lived in Austin, Texas. His mother was married to someone different, so he went by Zack Sinclair back then. Mitch got a call from someone out there who used to work at the school he attended. Zack made the same accusations against a teacher there."

I could hardly breathe. Had I heard my dad correctly? My shock quickly turned into a rush of adrenaline. "What does this mean?"

"It looks like it means that Zack and his mom were trying to scam the system. That teacher didn't fare as well as you and ended up in jail for a year. They also filed a civil suit against her and ended up making some money on the whole thing. If your case hadn't been dropped, they would have probably done the same thing to you."

"You mean people might actually have proof that I'm innocent?" Tears streamed down my cheeks. Would I finally have my justice? I'd assumed I'd never have it here on this earth, but maybe I was wrong.

"You can't tell anyone yet, Tara. They're still investigating, but we're hoping to have something solid for you soon. I just wanted to let you know."

"Thanks, Dad. I'm glad you called."

And I was. My heart felt lighter than it had in years.

Cooper picked me up at six. He was dressed in khakis and a button-up shirt. He looked gorgeous, as always. I'd borrowed some more of Lana's clothes—which was becoming a regular routine—and I wore a black skirt, high heels, and a red top with a modest V at the front. Cooper looked me up and down approvingly, and that was all the confirmation I needed. I felt nearly giddy as we set out for the evening.

I wanted to tell him everything. I really did. But maybe I could wait a few days until there was more concrete proof of my accuser's lies. Then when I told him, any doubts he might have would be put to rest. I'd be able to say, "Look! There's proof that I'm innocent!" I could feel whole again.

That's what I'd do, I decided. I wasn't sure what tonight might hold. Would our relationship move forward a step? Would it be confirmed that we were destined to be only friends? I didn't know. But, either way, there was an end in sight as far as telling Cooper everything. Some of the burden I'd been carrying around for so long eased off my shoulders, and the lightness I felt made me want to jump and leap and sing at the top of my lungs.

"You seem awfully smiley tonight." Cooper stared at me from across the table of a little hole-in-the-wall restaurant that Cooper claimed had the best food in the city. The place was dainty and clean with low lights, walls decorated with movie and sports paraphernalia, and a bar along one wall, complete with several TVs. He'd apologized for not taking me somewhere fancier, but I didn't care.

As strange as the thought might be, I was falling in love with him. I knew it by the way my heart fluttered when he was nearby, how my thoughts constantly drifted to him, how I wanted nothing more than to feel his touch.

Looking back, I hadn't really felt those things with Peter. I thought I had. But mostly we'd just made sense together. At least, I'd thought we had.

As I looked at him from across the table, I knew there was more to love than tingling skin and warm hearts. But Cooper was the kind of man who held on. That had been proven when his wife cheated on him. It was evident in the way he cared for Austin and in his steadfast grin and unwavering gaze.

But did he feel the same way?

Was I ready to find out?

Suddenly, my gaze focused on his hand. His wedding ring. It was gone. Pure giddiness surged through me.

He'd asked me about my sunnier demeanor tonight, I remembered. "My dad called, and we had a really good conversation. It helped to put some things in perspective."

"Sometimes you have to take a step back in order to see what you've got in front of you." Cooper pointed to the TV screen hanging on the wall. "Check that out."

I blinked at the familiar face on the screen. Miss Mystic.

A local news channel was covering the story about Danielle Miller's unsolved murder and highlighted Miss Mystic's role in the police's investigation.

"I told them that weapon still in house, but they no listen," Miss Mystic said.

"What else would you like them to listen to?" The reporter held the microphone up to Miss Mystic.

"I have strong feeling who killer is. I not say on TV, but I tell the police if they let me help."

The waitress appeared to take our order, and I didn't hear the rest of the interview. I quenched the urge to shake my head in disbelief at the psychic and instead ordered some lemon and garlic chicken with pasta.

Cooper did shake his head. "Ghost hunters, psychics, hauntings. This is like something straight out of a movie."

"Tell me about it."

I seemed to be surrounded by people like that lately. Was God trying to teach me some cosmic lesson about fame? I'd had my fair share of attention, but most of it had been negative.

Cooper took a sip of his soda and leaned back. "So Lana comes back soon. What are you going to do when she gets back? Stick around for a while or go back to Miami?" I thought I heard a catch to his voice, but maybe I was hearing what I wanted to hear instead of the truth.

"I'm not sure yet. So many things seem up in the air. I need to buckle down and make some choices, I suppose."

"You could always buy the house on the other side of Lana and look for a teaching position in this area."

I swiped a hair behind my ear and nodded. "I've thought about that. I really have." Well, maybe not the teaching part, but the staying in St. Paul part. "I know I want to spend some time with Lana when she gets back, so I'll be sticking around for a while."

He smiled. "Good. I'm glad to hear that."

I rested my chin on my hand. "Are you?" I kept the words light, even though I wanted to scream, *What does that mean, Ben Cooper?*

"I am. I've really enjoyed getting to know you, Tara." His gaze latched on to mine.

"Thanks, Cooper. Same here." *You've stirred up something in my heart—and not just romance. You've reminded me what it really means to serve Jesus, to love him.* I wasn't brave enough to say the words. "What's funny is that we may not have gotten to know each other if it wasn't for that stupid ghost at Lana's place."

"God has a funny way of working things out sometimes."

"You can say that again."

Our food came, Cooper prayed, and we dug in.

I really wanted to finish listening to what he was saying, but my attention was drawn across the room. The creepy man from across the street and his wife sat at a corner table there. She smiled across the table at her husband and, for a moment, I wondered if I was wrong and they were normal. Maybe I'd just caught them on a bad day.

"What is it?"

I nodded across the restaurant. "It's the neighbors."

Just then I saw the woman get up and head to the restroom. Quickly, I put my napkin into my lap and stood. "One moment, please."

I knew by Cooper's expression that he knew exactly what I was doing. He nodded. I was so glad he didn't try to stop me or tell me what to do. He was the kind of man I needed in my life, and I was thankful for him now.

I wove between tables until I reached the bathroom. Thankfully, the space was designed for three people, so I was able to slip inside and make my way to the mirror.

That's where the woman stood washing her hands and blotting her face dry. What was going on with her? Abuse at the hands of a psychopathic husband?

I lifted a quick prayer for wisdom and smiled at her. "You live on Elm Street, don't you?"

The woman glanced at me, soaking me in a moment before nodding. Her eyes looked weary and hollow. "You live across the street."

I finished washing my hands and pulled a paper towel out to dry them. "I'm Tara."

"I'm Melinda. I'm sorry. I'm all out of sorts today." She sniffed, grabbed a paper towel, and blew her nose. "I've been going through chemo. Stage-two breast cancer."

My heart pounded with sorrow for the woman. "I'm so sorry."

She nodded listlessly. "I'm going to beat it. I have to, for my husband's sake. If something happened to me, he would be totally lost."

Had I read the man wrong? Was his creepiness simply grief? "Cancer can take a toll on families, that's for sure." I waited to see if she wanted to talk anymore, giving her space. My heart honestly went out to her.

"All he does all day is watch birds out our window."

My spine stiffened. "Watch birds?"

She nodded. "It's his hobby. He can tell you what any kind of bird in our neighborhood might be. He wanted to be a zoologist, but his parents convinced him to go into accounting instead. Life is too short to do things you don't enjoy, you know? I wish he had pursued his passion. At least he can do it as a hobby now."

All the times I'd seen the man staring out his window...he'd been watching birds? I almost wanted to laugh but restrained myself. "If there's anything I can do for you, I'd be more than happy to help. On the days you have chemo, let me know. I'll bring over some food."

Her eyes widened. "You would do that?"

"Of course I would. Neighbors should help each other."

She grabbed my hand. "Thank you, Tara. I'm really glad we ran into each other. I don't have many friends in the area. Richard is such a homebody, and I just moved here a few months ago after we got married. I haven't made any friends yet, and then I got the cancer diagnosis. I've felt so alone at times."

I grabbed some paper from my purse and jotted down my cell phone number. "Call me if you ever need anything. I'll be in town for a while longer."

She took the paper and hugged me. "Thank you," she whispered.

I pushed the bathroom door open, squeezing Melinda's hand once more before walking back to Cooper. His perceptive eyes lit as I approached the table. "Everything okay?"

I filled him in on our conversation, my heart panging with grief. A new woman in a new town facing a life-changing diagnosis. I'd never been diagnosed with cancer, but somehow I still felt like I could relate to her.

"Sounds like a God-ordained meeting."

I smiled. "Yeah, it does, doesn't it?"

Our gaze met across the table. There was so much I liked about this man. He didn't necessarily fit the mold of someone I could see myself with. He'd lived a wild life as an Army Ranger. He had tattoos. He had a son. But I thought he was perfect. The thought of leaving Minnesota and leaving Cooper behind made my heart twist with sorrow. He'd quickly become part of my life.

As I stared at him from across the table, I wondered why none of those words would leave my lips. I was fairly certain he felt the same way, and that he couldn't deny the chemistry that crackled between us.

Maybe I couldn't say it until the Big White Elephant in the room was revealed.

Just a few more days, I thought. *Just a few more days.*

"What are you thinking about?"

I stared at him another moment, contemplating my words, not certain what might come out of my mouth. Finally, I said, "I'm thinking that I'm really glad I met you, Ben Cooper."

A smile slowly spread across his face. "I'm glad I met you, too, Tara."

It was nighttime again, and I was in a quandary. The thought of staying in Lana's house terrified me. The thought of staying at Cooper's seemed too tempting or too inappropriate, especially since Candy said she was staying with a friend tonight.

So, I decided to do the next reasonable thing and stay at a hotel. Cooper agreed to take care of Gaga for me, since most hotels wouldn't let the dog come with me. Cooper helped me pack my stuff and followed me across town to a decent establishment that was clean and affordable.

After I checked in, he walked me up to my room and stopped outside of my door to say good-bye. I had to be honest. Cooper and I had both known intimacy, so major boundaries were in order even though every part of me screamed otherwise.

I leaned against the door and swallowed a dose of strength. "It was really fun tonight."

He stepped closer. I could see it in his eyes—desire. He raked his hands through my hair, his fingers lingered in the tresses. His eyes were faceted on my lips.

I decided to stop thinking so much for once in my life. I reached up and wrapped my arms around his neck. In one motion, our lips met. All of my worries seemed to melt in that moment, and all the world seemed right.

We pulled away, but my hands didn't want to leave his neck. Something invisible seemed to draw me toward him. I rested my head on his chest, and we both breathed slowly, deeply.

It would be so easy to invite him inside. Just for a moment.

But a lot could go wrong in one moment.

"I should go," he mumbled into my hair.

It took all of my strength to nod and step back. "You're right. You should."

Our gaze connected again until I finally held up my room key and nodded toward the door. "I'll talk to you in the morning?"

He grinned, his arms still at my waist. "You know it."

I quickly turned, unlocked my door, and rushed inside. My heart pounded uncontrollably as I heard him walk away.

Hope was finally in sight.

32

"This is your big day, Candy. I'm really happy for you."

She grinned. "Me, too. I've wanted this for so long. Thanks for being here with me."

I looked around and saw several people from Candy's party crowd—including Mark. I'd stay far away from him. He didn't seem to mind, as he hit on a pretty little redhead. There were also some people there from The Mercy House. A strange mix of people if I'd ever seen one, but I liked it. I liked rethinking my idea of church. I had to rethink my idea of church. I loved my dad, and he probably wouldn't be thrilled about where this road had led. But at least it hadn't led me away from God.

I'd spent the morning at the hotel. I'd actually relaxed for the first time in a long time. I'd put a do-not-disturb sign up. I'd taken a long shower, and I'd watched some TV. Cooper had called to check in.

My thoughts had drifted to the mystery at Lana's house. All the pieces seemed to be coming together. Now I just had to make them fit. I was also hoping to hear something else today from either my dad or my attorney concerning my accuser's past. Maybe the truth would finally come out. When it did, I'd be able to tell Cooper, and our relationship would be that much stronger.

Speaking of Cooper, he stood beside me at the back of the room. Candy's favorite little café had decided to cater, and they had two tables set up on either side of the room. Wanda and her husband looked pleased to host the event here at The Mercy House and bring attention to the difference one person could make in a community.

I tried not to notice the way electricity crackled between Cooper and me as our arms brushed each other. But when his arm slipped around my shoulders and he kissed the top of my head, I thought I might burst with joy.

Commotion at the doors turned my attention that way. A news crew flooded the room, a glossy blonde leading the pack. She beelined toward Candy. Everyone seemed to quiet around them as they waited with anticipation for what would happen next.

"Pretty exciting, huh?" Cooper said.

I nodded. "Yeah, really exciting. I'm happy for Candy."

"You played a part in this, you know."

"Not really. In fact, it's usually when I step out of the way that God steps in and does his thing. I can't take any credit." At one time, I would have wanted to.

Maybe this was my new start. Maybe I was meant to come here and start over. Here in St. Paul, no one had to know what had transpired in Miami. It could be my secret, a part of my past that never had to be revealed.

Except that I had to tell Cooper. Why? Because I cared about him. And because I was beginning to trust him. I just had to figure out how to break the news. What I had to tell him was enough to shake even the most levelheaded person. I'd already seen that happen. I'd experienced the gossip and slander and backstabbing at my expense. I knew what it was like to be rejected, to be judged before even having a chance to explain myself. I knew what it was like to have friends turn on you, to have coworkers reject you, to have the public scrutinize your every move.

I'd survived. Now it was time to rebuild my life.

Everyone quieted when it came time for the news crew to film. They sat Candy in the middle of the room with her friends gathered all around her. They adjusted lights and microphones. The reporter chatted with Candy. I wasn't sure what she was saying, probably prepping her for what was to come. Finally, it came time to film. I leaned against the wall, watching with anticipation.

"A St. Paul woman has gained national attention and has become a part of the prestigious online celebrity club, the result of social media. Candy Cornelius, also known as iCandy, has been posting videos online for four years. It wasn't until she started a campaign with a local church that her channel exploded."

Today, Candy was like a 100 Grand Bar. Ten of them. She was well on her way to getting the fame and fortune she'd been seeking and working for.

They showed a clip of Candy giving "Hugs for the Homeless." She then talked about doing "Haircuts for the Homeless" and "H2O for the Homeless."

Cooper leaned in close. "I've got to go help Wanda over there."

I glanced up in time to see Wanda trying to manage two rowdy guys who'd come in through the back entrance and were bound and determined to make a scene. "Got it."

I glanced back over at the interview taking place. Candy basked in the limelight. This was her big day, the moment she'd been dreaming about for so long. I was really happy for her.

The reporter continued to hold the microphone in front of Candy. "Candy, is your friendship with accused child molester Tara Lancaster a part of your strategy?"

My heart dropped, and I stopped breathing. Had I just heard that correctly? No, no, no...

Candy's gaze fluttered up, surprise evident in her wide eyes.

Everyone in the room turned to watch me. Tears rushed to my eyes. My cheeks burned. My stomach roiled. I wanted nothing more than to sink back into the wall behind me and disappear.

"Excuse me?" Candy asked. Confusion narrowed her eyes, and her hands went to her hips.

The reporter stepped closer. "Tara Lancaster, also known as The Saint, was seen in one of your online videos. Paparazzi have been trying to locate her for weeks, and then she showed up on your video. A viewer tipped us off."

I grasped my throat, which felt like it was closing. Panic threatened to rip me apart. I couldn't bear to look up, to see anyone. Especially Cooper. I was going to tell him. I was going to. But this wasn't the way I wanted him to find out. What he must be thinking now. What everyone had to be thinking.

I could feel their gazes on me, and suddenly I didn't hear anything else. All I could hear was the voice of my accuser.

What was I supposed to do? Tell everyone that I was innocent? Tell them that new evidence had come to light to prove it?

They wouldn't believe me. Doubt had been planted. I'd be crucified before I even had a chance to defend myself.

I pushed myself from the wall. Tears blurred my vision as I ran toward the door. Before anyone could stop me—not that they would—I ran outside. I kept running. I wouldn't look back. I couldn't. I didn't want to talk to anyone.

Epic fail, I thought. *Epic fail.*

I curled up in a ball on my bed at the hotel and let the tears soak my pillow. I couldn't imagine a way that things could have gone any worse. Cooper had found out about my past in front of a crowd of his friends and on national TV. I'd stolen Candy's spotlight. The paparazzi now knew that I was in St. Paul. In one day, my relationship with Cooper was ruined, my friendship with Candy had ended, and my hope for a new start was squashed.

The tears came harder, saturating my skin, my shirt, my soul.

Maybe St. Paul wasn't for me after all. Maybe I would find a new town, a place where no one knew me. And I wouldn't get close to anyone. I didn't want to see their disappointment when they found out who I was. I didn't want to face those judgmental glances again.

But could I ever truly get away from all of that?

Someone banged at the door. Who was it? A reporter? An angry mob? I knew better. Only one person knew I was here—Cooper.

I'd turned off my cell phone, just in case he might try and call me.

Maybe I'd never turn it on again. After all, as soon as this hit the national news, my family would be calling. Peter and his family would probably be gloating, relishing the fact that my life had continued to go downhill. And my accuser would win—again.

He pounded again. I wiped my cheeks with my hands and said nothing.

"Tara, it's me. Can I come in?" Cooper's voice normally brought me comfort. Right now, fear coursed through me. Not fear of violence, but fear of seeing the accusation and disappointment in his eyes. I couldn't handle it. I couldn't handle having someone else I cared about reject me because of something I didn't do. Peter had been hard enough. But I couldn't bear seeing the doubt in Cooper's eyes also.

"Tara, I know you're in there. You're not answering your phone. Can we talk? Please?"

I sniffled but tried to remain still and quiet so he wouldn't know I was right on the other side of the door.

"I'm leaving to go out of town in the morning. I don't want to leave without talking."

That's right. He was leaving to pick up Austin. Maybe it was better that way. Maybe I'd just pack up all of my stuff and go to a different hotel for a while. He'd return from his trip, and I'd be gone. I'd get a new cell phone. I'd start a new life and put my time here behind me.

"I'll be awake if you want to call me tonight, Tara," Cooper finally said.

I heard him walk away, and my heart mixed with crushing sadness and relief. We wouldn't have to talk after all. I should be happy. But maybe there'd been a part of me that wanted Cooper to believe me with abandon. I had to kill that hope, though.

I walked to the window. I saw Cooper's truck pulling out of the parking lot.

Then I saw a lime-green Jeep pull away after him.

Mark Champion. What was he doing here? I remembered the crystals hanging from his rearview mirror and the New Age tattoo on his wrist.

Could he be behind all of this?

I shook my head. I didn't know, and it didn't matter. All that mattered right now was that I formulate a plan to get out of town with no car, no money, and no hope.

Tears flowed from me like someone had turned on a faucet and broken it. I had no idea my body was capable of losing so much fluid, or that my tear ducts could ache, or that I could feel so very empty inside.

At one a.m. my time, I called Lana, which worked out to be morning Tuscany time. She answered, her voice husky. I'd woken her up anyway. Go figure.

I told her about what had happened—about everything. I knew that I could always turn to my sister. She'd listened with surprising silence as I poured out how I'd always known that Dad had loved her more and how I hated myself. I'd never voiced those thoughts to her before, and, when I finished, I feared how she'd react to my honesty.

"Oh, Tara. I'm so sorry. Life just sucks sometimes." Her voice sounded sincere and compassionate. If she were here in person, I would have hugged her for actually thinking about someone other than herself for once.

"Sometimes I just want to give up. In the very least, I want plastic surgery for my soul." Wouldn't that be nice? Just get some anesthesia, go under the knife, and wake up changed on the inside?

"Look, I'm not an expert with the God-thing. You know that. But isn't that what repentance and redemption is? Plastic surgery for the soul as you said?"

Her words had a certain beauty to them, but I couldn't comprehend them now. "I just don't know sometimes."

"Tara, you're a beautiful person."

"I don't feel beautiful. I feel tarnished."

"Don't change. Don't really change, at least. I've always wished I was more like you."

"You have to be kidding." My voice held disbelief.

"I'm not, though. I mean, sure, you can be neurotic sometimes, but you're compassionate. You love people. You love working in the church. Your soul is already beautiful."

"All of that did me no good. I've lost everything from my past, from my present, from my future."

"There's always hope, Tara. That's what you would have told me." She paused. "You're one of the few people I know who truly wants to be good and holy with your whole heart. Don't change that, Tara. One day, I want to get to the place where you are."

My sister's words stunned me. She'd always seemed so content with her rebellion. Did she mean what she said?

We talked for a few minutes before I hung up. I continued thinking about what she said as I drifted into a fitful sleep.

I woke up the next morning with a new resolve. My tears had temporarily dried up.

My dad's words and Lana's words had echoed in my head all night. *You just have to be right with yourself. Isn't that what repentance and redemption are? Plastic surgery for the soul?* I'd been hiding and ashamed, all for something I didn't do. Mostly, I just wanted to be right with Jesus.

Though I regretted the way everyone had found out about my past yesterday, there was a certain relief in having my secret revealed. Now I would face my fears in the most public of ways.

I showered, dressed, and got ready. Though I felt depleted, a new calm had come over me. I gathered my wits and walked into The Mercy House. I knew they were having their weekly Bible study here this morning. I knew that Candy said she would be here, as well as Wanda and Larry. It was time to set the record straight.

My hands were sweaty as I stepped into the church. Larry's voice rang out from speakers on both sides of the stage. I spotted the group of people gathered in chairs and listening. Larry had his Bible open and was reading some Scripture when he saw me and stopped in mid-sentence. Heads swiveled toward me.

Would Larry throw me out? I was going to find out. My heart pounded in my ears.

He lowered his Bible. "Tara. What a surprise." His voice didn't necessarily hold condemnation or welcome.

Even though my legs wobbled, I wasn't going to turn around now. I walked onto the stage, the moment feeling surreal. "I was wondering if I could say something?"

"The floor's yours." Larry somberly sat down in a chair on the front row.

I looked at the group before me, trying not to lose my courage. They don't have any stones to throw, I reminded myself. Tonya was there with those big eyes that held so much expectation for me at one time. Candy stared at me, and I had no idea what she was thinking. That I'd ruined her big night? I recognized several other faces from my brief time here at the church. Maybe this wasn't the church where I should be saying this, but they were what I had right now.

I licked my lips. "Some of you know me, and some of you don't. My name is Tara Lancaster. For years, I perfected the act of looking and talking like the ideal Christian. I perfected it to such an extent that I even wrote my own rules. I published the rules and thousands of girls began following them. In the process, I became pious. I thought God loved me more than he loved other people because I was holy." I wiped my tears and drew in a shaky breath before continuing.

"I married the perfect man and got the perfect job, and I lived in my own little perfect world. But one day all of that crashed around me when a student at the school where I taught made false allegations against me. He told everyone that we'd had an inappropriate relationship." I stared at everyone's face. Some people's eyes widened in surprise. Some looked away in disgust. Others stared on curiously. "My world crashed around me. My husband left me. My school fired me. My dad's church was devastated."

I wiped at the fresh set of tears streaming down my cheeks. Tonya tiptoed on stage and handed me a box of tissues. "The fact is, I think God brought me through all of that so I could know him more. To really know him more. He wanted to change my heart. He wanted me to truly live out the gospel, not just my little American version of the gospel. In the process, I almost walked away from my faith, but God brought some very special people into my life."

I glanced at Candy, who remained expressionless. I couldn't stop now. "He brought me people who didn't care what other people thought of them. He brought me people who'd been through devastating circumstances but remained strong. He brought me people who'd truly been changed by God's love and who were living it out every day."

I tried to look at the crowd again but tears blurred my vision. My voice cracked as I continued. "I'm sorry if I've disappointed anyone. I couldn't bring myself to admit to anyone here what had happened.

In fact, when I came here, I was hoping that no one would have to know. But I'm here to tell you that I'm a deeply flawed individual. I'm anything but perfect. I'm a sinner saved by grace." I looked down at the ground. "I just wanted to share my story and to apologize for any embarrassment that I may have caused. Thank you for listening."

I didn't wait to hear any reaction. I fled the stage and raced back to my car. I was going to make things right before I left. Then I was going to figure out the rest of my life.

33

I went back to Lana's to wrap up a few things. I packed my bag and wrote a note to Cooper, explaining everything and asking him to take care of Gaga until Lana returned. Maybe leaving would be considered cowardly, but I thought leaving was best for everyone.

I also had a sweatshirt that he'd left here on the night of the ghost hunt. I ran my hand over it then brought it to my face and inhaled his scent. My heart twisted with grief at what could have been.

How would I make sure he got this note? Leave it on his door? A steady wind swept through St. Paul today and would certainly blow it away.

Winnie, I realized. I could leave it with Winnie. She didn't seem like the type who watched social media. Maybe she wouldn't have heard about what happened. Maybe.

I knocked at her door, fidgeting as I stood there waiting. My gaze wandered around me. Did anyone else around here know? Were they desperate for me to leave?

Winnie pulled the door open a moment later. The scent of cinnamon drifted out, and flour coated her checkered apron. The same pleasant grin that was always present there still today as she wiped her hands on a dishtowel.

I forced a smile, realizing I wanted to burst into tears. I couldn't do that, though. Instead, I extended my hand and offered her the sweatshirt and note. "Winnie, I've got to take off. I know that Cooper's picking up Austin, but I wanted to return his sweatshirt and ask him to take care of the dog for me. Could you give it to him for me?"

She frowned and pushed her tiny glasses higher. "He's sure going to be disappointed if you don't tell him good-bye."

I shook my head, remembering Cooper's kiss and our connection. Even if he believed my innocence, he'd never forgive me for keeping the secret from him. "I'm not so sure about that, Winnie."

"He's come to care deeply about you, you know. I can see it in his eyes." Her voice sounded so sincere and wise that I almost believed her.

"It's better if I stay away. I don't want to mess up anyone else's life." My chin trembled as I said the words, but I kept it raised.

"He's a good judge of character, you know. He knows you didn't do anything."

So she had heard? My cheeks heated, but I reminded myself that I had nothing to be embarrassed about. "You know?"

"It's been all over Facebook, darling." A motherly look of compassion stained her gaze as she tilted her head at me.

I pushed a hair behind my ear. "I didn't do it."

"I know." Her voice didn't waver, nor did she flinch as she said the words.

My breath caught. "How do you know?"

"Gut feeling. I don't know you that well, Tara, but I think it's terrible what happened to you." Her voice—although high-pitched—was steady and honest.

"Thank you, Winnie." My voice sounded strained, even to my own ears.

"You can let this experience break you, or you can let it make you stronger."

I nodded, my throat burning. I started to walk away when she called me back.

"Tara, one more thing I wanted to mention to you."

I turned around to look at her plump figure in the doorway. "What's that?"

She shifted, slinging the dishtowel over her opposite shoulder. "I was talking to an old friend who used to live in the neighborhood. We were reminiscing about the old days. She reminded me of an old rumor that used to circulate in the neighborhood."

"Okay..." I stepped closer so I could hear her better.

Her gaze latched on to mine. "It has to do with your house."

My spine straightened, and I was suddenly interested. "I'm all ears."

"Apparently, two sisters built houses side by side after they got married. This was back in the day when nuclear war was a big fear. Rumor used to be that there was a tunnel that used to connect their basements. They boarded the tunnel up because of city codes and such. But that tunnel might still be there." Wrinkles formed around her mouth as her lips came together.

Things began clicking in my mind. A tunnel? Connected to the house next door? "Thanks, Winnie. That does help."

On second thought, I did need to tie up some loose ends before I left. I was going to put an end to this mystery after all.

Before I even got back to my house, I turned my phone on. I ignored the eleven voicemail messages and uncountable missed calls as I dialed Candy's number. Maybe there was a way to make things right, to undo any damage my secret had caused, and to put this ghost in the grave for good.

"Candy, do you want something to film?" I unlocked the door and stepped inside this house that seemed to remind me of everything that was wrong in the world. For the first time in a long time, I didn't even shudder, not even when I saw the remains of the blood-like threat left on the wall.

"Bermuda?" Surprise tinged her voice.

I closed the door and leaned against it, not ready to go on any solo adventures. Not yet. At least, not until I told someone where my body could be found if something went terribly wrong. "Yeah, it's me, the island. But I don't want to be one of those anymore." I didn't have time to go into those details right now, though. "Candy, I've got something for your video blog. Are you interested?"

She paused. "I am."

I braced myself before asking the next question. "Are you willing to hang around me and possibly tarnish your reputation?"

"What's there to tarnish? And, no offense Tara, but any video with you in it is bound to get me more attention. For the record, I think you're cool. I don't think you would do any of those things."

"Thanks, Candy." My muscles nearly sagged with relief.

"Mark is the one who told the media, you know. I think that's the main reason they wanted to film me yesterday. They wanted the scoop on you. Mark's a jerk. He's just mad because you rejected him, and he never gets rejected."

"I'm still sorry."

"Don't be. Maybe God is trying to teach me a few things, also. Like don't always seek so much attention."

"Candy, I need your help. I need you to come over here with your video camera. We're going to figure out this ghost one way or another."

I had a feeling I knew exactly who this ghost was. Now I just had to prove it.

The doorbell rang at seven o'clock. I pulled open the door, and a balmy summer breeze wafted inside, along with the sound of crickets and cars passing by on the highway. It seemed so normal, though nothing was normal.

Candy and Mickey stood on the stoop. My eyes met Candy's, and I waited to see condemnation. I saw nothing but her normal mischievous sparkle.

She popped her gum and nodded toward Mickey. "He's going to videotape for us."

I ushered them inside, wishing Cooper was with them. But it was better that he wasn't. I'd come clean and now it was time for a clean break.

Clean, I thought. Clean hands, clean heart.

I turned to Mickey, and my voice sounded halfway apologetic when I told him, "I don't think we're going to find any ghosts."

He shrugged, looking like a beanpole in his extra-tight skinny jeans and form-fitting T-shirt. "That's okay. Anything horrific will do."

I motioned to them. "Follow me."

No way was I going to do this alone. I led them through the living room, into the kitchen, and down the basement stairs.

"Can you make this a live feed to your video blog, Candy?" I asked over my shoulder.

"Why would I want to?"

"Just in case anything happens. I want evidence."

Her eyes widened. "You're kind of freaking me out."

"Sorry."

"No, I like it. That said, no, I can't make this live. I don't have that kind of technology yet."

I paused once we cleared the stairs and turned toward them. "Where did you say you saw that burst of energy down here when you used your thermal heat monitor?"

Mickey went to the wall, waved his hands in the air for a moment, before finally pausing between the treadmill and the washing machine. "Right here."

I approached the area and knelt down and ran my finger over the floor. Could the low-pile carpet feel so clean because something had scraped across it recently? I stood and ran my hands over the walls, looking for something, anything.

"What are you doing?" Candy stared at me like I'd lost my mind. Maybe I had.

I turned toward her. "Rumor has it that there's a tunnel that runs between this house and the one next door. I think I know how our ghost is getting in without being detected."

Mickey snorted. "That's crazy. Who builds a tunnel between two houses?"

That was crazy but ghosts weren't?

"A father who's worried about his two daughters and the threat of nuclear war." I continued feeling along the wall. "I just can't figure out how it would open." Wood paneling ran up and down the walls. Did one of them come off?

"May I try something?" Mickey asked.

"Sure." I stepped back. What if I asked them over for nothing? No, I couldn't think like that.

He knocked on the walls until he found a space with a hollow echo behind it. Then, using his fingernails, he reached into the crevice and brought his arms toward him. Slowly, the wall moved. I held my breath, waiting to see if someone—or something—would jump out on the other side. He kept pulling until a dark space came into view.

Chills raced over me. "Wow."

Candy nodded. "Yeah, wow. That's just creepy."

We all looked at one another for a minute.

"Ladies first." Mickey extended his hand and held up the camera with the other. "Besides, I need to be at the back of the group to film this."

"Okay, okay. This is my mess. I'll go first." I grabbed a flashlight and stepped into the tunnel. The walls were lined with wood—not exactly protective in the event of nuclear war, but interesting nonetheless. Candy and Mickey followed behind me. The dank, earthy smell of the enclosed space filled my nostrils.

"This is straight out of a movie crazy. How could Lana not know about this?" Candy's gaze looked almost childlike. She crept along behind me.

"I guess after the sisters moved, they didn't feel the need to tell anyone."

Candy glanced back at Mickey. "Are you getting all of this?"

He held his thumb in the air.

"Well, someone knew about this. They were using this tunnel to get in and out." I had a feeling Candy was saying that for the camera more than for us. Her voice had even changed into her "entertainment" octave, a few steps below her normal speaking range.

I shined the light in the distance. "Look, there's the other house.

Suddenly, all the light from my basement disappeared.

Someone had just locked us in.

34

Darkness sank over the space, surrounding us, suffocating us. My breathing became labored and heavy as my pulse throbbed in my ears.

I swung my flashlight toward the door. The light illuminated a figure there. I gasped as a pale woman came into view—the same woman I'd seen from Winnie's house. She wore a long, white nightgown. Her skin was white, her hair powdery, her eyes hollow and her face expressionless.

"Danielle..." Candy whispered. She clutched my arm.

"Can you say 'big break'?" Mickey's camera was aimed right at the woman.

I gathered my wits and shook my head. "That's not Danielle. It's our friendly neighborhood psychic, Susan West or, as she's more commonly known, Miss Mystic."

At once, the woman's expression changed from hollow to devious. I halfway expected her to mumble, *And I would have gotten away with it if it hadn't been for you meddling kids.* Instead, she reached into the folds of her flowing white nightgown and emerged with a gun.

My gun.

I knew I shouldn't have had a gun, for a reason just like this—I was unlucky.

I raised my hands, hoping to calm her down. "There's no reason to pull that out. We're all stuck down here with nowhere to go."

Reason. I could reason with this woman, couldn't I? Did I have any other options, other than being shot and killed?

"This is one murder the police will give me credit for solving." All trace of Miss Mystic's accent was gone. She stepped closer, that gun still aimed at us. She was close enough that I could see the devious glean in her eyes. "Tragic that your little boyfriend snapped and killed all three of you."

Cooper? She was going to frame this on Cooper?

Even more resolve and determination built in me. I didn't have anything to lose. I'd reached the bottom of my pit, and I had nowhere to go but up. But I wasn't going to let Cooper's life be ruined by this.

"There's no way Cooper will be blamed for this. No way."

She raised her eyebrows. "He just arrived home. He dropped off his son and came here." She pointed that gun at me again. "You wrote a note that the police find, detailing boyfriend's temper. He's mad at you. You were around his son with your reputation. He was furious."

Her words washed over me. She was going to say Cooper killed us because he was angry after he found out about the allegations? What other evidence would there be? Him knocking at the door, trying to get to me? A note she would try to make me write? His prints might be on the gun from when he'd taken it from me. Would that be enough to convict him? I wasn't sure. I knew one thing—I would never, ever make a false allegation against someone. Never.

Think, Tara. Think.

We had this video. But would she figure out a way to erase it.

I sensed Candy behind me. What was she doing?

Hope surged through me as I realized that the woman who had the amazing ability to type with one hand with her eyes closed was updating her social media sites. No way would Miss Mystic get away with this.

Score one for social media, and the one and only iCandy.

"Put the camera down." Miss Mystic sneered at Mickey and pointed the gun his way.

"All right. All right. Don't shoot me, and I won't shoot you." He lowered the camera to the ground.

I sensed Candy putting away her phone, which she'd concealed behind me. *Nicely played, Candy. Nicely played.*

Miss Mystic tossed some rope at Mickey. "Tie your friends up."

He raised his hands in the air, all his urban coolness working in our favor and against Miss Mystic. Score another one for us. "I don't know how to tie people up."

"Figure it out!" Her voice sounded screechy and high-pitched, like a woman on edge.

I found comfort in knowing that she wouldn't get away with this, but I found grief in knowing that I might die in the process. No, she wouldn't frame this on Cooper. The mere thought had been one only someone in a deranged and desperate state of mind might conjure up.

"Okay, okay," Mickey mumbled. He grabbed the rope and turned toward Candy. "I'm sorry, Candy."

"Yeah, yeah." I couldn't see Candy, but I knew she was rolling her eyes.

I had to use every moment. "Danielle was about to report you to the police because you were defrauding your clients—and I'm not talking about defrauding in the normal psychic way. You could have gotten arrested."

She sneered again. "You think you're so smart."

"I saw Philip Whitehurst's blog entries. At first I thought he was talking about Danielle, but you were the psychic who made him buy the egg and the candles. You were totally exploiting someone with a mental illness. Philip went to Danielle for help, and she was about to go to the police. She confronted you about it, and you killed her."

"Nice work, Sherlock," Candy mumbled, her lips twisted in discomfort as Mickey tied the rope at her wrists.

"Then you had a brilliant idea that you could use this to your advantage. You could frame Jeremy Miller. They were having problems anyway, so it wouldn't be so hard to give him motive. But someone moved the body. I still don't know whom. So when you told the police where Jeremy had left the body—which was really where *you'd* left the body—you thought you would get accolades for your abilities. But the body wasn't there. Someone had moved it. The police were just annoyed with you for wasting their time, and they weren't about to give you another chance."

Miss Mystic scowled. "You think you're so smart."

"Then it was the anniversary of Danielle's death, so you thought it was time to revisit her murder. You'd kept the murder weapon. You knew about this tunnel because your client is the real estate agent selling the house next door. She'd told you about it, and you knew you had an opportunity. Somehow you got a copy of the key, and you set your plan into action.

"You planted the bloody knife in a place where police might argue they could have missed it two years ago. You gave me hints like the weapon was underfoot. You would have probably given me more hints, but when Candy dropped my sister's ring down that vent, you didn't have to anymore." I stared at the gun. This woman had killed before. She could kill again. Could I keep talking until the police got here? Exactly what had Candy posted? I had to have confidence in my friend that she'd posted something wise and usable.

Miss Mystic sneered. "I get my moment. One way or another, I get the credit I deserve."

"Credit for killing someone?"

"Stop talking." She pointed her gun at Mickey. "Tie her up. Now."

"So you're going to shoot us, leave us down here, and have a vision about it that you'll share with the police. You'll never get away with this." I cringed as Mickey tightened the rope around my wrists. Once I was tied up, what would I do?

As I glanced down at Mickey's camera, I noticed a light still on. Was he recording all of this still? Brilliant.

All of the sudden, I saw the hidden door move ever-so-slightly. The light in the basement had been turned off, and the only illumination was from my flashlight. But someone was there. Who?

At once, someone tackled Miss Mystic. She slammed to the ground, the gun skittering across the floor. I swooped down and picked it up, grateful that Mickey was not a Boy Scout. My hand trembled as I realized at that very moment how very much I hated guns.

I snatched my flashlight and shined the light upward.

Cooper. He kept a knee on Miss Mystic's back, pinning her in place as she mumbled literal curses at us.

"Are you okay?" he asked.

I nodded, just as the lights came on in the basement and police officers filled the space.

Yeah, I was more than okay.

By the grace of God, I was alive—inside and out.

The last three hours had been spent with the police. Everyone was sequestered at my place, being questioned. We had everything on video, so the police could do very little to dispute how events had played out—not that there was any reason they'd want to dispute it.

Cooper and I hadn't had a chance to talk. He'd maintained his distance—not in a chilly way, but in a professional manner. We'd talk later, after everyone else was gone.

Detective Hensley closed his notebook. "Good work, Ms. Lancaster."

I pulled my sweatshirt over my hands. I wasn't necessarily cold, but I found great comfort in the oversized Miami Dolphins hoodie. "There's one thing I still don't understand, detective. What happened to Danielle's body?"

He shrugged. "Miss Mystic claimed she buried Danielle in that empty field where she led us. She says someone moved it before we arrived, and that she has no idea who would do that."

My brain started whirring. Who liked to watch people without being seen? Who might have found Danielle's body and, worried about her soul, decided to move it because he loved her so much? "Talk to Philip Whitehurst."

The detective cocked an eyebrow. "Philip Whitehurst?"

I nodded. "He was in love with Danielle. What if he saw what happened, if he saw someone move her body? He might have moved it out of respect for Danielle."

The detective shrugged. "It's worth looking into. We'll talk to him."

I had a feeling it had been Philip who was at my house that first night also. Maybe he was on the lookout for Danielle's spirit, too?

The detective held out his hand. "Thanks for your help in the case.

Miss Mystic will be getting some of that attention that she sought—not exactly how she wanted it, but that's okay."

After the detective left, Candy and Mickey went back to a friend's place to edit their video. Tomorrow, I'd call Bryce Stephens and offer him the first scoop on the story. It was the least I could do since he'd helped me.

But now I had to face Cooper.

I'd almost rather face an entire medieval army bent on torture than risk my heart again. My throat burned as I turned to him, realizing there was no one else here to distract us.

"Can we talk?"

Cooper's gaze searched mine until he finally nodded. "Sure." He led me to the couch. He sat on one end, and I sat on the other. I pulled a pillow into my lap and wrapped my arms around it.

"I heard about what you did at church today. I think that was brave and courageous of you."

"Thanks." The timbre of my voice made me sound like an oversized frog who'd been singing too loudly at a Jimmy Buffet concert.

He was waiting for me to start. But I had no idea how to do that. There was no elegant way to say what I had to say. "I'm sorry I hurt you. I'm sorry I embarrassed you in front of your friends from church. I wanted to tell you everything. I did."

"So why didn't you?"

I stared at my legs, at the pillow, anywhere but at Cooper. "I was afraid that you'd believe the rumors instead of me. Or that there would always be this lingering doubt in your mind. I couldn't bear the thought of that."

"Do you want to tell me your version of what happened?"

I nodded, sucked in a deep breath of courage, and plunged in. I told him everything—about the accusations, how it affected my relationship with Peter, how people I'd loved had turned their backs on me. When I finished, I held my breath, waiting for him to respond.

"But they never found enough evidence to press charges. The media called you the Saint Turned Sinner."

I nodded. "Let me guess—you did an Internet search for me after you got home last night?"

He shook his head. "No, I knew who you were from the first day we met."

My heart stopped, or at least it felt like it did. "What?"

He moved closer, lessening the space between us. "I visited my parents in Florida, and it was all the talk. I also listened to your dad's radio show. I knew about everything that happened, Tara."

"Why didn't you run away then?"

He reached for my hand. "Why would I? The moment I looked into your eyes, I knew you were innocent."

My heart started again, going from zero to sixty in five-point-two. "How could you be so sure?"

"Your eyes tell me everything about you. Mostly, they let me see your heart. There's not an ounce of evil in you, Tara."

"I was married to Peter, and he didn't believe me."

"Then he's an idiot."

As my lips pulled upward, tears of joy streamed down my cheeks. "That really means a lot to me. Thanks Cooper."

"I was hoping you would trust me enough to tell me yourself."

"I thought about it a million times." I shrugged, wiping my cheeks with the back of my hand. "The thing is, this kid may have done the same thing to another teacher out in Texas. My attorney's trying to gather any evidence right now. I thought if I could wait until that was firmed up and tell you then that maybe you'd believe me. That you'd really believe me."

He reached up and wiped my remaining tears with his thumb. "I'm sorry you had to go through all of that, Tara. Think about what Jesus had to go through when he died on the cross. Betrayal. Accusation. I don't understand your pain, but he does."

"I know." More tears came a pouring. "I know that now. He's going to bring something good from this. Something really good."

Cooper smiled at me. "I think he already has."

Joy burst in my heart. "I think he has too."

Cooper scooted closer, until we were face to face. His hand caressed my cheek. "I just want you to know that you can trust me, Tara. I've got your back. Understand?"

I nodded. "Yeah, I understand."

His lips touched mine.

Plastic surgery for the soul, I thought. Yeah, Lana was right. All it took was some redemption, grace, and authenticity to get the sought-after results.

35

Lana and I had spent the three days since she'd been home catching up. I'd met her fiancé, Nate Sandler, a guy who played in an acoustic rock band and liked to wear sandals with socks and had dreads in his hair. He seemed like a genuinely nice guy, so I'd let the sandals and dreads get a pass for now.

A week had passed since the police found Danielle Miller's body. Philip Whitehurst had come to the house after Miss Mystic killed her. He'd arrived in time to see Miss Mystic pull away with the body in her car. When he'd seen her body, he worried that her soul would be forever tarnished—and that he'd be found guilty. So he'd moved her body to the woods to keep it safe. With someone else behind bars and without the fear of being framed himself, he told the police where it was. He said she could have a proper funeral now. I guess in his own sick, twisted way it had been the final kind act of an obsessive stalker.

Finally, Jeremy could get some resolution. Miss Mystic had definitely gotten her thirty seconds of fame. I only hoped she didn't get off on some mental plea, because to do everything that she'd done, she was off of her rocker.

Meanwhile, Zack Morris, who was now nineteen, had been arrested for grifting. As a part of a plea bargain, he rolled on his mom and confessed to everything. He'd told police that his mom had schemed the entire plan to get money. Finally, I felt free. Despite that, I had no desire to return to Miami. I knew that one day I'd be able to fully forgive the people who'd treated me poorly, but I needed more time to heal first.

Today was Candy's birthday, and she'd invited us all to the park to celebrate. I bristled slightly at the thought because the park seemed like such an odd place for Candy to want to have a birthday party.

Cooper was driving me there, and Austin sat in the backseat, the loveliest little boy I'd ever met. I'd so much enjoyed having him around. We pulled up to the park, and Austin ran on ahead to the playground. Before I got out of the car, Cooper grabbed my hand and pulled me back in.

He gave me a quick kiss. Even his touch sent fire through my blood. Instinctively, I reached up and caressed his cheek. "I'm glad you're going to stay around for a while."

"I'm glad I'm going to stay around for a while. You were right, Cooper. God brought me through everything that he did, but I'm a better person for it. My faith is stronger, my confidence clearer. And I met you and Austin."

He smiled and kissed me again. "We should go."

I nodded, reluctantly letting him go as we climbed out. Our hands instantly entwined together as we walked up a grassy hill. I saw Candy and some of her friends standing there.

Just what was she planning?

As soon as I reached the top of the hill, I saw a huge mud pit. I glanced over at Candy and saw the mischievous grin on her face. "Guess what we're doing for my birthday?"

"Cleaning up this atrocity in the park?"

Her grin broadened. "We're mud wrestling! I organized the whole thing as a part of a fundraiser to raise money for the homeless program at The Mercy House."

I have a new set of rules now. The rules of relationship, and there were really only two commandments: Love God, and Love People. I'm ending my love affair with the church and I'm moving in with God—

not just leaving my toothbrush at his house. I'm all in. Committed. Church...well, it's going to be a part of the equation, but mostly I just wanted to fall in love again with Jesus.

With that, I slipped off my watch and handed it to Cooper. Then I turned to Candy.

"Bring it, Jawbreaker."

"You got it, Bora Bora."

Acknowledgments

I'd like to thank my brother and his wife for inviting me to housesit in a creepy old Minnesota home filled with creaky floors, gates that mysteriously open at night, and windows without shades.

Thanks to everyone who has believed in this book over the years and who has encouraged me to keep pursuing this story.

Thanks to Roseanna, Dina and the rest of the gang over at Whitefire for giving this book a chance. I'm glad *The Good Girl* found a home with you.

To my loyal readers—thanks for sharing my dreams and embracing my stories. You all bring so much joy to the creative process.

Finally, thank you to Jesus, for His constant love and for giving me reason to hope and live.

Author's Note

Thanks so much for taking the time to read *The Good Girl*. This book was born way back in 2003 when I was housesitting for my brother out in St. Paul. The creaky floors of his old house, along with the exposed windows and some other strange happenings got my imagination going. I asked the magic question that every writer at some point asks: What if...?

Even more than those suspenseful elements, I wanted to explore the idea of grace versus works. Growing up in the church, I've always been more of a "works" girl than I wanted to admit. I caught myself thinking that if I just followed all of the rules, then I'd somehow get special privileges, maybe even avoid some of the hard stuff in life.

Within a short period of time, several things in my life went wrong and made me realize that there was nothing I could do to make God love me more or less. I had to stop trying to earn God's favor and accept that bad things happen to everyone. They're simply a part of this journey called "life."

I've come a long way in my journey for perfection. My hope is that if you're a good girl—someone who's constantly finding affirmation by doing things right—that you'll cut yourself some slack and rest securely in God's unending and unfailing love.

Life on earth can be hard and unfair. We can rest assured, however, that in all things God works for the good of those who love him, who have been called according to His purpose (Romans 8:28).

For "behind the scenes" look at *The Good Girl*, please visit my website at: www.christybarritt.com.

OTHER TITLES

If you enjoyed *The Good Girl*, you may also like these other titles from WhiteFire Publishing:

Paint Chips
by Susie Finkbeiner

What lies beneath the layers of hurt?

Jasmine
by April McGowan

She survived her past...but can she face it?

Love, Lace, and Minor Alterations
by V. Joy Palmer

This bridal consultant is sick and tired of everyone *else's* Happily Ever After.